Dilip Desai has written this book as a new venture after having worked for 43 years as a dentist, retiring at the end of 2018.

He has a wife, four children and five grandchildren.

My wife, Sharon, for her support, tolerance and patience while I was writing this book.

My parents, who made many sacrifices in order to give me the chance of a good education.

Dilip Desai

The Dark Side of White

Austin Macauley Publishers™
LONDON * CAMBRIDGE * NEW YORK * SHARJAH

Copyright © Dilip Desai 2024

The right of Dilip Desai to be identified as author of this work has been asserted by the author in accordance with sections 77 and 78 of the Copyright, Designs and Patents Act 1988.

All rights reserved. No part of this publication may be reproduced, stored in a retrieval system, or transmitted in any form or by any means, electronic, mechanical, photocopying, recording, or otherwise, without the prior permission of the publishers.

Any person who commits any unauthorised act in relation to this publication may be liable to criminal prosecution and civil claims for damages.

This is a work of fiction. Names, characters, businesses, places, events, locales, and incidents are either the products of the author's imagination or used in a fictitious manner. Any resemblance to actual persons, living or dead, or actual events is purely coincidental.

A CIP catalogue record for this title is available from the British Library.

ISBN 9781035814534 (Paperback)
ISBN 9781035814541 (ePub e-book)

www.austinmacauley.com

First Published 2024
Austin Macauley Publishers Ltd®
1 Canada Square
Canary Wharf
London
E14 5AA

Chapter 1

The sun was beginning to set, moving slowly across the cloudless sky as another day was ending and as it descended, the shadows on the ground elongated and the brightness and heat of the day were gradually being replaced by the dimmer light and coolness of the evening. As it lowered, its piercing light penetrated the back windows of the two-storey, wooden built houses on one side of the street and the front windows of the houses on the other side.

Each of the twelve detached houses, six on each side of the road, was rectangular in design and all were identical in appearance externally. Dusty, stone-lined, unmade paths led from the dirt road to each house, at the end of which were some wooden steps, which, in turn, rose up to the verandas of the houses that ran along the full width of the ground floor and there were matching parallel balconies on the level above.

The pitched roofs ran the length of the houses and a chimney could be seen attached to the right-hand walls, protruding above the rooflines, approximately two-thirds along from the front. One of the houses into which the sun was shining through its front window was the only one on the street that did not have any smoke curling out of its chimney, which indicated that today there was no cooking taking place in there.

The figure of a man would have been visible to anyone walking past the ground floor window of that house that evening but this was unlikely to occur as the house occupied a private location in the middle-class suburbs of Bombay; the street being a cul-de-sac with only those dozen houses on it, with this particular dwelling being at the end of the road and tucked away in a corner plot.

Ramesh Patel paced quickly along the length of the room, to and fro, with anxiety showing on his finely chiselled face and the perspiration rolling down from his forehead and into his eyes was causing them to sting and making them sore and red as he rubbed them. His collarless white shirt was partly unbuttoned, exposing some of his dark hairy chest and moist grey patches, where the sleeves of his shirt were attached to the bodice, marked the sweat from under his arms.

He pushed his hands deep into his trouser pockets as he walked, causing his button-down braces to stretch, which in turn caused his turn-up trousers to drop over his shoes and brush along the planked wooden floor. As he reached the window at the front end of the room, after about an hour of pacing up and down, he looked out onto the street.

The sun had now almost disappeared and the moon was rising. The road was empty except for the lamplighter, who was busy lighting the six gas lamps which he knew would, as he had seen this many times before, throw their own dancing shadows up and down the street as their flames flickered, in stark contrast to the static ones given by the moon.

He turned away from the window and then paused and looked around the ground floor of his home. The room was simply furnished; two armchairs, a two-seater settee a small coffee table in the front half and a dining table with four chairs tucked under, in the back section. Against the wall on the left, about halfway along, was an old, battered mahogany writing desk with a leather chair that did not match the desk, next to it.

To the right of the dining area was the cooking area, which consisted of a small wood-burning stove with a chimney pipe leading through the wall to the outside of the house and a large pail full of water, ready for the dirty utensils, pans and crockery, which was placed neatly next to the stove. A tall cupboard for storing food stood on the opposite wall, just further down from the writing desk. The dining table was laid out for two people. He started pacing again.

It was late evening on 7 December 1921. A man of above medium height, with shiny black hair, which was combed straight back, dark brown eyes, handsome features and a strong jawline, looking at Ramesh one would not have thought him a person who became anxious, but this was not an easy time for him. What was about to happen would have a great impact on the rest of his life, as it would for anyone experiencing the same situation.

He stopped pacing as he heard the shrill scream from the room above and looked up at the ceiling. He felt totally useless and helpless, a position he was not at all used to being in, but had no choice except to remain downstairs. He removed his hands from his pockets, walked to the front window and looked up at the sky, which was now studded with stars.

The beautiful sunset had now disappeared and a full moon that had created different shadows on the street gave a different scene to the one he had seen earlier. Ramesh knew that he would remember every detail of this night for the rest of his days. His thoughts were broken by another scream and he wrung his hands in despair and started pacing again. After a while, he collapsed onto the settee and sat down with his head in his hands.

This ritual of pacing interspersed by periods of sitting down continued.

After a very worrying and stressful period for Ramesh of approximately five hours of listening to the intermittent screaming, a longer silence filled the air, causing him to stop pacing, the phase he was in, and again look up at the ceiling.

Without warning, the sharp cry of a new born baby broke this prolonged silence and Ramesh knew that his first child had been born.

He looked at his wristwatch to register in his mind the exact time of the birth: 2. 27 a.m. on 8 December 1921. He then rushed out of the room, into the hall and up the stairs, two at a time, and waited impatiently on the landing for the doctor to come out of the bedroom as he knew better than to enter without permission.

After a few minutes, the bedroom door opened and the doctor emerged and upon seeing Ramesh waiting on the landing, he extended his right hand in an offer of a handshake, which Ramesh accepted and at the same time said:

"Congratulations, you have a son," and then added, "Both are well but your wife is very tired and needs rest. There were no complications, I will come back tomorrow to check on them."

Ramesh was relieved to hear that both his wife and baby were well and was ecstatic to learn that his new born child was a boy. He led the doctor downstairs, thanked him for his services and then, having paid him, politely and firmly ushered him out, shut the door, turned around and bounded up the stairs to see his son, whom he had yet to meet, and his wife.

He ran into the bedroom, knelt down by the bed and took his wife's left hand with his right one and laid his left hand on the back of his son who was wrapped up in a blanket and snuggled up in his wife's arms with his head cradled in the crook of her right arm. She gave him a tired, happy and loving smile.

'Well done,' he said and then gripped her hand a little tighter and added, 'Thank you for giving me a son.' Ramesh stayed in that position until both his wife and son had gone to sleep and then quietly left the room.

Ramesh did not go to bed that night but instead sat on a chair on his balcony staring out at the night sky without actually registering any of the sights. As he sat there motionlessly, with his mind full of thoughts, the earth slowly rotated on its axis, the moon and stars faded away, the sun rose to herald the start of another day and the coolness of the night changed to the warmth of the day. Even in December, the city of Bombay never really became cold.

After the immediate joy and excitement of having a boy, Ramesh spent the night thinking and visualising about the future glory that all men want for their sons. Vijay, the name they had decided on should they have a boy, was just over six hours old when his father finally drifted off to sleep in his chair on the balcony.

Ramesh was roused from his sleep by a knocking on the front door. He stood up and looked down over the balcony and saw two ladies standing on the steps to the veranda, both carrying what looked like dishes of food covered by cloths. This reminded him of when Sunila, his wife, had bustled around the kitchen cooking for them when their children had been born and how he had heard the disappointment in her voice on her return as she told him about the new babies because her turn as the recipient never seemed to come.

Thinking about Vijay now made him very thankful to God and happy that the long wait was over. He went downstairs and met the two women on the veranda, thereby not allowing them access to the house, and gave them all the information that he could about Sunila and Vijay; then accepted their food and thanked them for their generosity knowing that they were behaving in a way that had not changed for centuries and was probably very similar throughout the world. He placed the food on the table in the kitchen and then returned upstairs, this time going to the bedroom to check on his family.

Ramesh and his wife Sunila had been married for just over five years when Vijay was born, an unusually long time by which to not have conceived and they thought they would not be able to have children. They had met for the first time on their wedding day, their marriage having been arranged by their parents some years prior to the event, as had been the case for millions of couples over the centuries.

This was an age-old custom, where a friend of both families would arrange a meeting between the parents of the boy and the girl who was the prospective couple, at the home of the girl usually, where they chatted about and discussed their respective children, all four trying to glean as much information as possible.

In the case of Ramesh and Sunila, the meeting between the parents had taken place when Ramesh was fourteen and Sunila twelve. Ramesh's parents had wanted to find out about Sunila's domestic capabilities and her willingness to devote herself to her husband and Sunila's parents were mostly interested in Ramesh's prospects and his temperament.

Looks or love was never mentioned by any of them.

After another two meetings, it was decided that the wedding should take place and the two fathers then went to a private room to discuss the dowry, which was the amount of money Sunila's parents would give to Ramesh for agreeing to marry her. The figure having been settled, an approximate date for the wedding was decided upon; two years hence and the parents arranged to meet again a few months before the ceremony would take place, which was when the exact date of the wedding would be set and also the time when the planning for the occasion would begin in earnest. Ramesh was told about his betrothal, but not to whom, at the same time as the wedding plans were started.

They both came from small villages, a few miles apart in the state of Gujarat, which lies on the North West coast of India. Sunila, a small and petite girl, had been forced by her parents, against her wishes, to leave school at the age of twelve, having been told that her betrothal had been arranged but not to whom, so that she could learn to become a 'good wife.'

Although she learnt quickly and well, she constantly argued with her parents, especially her father, about the role she was being asked to train for, with the arguments usually being ended by him becoming exasperated and walking away, muttering under his breath about young people having no respect for their elders, whereas Sunila would have continued until she had worn him down and therefore, by default, won her case.

Her mother, upset by the bickering, would try to mediate but would never directly or publicly challenge her husband, although privately she did try to make him understand the viewpoint of their daughter, further aggravating him, although she reassured him that the decision they had made was right and that hopefully, Sunila would understand in the future. By the time she was fourteen, Sunila had become proficient in all domestic chores and had also, reluctantly, accepted her fate.

Ramesh, on the other hand, was encouraged by his parents to stay at school and achieve as good an education as he could and, consequently because of this, he was one of the oldest boys to leave, which was at the age of sixteen.

The wedding, which was attended by family and friends from both villages and was a small affair as neither of the families was wealthy, had been arranged to take place in Sunila's village; another decision based on tradition, with the local priest carrying out the religious part of the wedding which was the only formal part of the occasion.

The food and catering was prepared and arranged by Sunila's mother and any relatives who offered their help. During the formal part of the ceremony the women would sit in one area of the school hall, where the wedding took place, and the men in another part whilst the children ran around and played.

These events were usually also the time when further betrothals were engineered as the adults discussed amongst themselves which boys and girls were next available for marriage and if there was any 'scandal' associated with them. Again, the questions asked were all about temperament, future prospects, deformities, behaviour and the general personality of the boys or girls as no parent willingly wanted their child to 'suffer' in a marriage.

After the wedding, the couple went to live with Ramesh's parents, again another long-standing tradition and Sunila was now expected to do all the cooking and cleaning whilst Ramesh's mother would sit around and entertain her friends and relatives, the men being out at work.

This was the traditional and historic way of life for native Indians and had not changed for centuries; so Sunila, although not comfortable with this state of affairs, had no choice but to accept the situation.

By this time, Ramesh, having worked hard at school and therefore achieved very good grades, had secured a position working for a small textile factory in Bombay as a junior clerk, which, because of the distance, meant that he had to catch the late evening train on Sundays and return home on the afternoon train on Saturdays, as his working hours included Saturday morning as well as weekdays.

He had managed to secure a single room for his lodgings in the home of an Indian family and included in his rent was the provision of a daily 'tiffin'; his midday meal. Being on his own, he spent as much time as he could at work, sometimes staying on well into the late evening, which did not go unnoticed by his superiors and he soon was rewarded for his endeavours and duly promoted.

This made life very hard and lonely for Sunila back in Ramesh's village. She did make the occasional trip to Bombay to see Ramesh but this was not easy for a number of reasons but predominantly those of money and accommodation.

Fortunately, however, being very good at his job, it was not long before he moved to a larger company and made excellent progress there as well. His meteoric rise in this company was the envy of his colleagues and also enabled him and Sunila to afford to rent a house in the expanding middle-class suburbs of Bombay. He was twenty when they moved to Bombay as a married couple.

Life was good for Ramesh and he had prospered well over the years, becoming a senior manager for a large British-owned textile company, the Bombay City and Gujarat Textile Company, at the very young age of twenty-four, a position which made him the highest paid, non-white, employee in the company.

Ravi, a younger brother for Vijay, had arrived nine months earlier and as far as Ramesh was concerned, as he sat one day reflecting on his life so far, that day being in March 1924, with a devoted wife Sunila, two sons and a successful career, life could not be better.

As Ramesh watched Vijay develop, he believed that his progress was beyond and quicker than the thoughts and visions that he had had on the night of his birth. Walking at nine months, talking very soon afterwards and reading at a level two years his senior by the time he was six, his father told himself in his private moments, not that he ever expressed his thoughts to anyone, including Sunila, that Vijay would become someone special.

Vijay's first day at school gave Ramesh a very fond memory.

"Look, Daddy, I have been watching you put on your tie and have copied you. Have I done a good job?" asked Vijay, looking up at his father.

Ramesh beamed down at his son, straightened up his striped school tie and said, "You will be the smartest boy in your class." Vijay smiled but did not grasp the double meaning that his father had intended …

As Vijay grew and developed, Ramesh spent many an hour talking to him as much as he could about the politics and economics of India and also of the wider world. They played chess and card games when relaxing at home and cricket with the other boys and fathers in the nearby streets when outside.

As an upper-middle-class Indian family, Ramesh and Sunila could afford to send both Vijay and Ravi to a fee-paying school, one of the many set up by the East India Trading Company, so both boys were receiving a high standard of education.

Seeing their sons start school, smartly dressed in their uniforms, gave Ramesh and Sunila a great deal of pride; watching them grow both academically and physically gave them a great deal of satisfaction and, as far as they could tell, the boys were also very happy with their lives, which made them very happy as parents as well.

The boys were trilingual as they were taught both English and Hindi at the school and were fluent in Gujarati as well, that being their native language at home. A varied number of other subjects, including maths and science were also in the curriculum. Ramesh was impressed by the philosophy of the schools which was that these higher, middle and upper-class Indian schoolchildren would become 'Indians by blood and colour and English by taste.'

The rationale behind these schools, he was reliably informed by the headmaster, was to develop a tier of administrators who could act as intermediaries between the uneducated masses and the elite British.

Time moved on and the boys both progressed well in all aspects of their lives. Ramesh also maintained his advancement with the company and was involved in all major decisions, albeit for his advice and perspective only, as all final decisions had to be made by the British hierarchy, which he accepted without any animosity.

Chapter 2

With his importance in the textile industry and his dealings with trade in many countries, Ramesh had become knowledgeable about the political moods in those places. Also, with tensions rising between the British administration and leading Indian politicians, he could perceive that his own country was edging more and more towards revolution fever as time dragged on with the British occupation.

There had already been many incidents involving skirmishes and bloodshed between 'revolutionaries' and the British forces, which were causing fear and unrest on both sides. An increasing number of leading Indian politicians were publicly advocating peaceful means of pressure against the British but were privately accepting that this was not achieving the goals they were hoping for and that violence was now becoming an acceptable tool in the struggle for independence.

Ramesh was aware that Germany was trying to recover from the aftermath of the 'great war' and that unrest was increasing in that country at an alarming rate as resentment towards the international communities grew with regards to the way that they were being treated and he also knew from his own experiences at work that Britain was having major industrial problems at home, along with its political problems in South Africa and India.

Ramesh, along with many other senior and influential businessmen, had met Gandhi, Nehru, Jinnah and Patel some months previously when there had been a few secret discussions on how the textile industry, amongst others, might be used to help in the fight for independence. Although nothing definite had been decided as to his role in this action, it became very clear to him from those meetings that it was the fight for freedom that was binding all the factions and religious groups of India together and that revolution fever was strong.

It was also very obvious to him that the internal problems of India would have to be put to one side until independence had been achieved but he also felt convinced that civil war would follow very soon afterwards; he knew from his own history lessons that when countries are not at war, religious and racial prejudices come to the surface and replace national integration.

Man, by nature, likes confrontation and challenge, he had concluded to himself. However, Ramesh also knew that self-rule was always preferable to colonial rule; so as far as he was concerned, the outcome was inevitable, and time was the only variable factor.

His thoughts came back to the letter in his hand, the reason for his present contemplation on the situation in India and the dilemma he faced. Gandhi had written to him, as well as many others, asking that they join him in the fight for independence but not as Ramesh had envisaged, that is, using their position to influence the economic stability of the country but actually, in his case, asking Ramesh to give up his job and travel around India with him in order to rally the people in peaceful but disruptive demonstrations, which would cause considerable problems for the administration but, hopefully, not allow the authorities to become aggressive and violent when they tried to enforce their laws and rules.

After giving the matter some considerable thought and after discussing the letter with Sunila, Ramesh decided to decline the request and remain in his position with the textile company believing that his first loyalties lay with his wife and children who still needed him to provide for them, unlike Gandhi, whose children were now grown up.

He did, however, offer to organise any industrial action that would benefit the fight for independence as long as it did not involve violence and in this, he kept his word, with the outcome that there were more strikes in the textile industry in India during the late 1920s than in both the United States and England together but none could be directly attributed to Ramesh. Time moved on in this vein for Ramesh and his family for a few years, with him leading a double life of family man and provider and also an active but secretive 'revolutionary.'

Chapter 3

Vijay was eleven when tragedy struck.

He was growing up to be a fine specimen of a young boy and was an outstanding pupil at his school, achieving top marks in all of his examinations and even at this young age, bright prospects were expected of him by his teachers.

On one of his son's parent's evenings, Ramesh had been told by Vijay's headmaster that he, Ramesh, would go down in history as the father of Vijay. Ramesh knew this was an exaggeration but was, nevertheless, very pleased that his son was excelling at school.

Apart from his academic achievements, Vijay was also a fine athlete, with his favourite sport being the national game of cricket. His leadership qualities meant that he was chosen by the sports teacher to be the captain of the school team and the consensus amongst his fellow teammates was that he was also the best player.

It was following a game of cricket against one of the other schools in the city when, as he was walking home with his father, they heard a commotion near one of the barracks set up in Bombay by the British Army, although they could not see the buildings.

A great deal of shouting, cries of 'go home', and then the sound of splintering glass, as a rock or stone was thrown breaking one of the windows of a building, caused them, along with many others, to stop in their tracks to try and ascertain what was happening, with everyone gazing up the street in the direction of the noisy exchange.

Booming British voices shouting 'Stop him, and 'Grab him', could be heard and then the unmistakable sound of pistol fire seared through the air. This frightening noise of the gunfire riveted them both to the spot where they stood, as it did the other people on the street. As they stood there the slapping sound of sandaled feet running on a dusty road came nearer and louder, making the residents of the street transfix their gazes in the direction from which it came. The sound was accentuated by the noise of boots also running on the road and then, around the corner of the street appeared a young Indian man, his dirty white tunic billowing around his torso, with a growing blood stain on the right shoulder area of the garment.

He moved quickly down the road, shouting obscenities about the soldiers as he ran and was almost past Ramesh and Vijay when a British officer appeared careering around the corner and without steadying himself, the soldier raised the pistol he held in his right hand and fired in the general direction of the young Indian man.

The next thing that Vijay knew was that his father let out a small cry and fell to the ground, blood pouring out from the left temple region of his head.

Ramesh died within seconds of the bullet entering his brain. The bullet had ricocheted off the wall of the house next to where they were standing and had then entered his head through one of its most vulnerable areas, the left temple; thereby causing almost instantaneous death.

His death was so sudden and quick that he did not have time for any dying words. As Vijay dropped his cricket bag and fell down onto his knees, he vaguely noticed the boots of the officer stomp past him as he continued chasing the young man, who was now out of sight, around the next corner.

Kneeling by his dead father, his thoughts were directed to the soldier and he was not sure whether the officer was unaware or just oblivious to the fact that he had killed an innocent man by indiscriminately firing his pistol in a residential area.

As Vijay knelt by his father, watching a thick rivulet of blood oozing out of the wound and haloing his head, he became aware of a crowd forming around him, the men shouting loudly and angrily, the women screaming and crying and the children whimpering as they hid behind their mothers.

From behind him, he heard footsteps approaching and then he felt the gentle hands of a woman take hold of his arms, just below his shoulders and lift him from his knees. She turned him round and hugged him close to her chest. Vijay tried to control himself but the tears came, despite his efforts.

He was roused from his grief by the sound of British voices, so he half-turned his head away from the woman's chest to see what was happening. A dozen soldiers in regular formation had arrived on the scene, followed by a captain. The crowd was then quickly shepherded together and the captain then asked one of the less agitated and more elderly men of the gathering what had occurred.

As the events were being described, the young officer returned, still holding the pistol in his hand, dusty and breathless and the crowd, upon seeing him, again became aroused and started to shout and push forward to try and reach him. The army unit held firm and the soldiers retreated back to their barracks.

Vijay did not manage to see the face of the officer who had just shot and killed his father but he did register the fact that he had a single diamond-shaped badge on the epaulette of his jacket.

The woman who had taken care of him now eased him away so that they were face-to-face and asked him where he lived. She gave instructions to a man, Vijay assumed he was her husband, about moving and sorting out Ramesh's body and then she picked up his cricket bag, led him away from the scene of his father's murder and took him home. No conversation was had between them during the walk to his house, except for any directional instructions that he gave.

Sunila was devastated by the news of her husband's murder. She screamed for a short while and then sat down on the sofa crying, and beckoned her sons to sit down either side of her and then hugged her two children so hard that they found it difficult to breathe. Ravi cried along with his mother but Vijay did not.

He sat motionless and just stared at the wall in front of him with empty, unfocused eyes. The lady who had brought him home felt uneasy as she looked at his face and a shiver went through her body. After a few minutes, Vijay extricated himself from his mother's grip, stood up, thanked the lady for all her help and escorted her to the front door.

Tuesday, 13 June 1933 would be a date he would never forget.

Ramesh's body was taken back to his village a few days later, to the home of his parents, who were distraught at the death of their son and only child. Sunila had taken the death of her husband very badly and had been inconsolable since she had heard of the tragedy.

The ladies who lived on the street helped to look after the boys and Sunila's elder sister, Nalini, came to stay for a couple of days, until the day before the funeral, on which they all travelled to Ramesh's village. Vijay slept very fitfully that night, worrying about the funeral and his part in that ceremony.

The funeral was a very emotional affair with Vijay already knowing what was expected of him, having been given his instructions by both his grandfathers. Lighting the funeral pyre would, in the eyes of his community, declare the moment that he became the head of the family and had to take on the responsibilities that this position required. When that moment came he was trembling and had to hold the flaming torch with both hands to stop the shaking, as he pushed it deep into the wood.

His voice faltered as he tried to follow the religious chants of the priest and his legs felt weak and rubbery as he led the procession of men around the pyre, whilst the women and children gathered in a group further away, all chanting and crying at the same time making everything sound incoherent, not that anyone bothered or minded. He stopped trying to join in with the chanting and started to contemplate his future, which this tragic event had now irrevocably changed.

This burden of becoming the head of the family and the pressures that it brought and the anger he felt towards the British officer, now dramatically altered his perception of life and he knew this would have a great bearing on how he conducted himself for the rest of his days, knowing and accepting that what remained of his childhood had now been taken away from him.

He acknowledged to himself that until now he had been a very happy child living a very privileged life, especially compared to the majority of the native population of India, but he realised this would all change now and not for the better.

He became very anxious, frightened and worried.

That evening, after everyone had left and Ravi had gone to bed, Sunila, Vijay and Ramesh's parents talked about the future. Sunila had already decided, after discussing the situation with her parents, that she and her children would live with them and was pleased when there was no objection from her in-laws.

Having made their decisions and agreed on them, they all went to bed and lay awake having their own personal thoughts about Ramesh and then, gradually, one at a time, they all fell asleep as tiredness overtook them. The following morning Vijay left the house early, leaving a note of his intentions in order not to worry anyone and went back to the funeral site.

He gathered some ashes into the container he had taken and then walked the six miles to the coast, spending that time reflecting and thinking about his father, their relationship and what might have been their future together. He knew his father had loved him dearly and had been extremely proud of him and of his achievements during the very short time they had been together, always encouraging him to be the very best he could be at whatever he was attempting, be it academia, sport or anything else. He fondly remembered their leisure time together playing chess and wistfully regretted that he never managed to win.

His thoughts were broken as he reached the beach where he had been on a number of occasions with his family when they had visited his maternal grandparents, enjoying the warm waters and playing on the sand. Wading up to his waist into the ocean, he gently lowered the container into the water and removed the lid, allowing the seawater to swirl into the tin and wash out the ashes as the tide rolled in and out.

After a few minutes, no evidence of Ramesh's ashes could be seen.

Vijay walked ashore, lay down on the sandy beach and dried off in the sunshine before setting off for home, arriving there just in time for lunch. His young mind was in turmoil on the walk home as he tried to come to terms with all that had happened in the last few days because he knew that he was not old enough to make adult decisions but he also did not want to have his choices dismissed by grown-ups who could do so because of the positions and power that they held.

He resolved that he would always give his opinions on what he wanted to do even if it meant upsetting his mother and grandparents. After lunch, Sunila and her sons returned to Bombay.

Some days later, a letter arrived from the British Army informing them of 'regret at the occurrence of this unfortunate and tragic accident.' A separate letter came from the officer concerned, explaining the circumstances of the incident and intimating that Ramesh was 'a casualty of war.' He did not give his name or rank and had signed the letter as 'A British Officer.'

Three days after Sunila had received the letters, Ramesh's parents committed suicide by hanging themselves from the beams in their house. A double funeral was held but fortunately for Vijay, he was spared from having to take part in the ceremony.

Within weeks of Ramesh's funeral, Sunila closed down the family home in Bombay, which she could no longer afford to keep and took Vijay and Ravi to her parents' small farm in the village of Untdi, approximately one hundred miles north of the city.

Chapter 4

Life in a village was very different to that in a city and Vijay found it difficult to adjust. This village, like hundreds of thousands throughout India, was a collection of wooden buildings with one main street, their locations being close to either a railway station or a river or both. The house he had been brought up in when he was living in Bombay was now replaced by a much smaller single-storey, square wooden building with a pitched roof.

The inside of the house was a single room with no partitions, the rear part being the cooking area during the day, which then converted to a sleeping area at night; the front part being the sitting area in the daytime, which then also became a sleeping area at night.

His mother explained to him that he and Ravi would sleep at the back for the time being but that his grandfather was going to place some planks across the beams to create a sleeping area up in the roof space for him and his brother, with sides to stop them falling off. This was duly done a few days later and a home-made wooden ladder was tied in place. Vijay felt like he was sleeping in a coffin.

Weeks became months and Vijay was becoming unhappy because his life had been completely changed, for the worse as far as he was concerned. He wanted his previous life back and because he knew that this was never going to happen, he became sullen and moody.

As a consequence of this temperamental behaviour, Vijay was constantly being told off by his grandfather who now expected him to help around the farm, as he grandly called it; whereas, realistically to Vijay, he owned a small rice field and two cows, whilst all Vijay wanted to do was to attend school and play cricket.

He also started to resent Ravi, who was treated by his mother and grandparents like a child who had lost everything and therefore deserved all their sympathy, causing his relationship with his brother to deteriorate so much that they only spoke to each other for reasons of necessity and even then, he was very derogatory in his language towards him, calling him stupid when he didn't understand something or an idiot if he could not carry out any tasks or schoolwork.

Sunila could see what was happening but was powerless to do anything about it, having no means to support herself and knowing that she was unable to give Vijay back the life he had been living, she had to accept the situation she now found herself in. This resulted in a situation that caused more friction between her and her father because she blamed him for denying her an education when she was a child, thus preventing her from getting a job.

In order to improve matters for her son, she decided to speak to Vijay and thereby, hopefully, try and find an answer to his problems and therefore resolve the spiralling decline in his behaviour, which was evident to all who were involved in his life.

After a series of long conversations, which always ended with one of them losing control and then shouting at the other, they were still undecided as to the best way forward which made matters worse and Vijay became an even more angry and uncompromising boy, with the result was that he was very argumentative with everyone, especially anyone who, in his eyes, had any position of authority, and was sent home from school on a number of occasions for being disrespectful to his teachers or for fighting with his fellow students, which also meant that he was very quickly losing the few friends he still had.

So after some months of watching her son becoming a bitter and unhappy boy, Sunila decided to take some action. She discussed the situation with her parents and they came up with a plan which they thought might help Vijay to come to terms with his present life.

A day trip to Bombay, but to the area reserved for the untouchables, to show Vijay that his life, though hard and difficult, was not as bad as he thought it was, followed by a reasoned talk, explaining to him that at his age decisions he made now would affect the rest of his life and that he was responsible for his actions would, she hoped, be enough to make him accept that the loss of his father and paternal grandparents was not the fault of those around him but someone else and he had to make his own success story in life despite the difficulties that had been thrust upon him.

Vijay listened to his mother's planned course of action and the reason for it, his mind taking in the words she had uttered, making him realise that his life was miserable for himself and intolerable for his family.

When his mother had finished he said nothing, so after a short time his mother asked,

"Well, do you agree to the trip and do you think it is a good idea?"

"Yes to both," he finally replied, understanding that he needed to change both his attitude towards his family and friends and also his outlook on where he was heading; as his behaviour at this moment in time was not at all productive and was, if anything, destructive. A date was set for the trip and they both made sure their work was completed as much as possible to enable them to take the day off and make the journey.

They caught the early morning train and arrived in Bombay mid-morning, chatting about anything but the reason for the trip. After leaving the station Sunila guided him down streets and alleys that Vijay had never seen before, on which all the dwellings were ramshackle structures providing very little protection from the elements and absolutely no privacy.

After about three-quarters of an hour of walking through this squalid area of cluttered and disgusting residences, they exited onto a vast open space. The look of shock on Vijay's face at what he saw left no doubt as to the dreadfulness of the sight.

What he saw was a huge mound of rotting and decaying garbage, surrounded by men, women and children of all ages, with flies buzzing around in the air and rats running about on the ground, all searching for anything that would give them the chance of surviving another day. As he stood and watched, he noticed the threadbare clothing on the adults, the majority of the children being naked, although some of the older girls were wrapped in clothes that they had found amongst the rubbish in order to cover themselves to try and have some sort of modesty.

Those who had shoes did not have a pair that matched but most were barefoot. Sunila and Vijay stood in silence and watched, for a short while and at a safe distance and then, as if by some co-ordinated thought pattern, they both turned simultaneously and walked away, heading back to the centre of the city where they sat on a park bench in the affluent business district and quietly ate their lunch which Sunila had packed and brought, neither starting up any conversation, after which they made their way back to the train station.

They sat silently on the train journey home, each in their own thoughts, with Vijay thinking about what his mother had said prior to the visit and also now his mind kept bringing up the images of the slums of Bombay and the stench from the rotting rubbish would not leave his nostrils. The visions of the small children foraging amongst the waste of other people, for anything to eat, use or sell in order to try and eke out an existence revolted him.

As he resolved never to end up in that situation, he came to the realisation and understanding that his mother was right, which was that life has to be worked at and success is only achieved by your own actions.

Life-changing luck, good or bad, is for the very few, he concluded to himself. Daily life became a routine for Vijay; up at six in the morning, down to the well for buckets of water, then to sort out milking and feeding the two cows, more trips to the well for water to swill down the latrine-a small wooden building with a deep hole-about fifty yards away from the house, collect the pots [urinal] which had been used during the night and clean them, so that they were ready for the forthcoming night, time for a hasty breakfast and then off to school for lessons. Home from school, more chores, homework and studying and then to bed.

Life was hard and monotonous.

Sunila also found it hard because she had become used to servants coming for two hours a day to help with the domestic chores when she had lived in Bombay. Her daily routine at her parent's home was no easier than Vijay's, just different. Her day was spent cooking and cleaning. She now appreciated even more how hard it must have been for her parents to raise her and her older sister, Nalini, who now lived in the next village with her husband and two children, a boy and a girl.

During the nights when she could not sleep, Sunila often thought how cruel life could be and how one minute in time can result in years of pain and suffering; although, in times of reflection she appreciated that the reverse was also true, such as when after your children are born, they give you happiness and pleasure as you watch them grow and flourish, which then balances the bad times.

The weeks became months and as time moved on, the family became accustomed to their new lives and apart from the occasional incident, all five of them accepted the situation they were in and lived together in reasonable harmony. Vijay and Ravi became more tolerant of each other and actually started playing cricket together after school, when they could, and cards and chess in the evenings.

They all accepted that the lives they were now leading had been thrust upon them, rather than chosen by them. However, the cause of this would never be forgotten. The loss of a husband, son-in-law and father was a life-changing event. Ramesh had left such an unfulfilled promise.

As if the loss of Ramesh was not enough, further tragedy hit the family. Ravi attended the local school with his elder brother but due to the chores that Vijay had to do, they went to and returned from school separately. One day, on his way home, Ravi along with a few friends, as they had done on numerous occasions before, decided to go home through the fields and spend some time swimming in the pond, which was about halfway between the school and the village.

After a while, they all came out of the pond, shook themselves to remove the water and then lay down on the grass to dry off in the hot sun. After an hour or so, they decided to go home and Ravi put his left hand down on the ground in order to push himself up. His hand landed on the body of a snake, a Russell's viper, which being a nocturnal animal, had curled up and was sleeping in the long grass.

The sudden disturbance caused the snake to whip its head round and bite Ravi on the hand, sinking its fangs into the fleshy part at the base of the thumb, unfortunately meaning that the fangs were stuck and as Ravi sprung to his feet, the snake swung from his hand like the uniformly patterned multi-coloured tail on a kite.

Ravi shrieked in pain and shouted for help as his friends, on seeing what was happening, rushed towards him. One of them managed to grab hold of the tail of the snake and as he pulled, it let go of Ravi and the boy was able to fling it into the pond. Ravi's hand was already swelling as they started running back to the village.

They all shouted for help as they ran, which meant that by the time they reached the house there was a small group of villagers already gathered, all wondering what the commotion was about. Whilst Sunila rushed Ravi into the house and laid him down, her father sent Vijay off to the next village, some three miles away, where there was a doctor.

He knew it would take at least an hour for them to return, even though the doctor owned a motorcycle. He turned his attention to the boys and asked them to describe the snake and as they did, his heart started to sink. The snake was one of the more venomous types and the outlook was not very promising. He went into the house and looked at Ravi. Sweating, feverish and a left arm that was visibly thickening; there was an ominous feel about the outlook. Keeping him cool and calm was the only treatment they could offer.

The time dragged very slowly and a sense of panic started to grip Sunila as she realised that her second son and youngest child was about to die and that she was helpless to do anything to stop this. She knelt by his side, clutching his right hand, trying to hold back her tears. The villagers, adults and children, stood quietly watching through the open door.

After what seemed an eternity, the sound of a motorcycle filled the air and then the doctor and Vijay came rushing into the room. Vijay had run as fast as he could all the way to the village and was exhausted, even though he had rested on the way back as he was riding on pillion. As he looked at Ravi and understood that, in essence, his efforts had been in vain, he felt anger building up inside him.

The doctor administered some pain relief to Ravi and then looked up and shook his head from side to side as he faced Sunila. Her face drained as she registered his meaning and then she lay down next to her dying son, put her head on his chest and hugged him.

An hour later, Ravi slipped into unconsciousness and looked peaceful; two hours later his life was over. Sunila remained as she was throughout the final hours of his life. Her father had dispersed the crowd once the outcome was confirmed by the doctor and then he, his wife and Vijay had sat down in the house and silently waited for the final breath of their grandson and brother respectively.

Once Ravi had died, Vijay ran out of the house and down the road. He only stopped running when he was out of sight of the village and then slowed down to a walk. His mind was full of anger towards everything that was happening in his life. He hated God for allowing these deaths to happen. As if losing his father to a murderer was not enough suffering, his younger brother, with whom he should have shared so much in their future lives had now also been taken.

At twelve years old, he felt let down, with no explanation as to what he had done to deserve this. Betrayal, anger, grief, guilt, shame, in fact virtually every emotion possible that was negative, was experienced by him as he walked. He finally stopped walking and sat down on a rock at the side of the dusty track. He knew he had to get away from this life before it was too late.

His father had shown that ambition and determination could open up opportunities, which, in turn, could lead to a better life. As he sat there contemplating his future, a group of boys from the village approached him and told him that they had been sent to look for him as his mother was worried about him. He stood up and they all walked back to the village in silence.

17 September 1934 was another date now etched into Vijay's mind.

Again, Vijay had the unenviable task of setting the funeral pyre alight. He watched his mother sitting quietly, gazing into emptiness as the flames grew and swirled around Ravi's body, almost as if she had given up on living and he resolved that eventually, when he had made a success of his life, he would take her away from here and at least give her something to live for, although he would never be able to replace what she had lost.

He knew he was too young at the moment but the time would come. His mind started to drift as he thought of what might be his future life, whilst still continuing to lead the procession of men around the funeral pyre. Again, the following morning he made the trip to the coast and repeated the ritual he had performed only fifteen months earlier.

This time was no easier than the first time.

The next three years saw Vijay grow into a young man, taller than his father and due to the hard physical life he was having to live, a very muscular and strong one and also into a very determined but sadly, angry and bitter, person. Had it not been for that day trip to Bombay which now kept strengthening his resolve, he knew that he could very well have lost his way. He had finished school at the end of the summer term in 1937 and now spent all his days working on the farm, which was now doubled in size as his grandfather had bought two more cows and another small field on the basis that Vijay would be able to work all day and every day.

He was not happy about this action that his grandfather had taken and made his feelings strongly known to his mother who, however, in order to keep the peace, asked him to be patient and understanding, rather than supporting him as he had expected.

On his sixteenth birthday, Vijay took his mother to one side and told her that he wanted to make a different life for himself by explaining to her that he could not see a future for himself here in this village as he did not want to be a farmer and take over his grandfather's farm.

He also tried to convince his mother that his only chance of success would be to leave the village and acquire a good education from a 'big city college', such as Bombay, which could then, hopefully, give him an opportunity to obtain a scholarship to a university in England. Although there were many universities in India, including one in Bombay, he felt that he could achieve greater success in England.

His persuasive and passionate pleas meant that his mother, eventually, had to reluctantly agree with him and give him her blessing. Vijay then set about putting his plans into motion to start college in September 1938, the start of the next academic year.

His entrance requirements academically would not be of concern to him as he knew that his schooling had been good and he had excelled in all his subjects once he had changed his attitude but financing the move was of major concern as his grandparents and mother were only just barely scratching a living, so there was no chance of any financial help from them.

He decided that the most viable way for him to solve this problem would be to work for a British family, so that he would have lodgings, money and an insight into the British way of life, thus allowing him to be prepared for when he went to England.

He knew that finding such a position was not going to be easy as he also needed to have time off for his college work but he had heard of others, although he did not know anyone personally, who had managed to achieve this, so he felt some optimism.

Vijay decided the best point of contact for him to start along this plan of action was through his father's old place of work, so he arranged an appointment with a colleague of his father's for Friday, 17 December 1937 at 11.30 am, which allowed him to catch the early morning train from Surat to Bombay, a journey of just over three hours and then following an hour's walk from the station to arrive at the head office of the Bombay City and Gujarat Textile Company at approximately eleven o'clock.

Arriving there, he looked at it remembering the building well, having been there on a number of occasions with his father, and noted that it had not altered over the last few years. A large establishment with five floors, he recollected that his father's office had been on the fourth floor. He went in and informed the receptionist of his appointment and was asked to take a seat.

After a wait of just over half an hour, he was taken upstairs and ushered into the office of Gurwinder Singh, an old friend and colleague of his father, who was now also on the fourth floor showing that he had been promoted since the last time they had met and was now at the pinnacle of his career as only the British had offices on the fifth floor.

Mr Singh's office was a small square room with a rectangular-shaped wooden desk in the middle of it, and two chairs, one on either side facing each other. A small square window behind Gurwinder's chair allowed some natural light into the room and a single pendant light fitting with a naked bulb hung from the ceiling.

A wooden set of shelves against the right-hand wall housed a large number of files and documents. Vijay looked at Gurwinder, who gave him a huge beaming smile as he shook his hand. He looked no different to when he had attended Ramesh's funeral and had quietly told Vijay to contact him without hesitation if he ever needed any help, an offer he had repeated when he had come to Ravi's.

He was dressed in the traditional clothes worn by Sikhs and had a white turban on his head. A large man with big hands, he crumpled Vijay's hand with his grip when they greeted each other, causing Vijay to wince through clenched teeth. The usual greetings were followed by a short question and answer exchange, Gurwinder asking the questions and Vijay answering, on how the family was coping.

That being completed, Vijay explained his situation and asked Gurwinder for his help to find someone who might be able to solve his problem. He specifically requested that the details of his father's death were not to be mentioned but all other information could be passed on to anyone who might be able to help. His pride would not allow him to be treated either sympathetically, pitifully or both.

Once the conversation was over, they said their goodbyes and Vijay left the offices and walked back to the station, caught the late afternoon train and arrived home at approximately 9:30, very tired and hungry but pleased that some progress had been made.

To Vijay's great surprise, two weeks later a letter arrived from Gurwinder informing him that he had found a person who might be suitable for him and explained that it would take a few weeks to make the definitive arrangements but he was very hopeful that it would all work out and therefore, because of his optimism, tentative contact could be made between him and this lady and that this lady, although born in England, had lived in India for over thirty years.

Gurwinder had included the name and address of the lady in his letter. Vijay wrote two letters, one to Gurwinder thanking him for all his help and another to Mrs Florence Baldwin, arranging a date and time, which he hoped would be convenient, 10 February 1938 at 3.00 p.m., for them to meet and he also included in her letter some information about his appearance, so that she would recognize him when he arrived.

Chapter 5

Mrs Florence Baldwin had been a widow for fourteen years. Born in 1900, she had come to India at the age of six with her father, Jim Hunter, who was a civil engineer and her mother, Doris, a qualified schoolteacher, who had given up teaching when Florence was born. Working for the railways, her father had accepted a job in India and had travelled out in 1906, taking his wife and daughter with him.

Florence did not see much of her father as he worked away from home for weeks at a time, so spent most of her time with her mother and her nanny, an Indian lady called Kantaben, who had raised her.

Because of this dual attention, she was bilingual, speaking both English and Hindi fluently and was also well accustomed to both British and Indian cultural ways of life.

At the age of twenty-one, Florence had married a young British army officer, whom she had met at the British Club. Captain Clive Baldwin was posted to India in 1919, at the age of twenty-four, having returned to England after serving in Belgium during the 'Great War'; although Clive could not understand why it was called this as there was nothing 'great' about it; to serve as an officer in charge of protection for the workers on the railways and also to prevent any sabotage to the railway network by the so-called 'revolution army.'

His posting was given to him as a reward for his time in Belgium where he had bravely led his soldiers. Like other officers, he had joined the British Club on his arrival in India.

Florence would go to the British Club on Mondays to play bridge, on Wednesdays to 'knit and chat' and on Saturdays to the weekly dance. It was on a Monday, when Florence's bridge partner sent a message saying she could not play that evening that Clive, on overhearing the conversation, gallantly offered to stand in.

They had an enjoyable evening and Clive offered to stand in whenever Florence was short of a partner. Whether by luck or design, two weeks after that evening Florence was informed by her bridge partner that she was no longer able to play bridge on Mondays so Florence asked Clive if he would become her regular bridge partner from now on, to which Clive responded with an emphatic 'yes.' After a few months, Clive approached Jim and asked him if he could court his daughter.

Following a traditional courtship, with Kantaben having the dubious honour of being their chaperone, Florence and Clive announced their engagement during the summer of 1920, with an intention to have the wedding sometime in March 1921 in England.

In order to be well prepared, Florence and her mother travelled back to England in September 1920 to start all the planning. Being an only child and a daughter at that, her parents wished for her to have a wedding to remember, so they tried to arrange everything to be as perfect as possible.

Florence was born in Worcester, a small cathedral city approximately 20 miles southwest of Birmingham and her parents still owned a house there, which is where they would stay until the wedding. The wedding ceremony was to take place in their local church, followed by the wedding breakfast which would be held in a country house in the village of Chaddesley Corbett, a few miles away.

The local country squire owned the house and as Florence's father had been an active member of the local hunt and a close friend, he had offered the house as the venue for the reception and wedding breakfast with a local band being engaged to play the music for the evening. The house was a large Victorian building with formal gardens and a lake, which allowed for some wonderful photographs.

The wedding went smoothly, with the March weather being cold but dry. The previous week had seen a large amount of snow, the narrow country lanes being impassable and Clive and Florence had feared the worst but luck was on their side and all went well. After a brief honeymoon in London, they then went back to India, sailing back with Jim and Doris who met them in Southampton.

With the long sea journeys and the time for the wedding and honeymoon, Clive had been away from India for almost two months and Florence and her mother for just over seven months. Jim and Clive had arranged to travel back to England together, arriving a few days before the wedding.

Clive stayed with the Hunter family until the day before the wedding, then booked into a hotel in Worcester, staying there with his younger brother who was his best man, so that he would not see Florence on the day of the wedding until she arrived at the church.

Whilst all the family were away, Kantaben had been left in charge of the house and was also given the responsibility of preparing it, as it had been agreed that Clive and Florence would live there until Clive's tour of duty finished in 1925, after which they would move to wherever his next posting would be.

The next two years passed without much change in their lives. Florence and Clive had decided to start a family but nature was not taking its natural course, so the patter of tiny feet was not heard in the Baldwin household, causing much disappointment for them all.

Having been told about the beautiful scenery and landscape of Kashmir, the family decided to take a trip there so in May 1923, Clive, Florence and her parents Jim and Doris, packed up their cases and took the long train and bus journey from Bombay to Srinagar, the summer capital city of the state of Kashmir.

The train journey passed through the rice fields of North West India and then on to the Himalayas, a mountain range in northern India, taking over thirty hours. The landscape changed from flat fields to rolling hills and then mountain ranges, with the weather also cooling the further north they travelled.

The final few miles involved taking a bus along a narrow, winding road which gave them spectacular views of the snow-capped peaks of the mountains and also of the rushing icy blue water cascading over the rocks in the valleys below, as the rivers flowed over them, which made them gasp in awe at the sights they were experiencing.

They had arranged to stay on one of the houseboats on the banks of Dal Lake in Srinagar and as they arrived there, they were greeted with the delightful smell of home-cooked chapattis and the many different dishes of Kashmiri cuisine. The staff on the boat served them their meal and afterwards, feeling completely exhausted after their long journey they retired to bed.

The next two weeks were spent touring around the beautiful state of Kashmir, which included canoe rides on the lake, donkey rides into the mountains and relaxing on the houseboat. The holiday gave them all the time to rest, relax and talk about the future. Most evenings were spent playing bridge, with Florence and Clive excelling by scoring better than Florence's parents, Jim and Doris;

showing that, in Florence's case, she had surpassed her teachers, a sentiment that did not go down well with Jim, although he did accept his defeat with good grace. After the ladies had retired, Jim and Clive would sit on the deck enjoying a cigar and talking about numerous topics, politics and sports being the most popular.

The time eventually came when they had to return to Bombay. They set off from the houseboat, their luggage having been strapped onto five donkeys, all led individually by young boys from the town, whilst Jim, Doris, Clive and Florence climbed into a small horse-pulled wagon, travelling to the bus station in a convoy.

Unfortunately, when they arrived at the bus station, they were greeted with the news that there had been a small rockslide on the road which would take a few hours to clear but the good news was that the bus was on the other side of the blockage, so they could travel down to there and then transfer everything over to the bus and still be in time to catch the train.

They set off and made good time to the obstruction. The passengers on the bus who were travelling to Srinagar had already made their way around the rocks and their luggage and belongings were being passed over as the passengers from Srinagar arrived.

Jim and Clive climbed down from the wagon and helped the boys unload their baggage from the donkeys and then load up the bags of the new arrivals to hasten the transfer, whilst Doris and Florence made their way across the rocks to the bus. The other passengers had walked down behind the wagon, carrying their own baggage and they also climbed over the rocks and boarded the bus.

As one of the boys was tying a bag to his donkey, it started shuffling to the side, pushing him towards the edge of the road, over which there was a sheer drop into the valley below. The frightened boy started shouting and tried to stop the donkey but he was no match for the much heavier animal and his bare feet kept slipping on the dusty, gravelly road.

The donkey just stopped at the edge, which meant the boy slipped off and was left dangling over the valley, still gripping tightly onto the rope he had been using, stranded about ten feet down and screaming for help.

Clive, who had witnessed the demise of the boy, ran over as quickly as he could and managed to grab the rope and started pulling the boy up when the loose unfinished knots on the ropes holding the luggage became undone; the baggage slipped off the donkey and careened onto Clive's back, which sent him, the boy and the bags into the depths of the valley, never to be seen again.

Florence and Doris, who along with the other passengers had been watching the commotion, stood in shock, not being able to move, their mouths open in aghast but no sound could be heard emanating. Jim ran over and stood at the edge of the track looking down into the abyss, hoping, although not really expecting that, by some miracle, either Clive or the boy or even both, had managed to hold onto an outcrop, but saw neither.

The other four boys panicked and left their donkeys and ran off back towards Dal Lake. No one knew what to say or do for a few minutes until the driver of the bus broke the silence by saying that nothing could be done and that the train would be missed if they did not leave. Doris, by this time, had gathered herself together and was busy consoling her daughter, who had sunk to her knees and was crying uncontrollably.

Jim reluctantly agreed with the driver and went over and started ushering Doris and Florence onto the bus. The locals who were also travelling on the bus avoided looking at them and sat well away from them, talking quietly amongst themselves about what had just happened. When they arrived at the train station, the driver offered to inform the authorities in Srinagar of the tragic accident when he returned the following day and asked Jim if he could do the same when he returned home to Bombay, to which he nodded his head in acquiescence to the request.

When they arrived back in Bombay, Jim carried out all the necessary administration, including sending the tragic news back to Clive's parents in England.

A memorial service was held at the British Club and then, as is always the case, life went on as normal for everyone except for those directly affected by the tragedy.

After a few months, Florence announced to her parents that she wanted to become a teacher at the army school looking after and teaching the younger children. She had decided that she wanted to fill her time doing something that would benefit the children of the officers and also allow her to begin to build a new life for herself. She had, at this moment in time, no wish or desire to re-marry.

Life in the Hunter and Baldwin house did not change much over the next few years. Florence flourished as a teacher and was held in high regard by both her colleagues and the parents of the children she taught. The children adored her and often cried when they had to leave and change classes.

She was very happy with her life as it was and had decided not to marry again and made it clear to everyone that this was the case in order to avoid any embarrassing situations and because of this clarity, she had both male and female friends with whom she could socialise without gossip or worry.

Although Kantaben was no longer needed as there was no prospect of Florence now having children, she had been kept on, being told that she was part of the family. Kantaben realised how kind Jim and Doris had been to do this as she knew of other friends who had been dismissed after many years of service, leaving them homeless or having to return to their villages with no means of support.

She felt valued and was very grateful for their kindness and generosity. The four of them were living an easy and comfortable life with no great problems to worry about.

Ten years after Clive's death, Jim announced that he was retiring and that he and Doris would be leaving India to return to England. He had assumed that Florence would go with them and was rather taken aback when she informed him that, as she was very happy with her life in Bombay, she had no intentions of leaving.

After a very heated discussion, Jim finally accepted the decision as he was outnumbered because Doris, although very upset by Florence's choice, was more understanding and supportive of her daughter, telling her husband in no uncertain terms that Florence was old enough to make her own decisions. Jim and Doris Hunter packed up their belongings and after a farewell party at the British Club, left India in July 1933.

Florence and Kantaben became even closer as the next few years passed, discussing and chatting away about whatever was happening at the time, having the occasional holiday but spending the majority of their time on housework and gardening. Their house and garden were, by far, the best kept on the street.

Kantaben was more of a mother-like figure and friend to Florence than a servant and they talked a great deal about their personal lives and what the future would hold for them. As neither of them had any children, Kantaben because she had never married and Florence due to natural causes, they often chatted about what it would have been like to have had children and what sort of mothers they might have been, although Florence reassured Kantaben that, as far as she was concerned, Kantaben had been like a second mother to her and a good one at that.

Time was passing along happily for them and they were content with their lot, enjoying their slow pace and leisurely lifestyle. Florence had travelled back to England once in 1937 for a month, to see her parents but could not face seeing Clive's family, so sent them an apologetic letter saying she did not have enough time on this short trip, so would visit the next time she came even though she did have plenty of time, having retired from her teaching position after fourteen years of working at the army school and had settled into a quiet and relaxed life, with hardly any worries or concerns.

Chapter 6

Vijay stood at the end of the cul-de-sac street, looking at the beautiful houses, with their little white picket fences, carefully manicured lawns, ornate woodwork and paved paths. There were three houses on each side of the street and a very large house at the end, which faced back down to where Vijay was standing.

Bicycle and carriage wheel tracks could be seen on the dusty road surface criss-crossing up and down the street. It was 2.30 p.m. on Thursday, 10 February 1938. He knew he was early for his appointment to meet Mrs Florence Baldwin, so he waited and watched, trying to improve his appearance by brushing his hair with his hand to smooth it down, although he could do nothing about his bedraggled look or the shabbiness of his clothes.

As he stood there, an English gentleman in a light brown suit, a white shirt and a broad blue and brown striped tie walked out of the middle house of the three on the right and came towards him, a firm step in his stride and an intense look on his face, indicating that he was not coming for a friendly chat. Vijay anxiously stood his ground and waited.

William Grundy was a few inches shorter than Vijay, of stocky build, thinning brown hair and a small, thick moustache, which was flecked with a number of grey hairs. He had bushy eyebrows, piercing blue eyes and a wrinkled forehead, which gave the impression that he frowned a lot. Vijay guessed his age to be approximately forty five.

When he was about a foot away, he stopped, made eye contact and asked in an aggressive manner.

"What business have you coming to this street and why are you loitering in an area that is reserved for British families? Unless you have a good reason for being here, I suggest you move away quickly."

Vijay, feeling uneasy and slightly intimidated, just stood there, not sure which tack to take and said nothing. William Grundy repeated his question in a much louder and more aggressive tone, adding that if no response was given, he would physically remove Vijay from the street. They glared at each other and Vijay saw the wrinkles on William Grundy's head furrow more deeply as he frowned.

After a few seconds, Vijay, having composed himself, enquired, in his most politest voice,

"Which house belongs to Mrs Florence Baldwin?" even though he already knew which it was from the letter that he had received from Gurwinder Singh, that letter being in his pocket. This was not the response William Grundy had expected, so he took a step back and a puzzled look appeared on his face as he tried to fathom out how, in his way of thinking, this poorly and scruffily dressed young vagabond of a boy knew the name of one of the residents on the street.

Vijay used this moment to deftly side-step past him and briskly walked up the street towards the house, third on the left, which he already knew belonged to Mrs Baldwin. William Grundy quickly gathered himself together, turned round and set off in pursuit of Vijay, catching up with him just as he had opened the gate and let himself into the garden and stepped onto the paved path.

Vijay turned around and closed the gate and stood there facing William, almost challenging him to dare to try and follow. As they faced up to each other, the front door of the house opened and Kantaben came out onto the porch.

"You must be Vijay," she said in a loud voice.

Vijay turned round and nodded his head and started walking up the path towards her. Kantaben looked past Vijay as she walked down the path towards him and gave a polite bowing of the head, followed by a smile, to Mr Grundy and then took Vijay by the hand and led him to the front door of the house. He took off his sandals and followed her inside.

A quick glance back as he shut the door told him that Mr Grundy still stood at the gate with his hands on his hips and a perplexed look on his face. He turned around and looked at the lady in front of him. Kantaben reminded him of his grandmother in her appearance; a small, wrinkled face, hair combed back with a centre parting and a plaited ponytail which had been curled into a bun and secured with hair grips, small rounded shoulders and thin arms.

She was wearing a fitted blouse under her colourful sari. Very tiny in stature, the top of her head was only just level with the roll on his shoulders.

He looked past her into the hallway of the house and beyond. It was more magnificent than Vijay had imagined when he had laid awake at night thinking about his visit. His distant memories of his father's British boss's homes, which he had visited on some social occasions, had given him some inkling of how grand it might be but he was open-mouthed and dumbstruck at the sight he now beheld.

He was standing in a large hall, a round mahogany table, beautifully sculptured and carved, standing on a round, symmetrically patterned Persian carpet, was directly in front of him. Brightly coloured flowers that gave off a delightful aroma, had been beautifully arranged in a glass vase, which stood on a white crocheted doily, which in turn sat on the centre of the table.

Looking beyond the table, he saw a wide staircase, which then fanned out to both the left and right leading to galleried landings. From the hall in which he stood, he could see doors to both sides, which he presumed led to rooms such as a kitchen or drawing room.

Kantaben brought him back from his amazement by introducing him to Florence who had emerged from a room to his left.

If the house had astounded him, then the vision before him took his breath away. Vijay had never seen such beauty. Florence stood there in a calf-length, brightly coloured floral dress, a dainty pair of tan shoes and a thin white cardigan. Her auburn-coloured hair was combed back from her face and tied in a bun, secured by a pretty white and pink clip, small pearl earrings studded her ears and a matching pearl necklace adorned her neck.

He knew that Florence was of a similar age to his mother but there the similarity ended, because his mother, due to the hard life she had lived, appeared a great deal older than Florence. As he looked at Florence, he could see the benefits of wealth and class.

Florence walked towards Vijay and welcomed him to her home, extending her right hand as she approached him and shook his right hand, which he had similarly extended in response to her action. Again Vijay was taken aback, this time at the smoothness, softness and gentleness in the hand.

In contrast, his mother's hands were rough, hard and calloused. Florence let go of his hand and motioned towards the drawing room, the room from which she had just emerged and said.

"Follow me, we will sit in the drawing room whilst Kantaben makes some tea."

Kantaben went the other way to the kitchen which was to the right and Vijay followed Florence into the drawing room, discovering as he entered that it was a large rectangular one with two square Persian rugs laid on the highly polished wooden floor. Two double seater leather settees and a single leather armchair made up the seating arrangements and a mahogany coffee table stood on each rug in front of each double settee and a matching mahogany display cabinet, full of exquisite ornaments and glassware, completed the furniture.

The walls were covered with a pale blue and light cream striped paper with pictures of flowers hung on either side of the oblong-shaped mirror which hung over the fireplace and scenes from England on the opposite side. Windows at the front and back, both having full-length light brown curtains, looked out onto the gardens. A piano stood in the far right-hand corner, angled to allow a view of the back garden through the window for anyone who was playing.

"Would you like to sit down?" asked Florence, gesturing to the armchair.

Vijay, feeling embarrassed about his shabby and dusty clothes said,

"I don't think I should as my clothes are dusty from the journey and I don't want to spoil your armchair, so I am going to sit on the floor."

He walked to the side of the settee nearest the back window and sat down on the floor, away from the rugs.

Florence immediately went over to him and said,

"It will be very rude of me to sit on a settee and to leave you to sit on the floor, so either we both sit on the floor or we both sit on the chairs and as I do not want to sit on the floor, please will you get up and sit on the armchair." She smiled at him and offered him her hand to pull himself up.

Vijay took her hand and pulled himself up, walked to the single armchair and sat down, not understanding the amusing smile that appeared on Florence's face. Someday, I will ask her about that, he thought to himself. He turned his head towards the door as he heard it open and saw Kantaben come in with a tray of tea and biscuits, which she put down on the coffee table nearest Florence.

Vijay sat still, not sure what to do.

"Do you take milk and sugar in your tea?" asked Kantaben.

"Yes please," said Vijay.

Kantaben gave him a quizzical look. "How many sugars?" she asked.

"None," he said, nervously.

Kantaben gave him a knowing smile as she handed him his tea in a china cup and saucer and three biscuits on a matching china side plate. He placed the plate of biscuits on the arm of the chair and held the cup and saucer in his right hand.

Vijay watched carefully and followed Florence in the way she took her tea and biscuits, thereby ensuring that he did not embarrass himself.

He had never been to tea before.

Florence asked Vijay to tell her all about himself and explain why he wanted to live with her and what he wanted to do whilst he was in Bombay. He gave her a short life story, omitting the cause of his father's death and then gave her a pre-prepared speech about his plans for his future, enthusiastically talking about his wish to go to England to study in order to better his life and, if possible, his family's.

Kantaben also listened intently, nodding occasionally as if she understood the difficulties he was having to overcome. He then explained that he was very willing to do anything that he could to earn his keep and that he would be very respectful towards both them and their property. After about half an hour of conversation, Florence brought the meeting to an end and told Vijay she would write to him with her decision, stood up and walked to the door of the drawing room and went out into the hall.

Vijay followed her, thanking her profusely for giving him her time and said that he hoped that he would meet her again. As they reached the front door, the impatient behaviour of a teenager overtook Vijay and he asked Florence why she had given him that 'funny' smile when he had sat down. Florence turned to him and said,

"Gentlemen allow the ladies to sit down first before sitting down themselves," and then with a warm and encouraging smile continued, "But we will teach you all that you need to know." With that, she turned away from him and opened the front door, indicating that it was time for him to go.

Vijay walked down the path, opened the gate and let himself out and then shut the gate behind him. A quick glance in the direction of William Grundy's house confirmed that he was being visually escorted down the street by him from his front window. He was not sure what to make of Mr Grundy.

What he did not know was that both Florence and Kantaben were also watching him from the front window of their drawing room.

The decision was easy for Florence, as the prospect of having a young man around to whom she could give an opportunity to better his life and the fact that he seemed to be the sort of person who would make the most of that opportunity excited her but she asked Kantaben for her views because she knew that Kantaben would give a more down to earth and less romantic perspective.

Kantaben was a little more concerned about the practicality of allowing Vijay to stay, pointing out that there was no real way he could earn his keep, that the neighbours would make up all sorts of rumours and gossip and that with war looming in Europe, the fight for independence in India and the general increase in both the cost and the amount of housework in having another person living with them meant, in her opinion, that it was not the right choice although she conceded that he seemed a very nice and genuine boy and that life would certainly be more interesting, exciting and possibly rewarding if all worked out as it should.

Florence listened carefully to Kantaben, thought about the matter overnight and then concluded that inviting Vijay to come and stay was, on balance, the decision she should make.

She wrote a letter to Vijay, offering him the opportunity and asked that he should arrange to arrive in mid-August if he still wanted to come and stay. She also wrote to Gurwinder Singh, thanking him for giving her this chance to help Vijay and also for considering her to be a suitable person and hoping that she would be able to meet the challenge. She knew she was taking on a serious responsibility and not some charitable cause.

Vijay's future was now, partly, her responsibility also.

Chapter 7

Sunila tried to be enthusiastic when Vijay gave her his exciting news, although a large part of her was sorrowful at the thought of losing her son because she was convinced that once Vijay went to England it was highly unlikely that she would see him again as she was getting older and by the time he had made a success of his life, if indeed he did, she would no longer be alive.

Vijay, on the other hand, could not contain his pleasure and excitement and went about his daily life with renewed vigour and a great deal more happiness and positivity.

He decided that electrical engineering would be his career choice as he was fascinated by the workings of electricity and electrical appliances, especially communication such as radios and telephones, although as there was no electricity in his village and only one person had a battery-powered radio, which worked intermittently, and there were no telephones, he knew his decision was based on dreams rather than informed knowledge.

The next few months passed uneventfully, apart from his grandfather's constant complaining about how he would manage once Vijay had left and that he would never have expanded his farm and livestock if he had known this would happen, after which, on 15 August 1938, Vijay packed all his meagre belongings into a small, battered old bag, which his grandfather had managed to procure from one of his friends, and left for Bombay. His mother and grandparents, auntie, uncle, cousins and some villagers all came to the station to see him off and wish him well.

His mother cried.

He arrived at Florence's home as the sun was setting, again being visually escorted along the street, from his window, by William Grundy. Kantaben, who had also been watching him walk up the street, had come out of the house and was stood on the porch with the front door closed behind her, ensuring that he could not enter, her arms folded across her chest and a stern look on her face.

Once he was in front of her, she looked up at him with a stern and steely eye and in no uncertain terms made it clear to him that if he, in any way whatsoever, behaved in a manner that would bring shame on Florence or her good name, he would be in serious trouble. She explained quite forcefully that the opportunity that he had been given was one to be taken very seriously and not to be squandered as he would never have this chance again.

She then smiled, turned around, opened the door and let him in. Vijay walked in but his thoughts were on what he had just heard. The firmness and intent of Kantaben's monologue had left him in no doubt that she was a lioness protecting her cub and anyone who, in any way, was a threat to Florence would have to deal with her as well.

He was pleased that Kantaben had taken it upon herself to tell him how she felt because he was now also more aware of the rules regarding his stay, not that he had any intentions of abusing the hospitality and generosity that had been extended to him by Florence.

Vijay placed his battered old bag on the floor and then walked through the hall and followed Kantaben into the kitchen, which was full of the wonderful smell of freshly baked buns, all neatly arranged on a plate. Kantaben told him that Florence had spent the day baking in anticipation of his arrival and as he looked at her face, it was clearly evident that she was delighted to see him.

He gave her a big smile and thanked her for all the effort she had made for him and also for agreeing to allow him to live with her whilst he was studying. He assured her that the trust and faith she had placed in him was very much appreciated and that he would not let her down, giving Kantaben a confirmatory smile as he spoke.

Florence welcomed him to her home and then asked him to go to the drawing room. A few minutes later, the two ladies followed with the buns and some tea, which they all then consumed.

Florence asked Vijay about his journey to which he replied that it had been uneventful, explaining that the train was crowded and noisy and he had to stand all the way. They chatted for a little while about what was expected of him and Florence told him a few of the house rules and then she asked Kantaben to clear away and wash up the plates and dishes whilst she took Vijay on a tour of the house.

Vijay followed Florence out of the drawing room, picked up his bag, as Florence had asked him to do and then caught up with her at the foot of the stairs.

They went up the central stairs together, then turned to the right, up a further set of stairs and reached the galleried landing. Florence walked along the landing past one door and on to a door further along, which she opened with her right hand and walked through, beckoning Vijay to follow her in.

"This is your room," she said. "Our rooms are on the other side."

Vijay looked around the room. He had never expected to have his own bedroom. He had assumed that there would be servant's quarters somewhere away from the main house; actually, the building he had seen from the back window when he had been in February was where he thought he would be staying. As he would find out a few minutes later, the building at the back of the property was in fact the latrine.

Vijay's bedroom was a large square room, with a window overlooking the immaculately kept front garden. The room was decorated with blue and green hexagonal patterned wallpaper and plain, full-length matching blue curtains. The wrought iron bed had a bedspread covering the sheet over the mattress, with a pair of matching pillowcases for the two pillows. A far cry from the thin mattress he had at home, laid on the planks his grandfather had fixed to the beams, with a rolled-up towel as a pillow, he thought to himself.

A dark oak double wardrobe and a matching dressing table made up the rest of the furnishings and a patterned rug covered part of the polished wooden floor. A small desk and chair, the newness suggesting they were a recent addition to the room, were against the wall next to the door. Vijay stood rigidly still, unable to rationalise the good fortune that had come his way. He was brought back to the present by the sound of Florence's voice.

"Leave your bag here and come with me, I will show you the rest of the house."

They left the room and went back towards the stairs. Florence stopped by the door they had passed and opened it.

"This is the bathroom," she said, gesturing with her hand. Vijay looked inside at the white enamel-coated cast iron bath with four ornate legs and the matching cast iron pedestal wash basin, which had white porcelain tiles embossed with a wave pattern as its splashback. A mirror was fixed to the wall above the sink.

On the wall facing the door was a shelf on which there was a neatly stacked set of white towels and in the far corner of the room, he saw a square hole in the wall with a shelf and some ropes on a pulley system.

"What is that?" he asked.

"That is called a 'dumb waiter'," said Florence, "It is used to send the hot water up from the kitchen, so that we do not have to carry it up the stairs."

This was a completely new experience for Vijay and as the tour continued, he marvelled at the way of life that Florence and presumably her friends and colleagues, were leading. If I achieve half of this, I will have succeeded, he thought to himself.

Florence finished the tour by taking him outside to the latrine.

The building was almost a quarter of the size of his grandfather's house and as he went in, he was surprised to see two latrines next to each other, one was level with the ground and had two 'footrests', one on either side, so a person could squat and the other was a raised 'box-like' contraption that allowed a person to sit.

"How do you clean them?" Vijay asked.

"There is a water pump at the end of the street which continually takes water from the river upstream and then flushes the water down a sewer pipe on each side of the street and back into the river downstream. The sewer pipes are connected to each house and are about twenty feet down below the latrines," Florence explained.

Vijay accepted the explanation but was not sure that he fully understood how the system worked; however, as there was no pungent smell of human excrement, he was pleased that it did work. They went back into the house and back to Vijay's bedroom.

"Would you like some help to unpack?" Florence asked.

"I do not have much," said Vijay and proceeded to take out one shirt and one pair of trousers from his bag. The remaining contents of his bag were his books, pencils and paper, which he would need for his college work.

Florence felt a lump develop in her throat as she looked at his meagre belongings, so she turned and left the room. Halfway down the hall, she shouted, "I will arrange for Kantaben to send up some hot water for you to have a bath and then come down to the kitchen when you are ready."

Florence went downstairs and asked Kantaben to heat some water so that Vijay could have a bath. This was the first time that Vijay had ever been in a proper bath. When he had lived in Bombay, they had a metal bathtub which was kept in the outhouse and brought in on a daily basis for him and his brother to bathe in before they went to bed. In his village, the boys bathed in the pond.

He wallowed in the water until it became too cold for him, then dried himself on one of the white fluffy towels, put on his clean clothes and went downstairs. He went into the kitchen and saw the two ladies of the house busy preparing a meal.

His offer to help was politely rejected and was followed by an instruction for him to sit down at the table until dinner was ready. They had their food and then Vijay insisted on doing the washing up, ushering them into the drawing room. After washing and putting away the plates, pots and pans, he went to join them.

Florence was sitting on one of the settee's knitting and Kantaben sat on the other reading a book, which he noticed was written in Hindi. They looked up and acknowledged him and then continued their respective activities. Vijay went to the bookshelf and chose a book written in English, sat down in the armchair and opened it.

His eyes saw the words but his brain was not registering them; instead, it was trying to understand and rationalise the situation he found himself in and then apply those thoughts so that he could behave in the best way possible in order to adjust to this new way of life; a life almost completely alien to him and not at all what he had envisaged when he had made his decision to leave his village and move to Bombay.

Excitement and trepidation were only two of the many emotions he was feeling. He mentally made a promise to himself that he would make the most of this opportunity, make his mother proud of him and take her to England to live a life of comfort.

After about an hour, Florence rose from her settee, packed away her knitting and announced that she was retiring to bed. When she had stood up, Vijay stood up too and was pleased to see Florence give him a knowing and appreciative smile, acknowledging that he had made an effort to learn some etiquette before he had arrived.

A few minutes later, Vijay also decided to go to bed. He could not wait to sink into the mattress, pull the sheet over him and dream of his future. For the first time since his father had died, Vijay felt optimistic about his life and where it could lead.

He bid goodnight to Kantaben and went upstairs to his bedroom, got undressed, removed the bedspread and climbed into bed, wrapping the thin top sheet around himself and laying his head onto one of the fluffy pillows.

He soon fell into a deep sleep.

He awoke the following morning and found himself disorientated in his new surroundings. He gathered his thoughts, jumped out of his bed and quickly dressed, rushed downstairs and almost fell into the kitchen. Florence and Kantaben were busy working away at their daily chores and were startled by his sudden and noisy entrance and stared at him, questioning his behaviour.

He profusely and energetically expressed his apologies for oversleeping and promised that it would never happen again to which the ladies just smiled at him and then Kantaben, in a grandmotherly demeanour, told him to stop babbling, sit down at the table and wait for her to make him some breakfast, which this morning was going to be porridge, which she was sure he had not had before.

She was right.

Chapter 8

Vijay was keen to show that he had meant what he had said and volunteered for any and every job that needed to be done. He washed the external and internal paintwork with exuberance, tended to the gardens, under close scrutiny from Kantaben so that he did not dig up the wrong plants, helped in the kitchen by washing up, sweeping and mopping the floor and just about anything he was asked to do and was capable of doing, he did. The ladies were delighted with his enthusiasm.

After a few days, Florence announced that she would be going shopping that afternoon and had arranged for her regular carriage driver from the British Club to pick her up at 2 p.m. She suggested to Vijay that he went with her so that he could go to the college where he would be studying and sort out his timetable and then meet her later at the British Club from where they would then return home.

Vijay was duly dropped off at his future college and given directions to the British Club, which was about a mile away. He went into the college and to the administration office where he introduced himself and explained to the man behind the desk that there had been communication between his school and the college, which had resulted in him being offered a place to study mathematics, physics and chemistry for two years after which, if successful, he would be able to go to England to a university to become an electrical engineer.

The office administrator, a bald-headed middle-aged Indian man wearing thin wire spectacles, withdrew Vijay's file from the filing cabinet, checked the details, confirmed that all the information he had provided about himself was correct and tallied with that given by his school and then informed him that the term started on Monday, September 5th at 9.00 am and that his first class would be physics.

A full timetable would be available on the notice board in the entrance hall from September 1st, so if he wished to, he could come in earlier and make himself a copy. Vijay politely thanked him for all his help and breathed a sigh of relief that everything was in order. He left the building and started to make his way to the British Club.

The streets were busy with men going about their daily business, with the occasional motor car on the road but mostly with horse-pulled carriages travelling in a ramshackle way up and down and beggars sat at all the corners. There were also a few small stalls selling hot prepared food.

The journey took him about twenty minutes and took him past the offices of The Bombay City and Gujarat Textile Company and Vijay, for a moment, contemplated quickly calling in to thank Gurwinder Singh but then decided against the idea, as he did not want to be late and keep Florence waiting.

When Vijay arrived at the British Club, he recognised and remembered it from when he had travelled around the city with his father. A grand building with a chest-high fence and two armed soldiers at the gates, Vijay knew that he was not going to be allowed anywhere close to it, so he waited about fifty yards away but in full view of the soldiers, showing that he posed no threat. There was no sign of Florence or her carriage, so he assumed, quite rightly and thankfully, that he was early.

As he waited, William Grundy appeared from the gates of the club, nodded to the soldiers and then turned to his right, saw and recognised him and strode over to him.

"What are you doing here?" he asked in a brusque voice.

"I am waiting for Mrs Baldwin," he replied.

He then asked Vijay to explain himself. Once Vijay had briefly explained where he had been and what he was hoping to achieve, William Grundy's attitude softened, so much so that he offered him his help if there was anything he could do when the time came for him to apply for a university place in England. Again, Vijay was unsure about Mr Grundy but thanked him and said he would bear this in mind.

At that moment, Florence shouted to him from her carriage as it pulled up outside the building, so he bade his goodbyes to William and ran to the carriage and climbed into the coach. Florence offered William a lift home but he politely refused, saying he would enjoy the stroll in the fresh air and the exercise would be beneficial for him.

As they pulled away, Vijay asked Florence what she knew about William Grundy, to which she replied that she did not know very much about him. The little she did know was that he was the son of a vicar and his wife, from a small town in Lincolnshire, had attended the local grammar school and then went to Cambridge University from where he had graduated with a 'first' in History.

He then became a journalist working for the Times, starting by writing the obituary page and setting the bridge challenge and then becoming the foreign correspondent in Rome. After that post, he became the assistant correspondent in India. The chief correspondent, she explained, lives in Delhi. He could have chosen either Madras or Bombay as his base and chose Bombay but she did not know why he had made that choice.

He had been in India for about ten years, was single and had no intentions of changing that status. He was one of the best bridge players at the club, did not dance but always attended the dances and was teetotal. She then asked him how he had fared at the college, to which he replied that his first impressions were that it was a nice and friendly place and he was looking forward to starting his course. He also told her that all was in place from an administrative point of view for him to start on September 5th.

When they arrived home, Florence asked Vijay to follow her into the drawing room and then handed him the large package she had carried in with her, which was wrapped in brown paper and tied up with string, and politely asked him to open it. Vijay untied the string and carefully opened the parcel.

Inside it, he found five shirts, two pairs of trousers, a jacket, two ties, five pairs of socks, five sets of underwear and two pairs of shoes. He had never been bought new underwear since his father had died and had, in fact, not worn underwear since his old ones had perished a few years ago. His present clothes were hand-me-downs from his older cousin, Hemant.

"Go upstairs and try them on; the shopkeeper said he would change anything that does not fit," said Florence.

"I can't accept these," said Vijay, "I have no money to pay you."

"When you are successful, you can pay me back," said Florence, with a twinkle in her eye, intimating that she would never accept. "Just take them as a gift for the time being."

Vijay excitedly ran upstairs and tried on the clothes. He relished the feel and smell of the new clothes and took his time. He had not worn a jacket since his school blazer when he had been at the fee-paying school in Bombay. His new clothes fitted him well and Florence had made good choices in style and colour, not that either of those elements were of any interest to him as he had no knowledge of fashion, current or past; he was just elated to have new clothes.

He went downstairs and thanked Florence profusely, overwhelmed at her kindness and generosity. Florence told him to calm down and accept the gifts.

"A simple 'thank you' is sufficient," she said. Kantaben, who was stood behind her, smiled at him.

Chapter 9

Vijay started college on the 5th of September and had a rude awakening.

He had always been the brightest boy at his village school and was top of his class every year. Even in the early years after his father's death, when he had been unruly and troublesome, his natural intellect and his previous schooling had been enough to make sure his work was of the highest standard.

He knew this had helped him to keep his place at the school; whereas, he suspected, other pupils of lesser academic ability may well have been expelled for similar behaviour to his because he also knew, by observing how the teachers behaved, that they are always more forgiving with the brighter pupils.

At college, all the students had been in the top five places at their schools and they all wanted to succeed, their intellect being of similar or better standard than his. He no longer was 'the big fish' in a small pond but 'just another fish.' He quickly came to the realisation that he would have to work even harder to achieve the grades he needed to secure a place at a university in England.

With this acknowledgement to himself, his ambition, drive and determination soon ensured that he was among the top students and after a few weeks he settled into college life, feeling relieved that he was coping after the initial shock. His father's observation of many years ago:

"It is better to have a second-class brain and a first-class effort than a first-class brain and a second-class effort to succeed in life," had certainly been of value to him in his present situation.

Meanwhile, Florence and Kantaben discreetly lessened his chores and duties to allow him to spend more time studying.

Vijay also met two boys who had been at his private school when he had lived in Bombay and they rekindled their friendships. The three of them spent time studying together at each other's homes, although Vijay did keep the visits to Florence's house to a minimum as he felt awkward about inviting them to a house that was not his home and also, because they were aware of the circumstances regarding his father's death, he did not want them to accidentally or inadvertently disclose them.

From them, he learnt a great deal about studying techniques and how to make the best use of his time. Again, he recognised the enormous value of wealth and the choices that it gave and pondered on how different his life would have been had his father not been murdered, leaving his family penniless. He may well have ended up in the same college on the same course but the journey would have been much easier and more pleasant with much more recreational fun along the way, he assumed.

Vijay's timetable allowed him Tuesday afternoons free for relaxation and studying. After attending trials, he was chosen to play cricket for the college's first team, which involved him having to be available on Saturdays, which he only agreed to after having obtained Florence's permission, which she readily gave and became, along with Kantaben, one of his regular followers, missing only the occasional game. Both Florence and Kantaben had watched Clive play cricket for the army and were, therefore, well acquainted with the game.

Life was good for Vijay and he started to become more mellowed and his anger and bitterness subsided which made him a better person, although he never forgot what had happened to his father and the plans he had made in his mind to exact revenge on the perpetrator of that crime were still very much in his thoughts, especially at nights.

He knew that he would have to be patient and that it could take many years for them to come to fruition but he was determined that he would succeed. Discovering the identity of the soldier would be the most difficult part but, once that objective was achieved, he believed he could refine his plan to fit in with the situation of the perpetrator, he reassured himself.

After a few weeks, Vijay suggested to Florence that they should spend Tuesday afternoons exploring Bombay so that he could learn more about the city and she could teach him about the 'British' way of life in the city, which, no doubt, would benefit him in the future should he be successful in achieving a place at Birmingham University, which is where he hoped to go. She agreed without hesitation.

For their first Tuesday afternoon trip, Florence arranged for them to visit the dock area. Although Vijay did not say anything to her as she seemed so excited, he did know the area reasonably well, as he had been there with his father on the many occasions when, as part of his job, he had been in attendance to supervise shipments of fabrics to foreign lands.

Florence told him about the passenger ships that travelled the world and her descriptions were so colourful and glamorous that he could only try to imagine what it must be like to travel as a first-class passenger, although she did emphasise that she had never travelled first class herself.

On the third Tuesday afternoon trip, the second one being around the business district, Vijay asked Florence if they could go to a small cricket ground he knew about, where schools played against each other and where he had also played when he had lived in Bombay, and watch the game. Florence agreed, so they set off with Vijay taking the lead.

They arrived about three o'clock, just in time to see the start of the visiting school team begin their innings, who were chasing a total of 126 runs scored by the home team who had batted first. They sat and watched the game for approximately an hour, by which time it became evident that the visiting team would more than likely win as they had scored 87 runs without the loss of a wicket.

Vijay led the way when they left saying he knew of a different route home, which might be shorter. He retraced the same journey that he and his father had taken on the day that he had been one of the visiting team players, also having won the match that day, as they made their way home after the game, not knowing the fate that awaited them. As he turned the corner and walked up the fatal street, he felt his heart beat faster and a cold tingling feeling enveloped his body.

He tried not to shake but was unsuccessful in his efforts. Vivid visions of that fateful day filled his mind and he felt weak and light-headed and his legs started to buckle under him. He only managed to gather himself together by leaning against a house wall for a few seconds and avoided falling over. Florence, who was a little distance ahead of him, did not notice his distress and carried on walking.

When he neared the place of his father's murder, he looked closely at the area.

The groove in the wall of the house where the bullet had struck was now weathered and indistinguishable from the numerous other markings of trauma the building has suffered over the years.

The bloodstain on the ground was also lost amongst the stains of excrement that animals, such as cattle, dogs and cats had deposited over the years and which had been scrubbed away by the residents, leaving just a general discolouration along with similar patches along the street, where the same had happened, apart from the murder.

To all intents and purposes, his father's death could not be related to that spot any more, as all physical evidence of it had been concealed over time by the actions of the residents as they went about their daily lives.

They reached the end of the street and turned right at the corner, heading back in the general direction of the more affluent area of Bombay, where Vijay had been born, beyond which lay the British section. As they walked, they reached a grand building, surrounded by a stone wall which was the height of a small boy. Vijay could see the windows on the front of the house and he tried to imagine which one had been the broken one and whether a pane of glass equated to the price of a life.

"Who lives there?" he asked Florence.

"The Chief of the army, usually a General, who spends approximately two years in India before moving on, and there is a small barracks in the grounds," she said.

"How long do the soldiers stay?"

"It varies on what they are doing but an average term is about three years and then they are posted elsewhere."

"What happens to them when they leave the army?"

"Some go back to their lives in England, others choose to stay and try and find work in India or wherever they are. Mr Grundy would know more about this as he has regular contact with the army so that he can write his pieces for the Times. Perhaps you could ask him if you are interested."

"No, I was just asking, it's not important," said Vijay, not wanting to arouse any suspicions.

They were past the end of the street and were heading towards where Vijay had been born and again his heart began to beat a little faster and his mind started to think as he began formulating yet another plan to try and discover the identity of the officer who had murdered his father and then once that soldier had been found, how to exact his revenge even though he knew that all his thoughts were actually only ideas and not plans as he had no definitive information about his quarry.

His thoughts were broken by the sight of William Grundy walking towards them. They all stopped and exchanged pleasantries after which William explained that he was visiting the general for a chat and an update on the current situation with the military with regards to developments in Europe.

Vijay used this opportunity to ask him if he could visit him sometime and discuss the educational system in England in order for him to prepare for his, hopefully, future studies at university in England.

"I would be delighted," replied Mr Grundy, "I will drop off a note to let you know when I am available after I have checked my diary." With that, he marched off.

As he left, Vijay shouted,

"What rank in the army has a single red diamond-shaped pip on the shoulder?"

"Second Lieutenant," replied William, still in motion towards the General's mansion.

"Thank you," shouted Vijay. Florence and Vijay continued on their journey home and were pleasantly surprised to see that Kantaben had baked some butterfly buns and brewed some tea for them. As he enjoyed his 'afternoon tea', Vijay decided he needed to revisit his father's murder scene.

The following day, he skipped his mid-morning lessons and returned to the street of his father's murder, walking slowly as he tried to recognise anyone he had seen on that fateful day but did not, so he asked one of the residents who was cleaning the area in front of her house if there was anyone around who had lived on the street for more than six years and was shown to a house approximately twenty yards back down the street.

He firmly knocked on the door of the house and waited.

He saw a plump woman appear as the door opened.

They both recognised each other almost immediately and then the woman stepped back with a look of shock on her face and stared at him for what seemed an eternity, before she recovered herself and invited him in, calling to her husband who was sitting inside consuming a drink, as she made way for him to enter her home.

After taking a seat, Vijay started the conversation by thanking them both for the care that was given to him by them on the day of his father's murder and then asked them to relate the events of that day as they remembered them and their sequence. After about an hour he left, having obtained as much information as he could about what had happened and the circumstances of that day, Tuesday 13 June 1933, the day his father was murdered.

He asked if he could come again if he thought of any more questions. They agreed to his request, although they said that they felt sure that they had told him all that they could remember.

He never did return.

Chapter 10

The weeks became months and December was upon them and the talk in the house turned to how he was coping with his studies now that he was nearing the end of his first term, his birthday and Christmas. He told Florence and Kantaben that he thought his college work was progressing well and he felt confident that his aspirations of going to university in England were achievable.

A small celebratory party had been prepared for him by Florence and Kantaben for his birthday, which was another event in his life that had not been marked for some years and again Vijay felt uplifted and happy. Mr Grundy had been invited as he was the only person on the street who had not shown any disapproval regarding Vijay living with them, once he had understood the generous and gracious opportunity Florence had given to him.

The other residents of the street, though polite, kept their distance and showed that they would not condone or encourage the situation of a young man living under the same roof as a widow and would have preferred him to have been accommodated elsewhere, with Florence just providing some form of sponsorship, if she felt that way inclined.

After the meal, Florence gave him her present; a brown leather briefcase with his name stitched inside the flap, to replace the sackcloth bag that he had brought with him, to carry all his books and writing paper when he attended college. As her present, Kantaben had cooked him his favourite Indian meal; Bhindi [okra or lady's fingers], chapatti and mango pickle, followed by rice and dal.

William Grundy gave him a fountain pen and ink. Vijay thanked them all profusely, not believing that he had been so fortunate. He knew that he could have been with a family that would have not been as considerate, caring or as generous as Florence. He now fully appreciated the 'talk' he had been given by Kantaben and her 'threat', should he misbehave.

After the meal, they played card games such as whist as Vijay could not play bridge. The evening went so well that, at Florence's suggestion, they decided, allowing for flexibility with regard to their individual commitments, that they should all get together once a fortnight, either at Florence's house or William's, to play bridge so that Vijay could learn.

This arrangement suited everyone and over the coming months, many a pleasant evening was spent by all, with Vijay picking up the game of bridge very quickly, although he was never a match for William. He always partnered Florence with William partnering Kantaben, who had been taught by Jim and Doris at the same time as they had taught Florence.

But, as seemed the way that Vijay's life was evolving, nothing remained stable.

Chapter 11

Florence received letters from her parents on a regular basis, informing her about how life was in England, but in the more recent ones she could glean from the tone and general language that her parents were worried about the political situation in Europe and that a probable war was looming. They urged her to come back to England as they felt that the situation in India was also deteriorating and that her safety would be compromised, especially as she was a woman on her own.

She talked over the problem with her friends at the British Club and discovered that many of the women and children were going back to England, leaving the men behind, so after much thought, deliberation and discussion, especially with Kantaben and William, and witnessing all the turmoil in Bombay and the general unease of the British administration in trying to guarantee the safety of its subjects, Florence reluctantly decided to return to England.

The wrench for her to leave was even harder than she had imagined.

After much thought about the logistics involved, a decision to leave on the first available ship in June 1939 was made and the mammoth task of packing up her belongings was started. A lifetime of memories was stored in that house; childhood, adolescence, marriage and Kantaben.

Florence decided to offer Kantaben the option of going to England with her but knew deep down that this offer would most likely be rejected, as she was getting on in years and would not easily adjust to a new life in England. After a long discussion interspersed with many emotional tears and hugs, the solution they arrived at was for Kantaben to continue living in the house with Vijay until he finished his studies and then the house would be sold and the proceeds transferred to England.

On the assumption that Vijay secured a place at a university in England, Kantaben would then return to her village and Florence assured Kantaben that funds would be made available for her in her 'retirement.'

Vijay was very happy with these arrangements as they gave him security and kept alive his dreams for his future. However, he did wonder how Florence could afford to do all she did for both him and Kantaben, resolving it in his mind by assuming that all British people were rich and that, indeed, the streets of England were, in fact, 'paved with gold.'

He could not wait to go there.

The day of separation arrived and the tears of Florence and Kantaben flowed freely, mingling together as they kissed each other on their cheeks. The prolonged hugging became more intense as the time moved on towards the departure. Reassurances of regular communication were promised and the final hugs were exchanged just before the carriage arrived to take them all to the port.

William, along with many of her friends from the Club, the school and the bridge group, had come to the port to see Florence off. After a final hug from Kantaben, she boarded the ship along with the other passengers and then found a space on the promenade deck from where she could see William, Kantaben, Vijay and her friends. The luggage having been stowed away, the ship set sail after all the passengers had boarded and as it started to move, the waving of hands from both land and sea took on a vigorous fervour.

Once the ship became a distant speck, Kantaben and Vijay returned home and William went back to his office.

Chapter 12

The journey took three weeks to sail from Bombay to Southampton, via the Suez Canal, which connected the Mediterranean Sea to the Red Sea, with Aden, Alexandria and Gibraltar as some of the ports where the ship docked to refuel and replenish its supplies. Florence was travelling second class.

Jim was waiting for her at the port of Southampton and together they travelled back to Worcester by train via Birmingham. From Worcester, they caught a bus to Bromsgrove, which is where Jim and Doris had moved to two years earlier, just after Florence's last visit. Arrangements had been made for her luggage to follow by road which would take three days as the haulage firm would be making a number of other drop-offs on the way north from Southampton.

Doris was overjoyed at seeing her daughter again and, like all mothers, assumed that no matter what age their children are, they are unable to look after themselves and therefore had spent the last few days baking and cooking in preparation for her daughter arriving home.

Jim and Doris lived in a detached house on a small housing estate a mile from the village centre, with a small front garden and a drive, which had a car parked on it. The house had an entrance hall with stairs which led to three bedrooms and an indoor bathroom and toilet whilst the ground floor had a front room, a dining room and a kitchen from which there was access to the large back garden.

On the train journey, Florence had talked to her father about her future and had explained that, although Clive's army pension was more than sufficient in financial terms to provide for her, she needed to find employment of some kind to keep her occupied. Jim explained to her that work was not easy to find at present as the country was going through difficult times but her teaching experience would stand her in good stead and as Bromsgrove was an expanding town, a teaching job should be relatively easy to find.

However, the outbreak of war in Europe changed all their lives.

Chapter 13

The immediate impact on Vijay when war was declared was minimal.

Although the talk on their street was all about the war, with William Grundy becoming more and more the man of all knowledge because of his regular communications with England, Vijay's life continued as before. He went to college as usual and continued with his daily chores, with the most significant change being that he no longer had the same opportunity to question William about the army, and without arousing suspicion, to try and ascertain the identity of the soldier who had murdered his father.

Over the next nine months, other changes did take place. William Grundy spent more and more time in his office, reporting back to England on the war in Asia (Japan and China had been in conflict for two years and this was now escalating) and to the British in India about the war in Europe and how, as a British colony, Indians were becoming the 'second' army and Indian resources were being used to make armaments to support the war effort.

Kantaben became ill with suspected chronic lung disease and was struggling to maintain the house and Vijay's grandfather had died following a heart attack. Vijay's uncle, Bhupendra, his auntie, Sunila's elder sister Nalini, and their two children, Hemant their son and his younger sister Gita, all moved back to Untdi. Bhupendra continued his employment as a guard on the railway and the two sisters ran the farm, which was a relief for Vijay as he had thought that he would be expected to pick up the mantle and return to tend to it.

Vijay completed his studies and passed out of college in May 1940 with grades good enough to study in England. He asked two of his tutors for references with the intention of applying to Birmingham University to study electrical engineering and without hesitation, they both gave him glowing reports. He then contacted William Grundy for advice with regard to his application, who suggested that he wait as the war in Europe was escalating and he felt that this would not be a good time to apply.

Reluctantly, and with great disappointment, Vijay accepted the advice but another blow had been struck to his belief in God. He felt that the small amount of faith he did have left, having been brought up in an actively religious family, was now barely a minuscule and he struggled to accept and understand how his mother had continued for so long and so strongly with her faith.

He discussed his predicament with Kantaben who, in his perception, always spoke objectively and wisely and, he believed, would not make judgements on a selfish or sentimental basis but, after their discussion, sadly for him, she agreed with Mr Grundy, so Vijay let the matter drop for the time being, hoping that the wars across the world would end quickly and life could resume as he had planned and envisaged.

Chapter 14

Vijay went to see Gurwinder Singh in order to find some employment as he was now a person with time on his hands and no formal plan for his future, that having been floundered and dashed by the outbreak of war. Unfortunately, he informed Vijay, there were no jobs available within the Bombay City and Gujarat Textile Company but he promised to make enquiries through colleagues and friends and would contact him either way in two weeks' time.

The only jobs that were forthcoming were labouring ones at the port and Vijay started to become despondent and disillusioned with his future life, although he did accept a position at the port loading ships. At the same time, Kantaben was becoming more ill and a visit to the doctor, followed by chest x-rays and blood tests, resulted in the devastating news that she had terminal cancer with only months to live.

Vijay cried for the first time since the tragic death of his father, which made him feel even guiltier as he had not cried at the death of his brother, being so angry at the time, or of his grandfather with whom his relationship had been volatile initially, followed by acceptance latterly. Vijay wrote to Florence with the sad news, adding that he would look after Kantaben.

A few weeks later he received a reply saying that she would not be able to come to India because of the dangers involved, that he must keep her informed as much as possible and that William Grundy would sort out any problems, financial, medical and administrative, to whom she had also written, knowing that he would need help.

Vijay gave up his job after only a couple of months and took on the task of looking after and caring for Kantaben and also cooking, cleaning and gardening. She gently scolded him on a daily basis, saying he was better at academia than domesticity and that he should make sure he chooses his future wife well.

They talked openly together, mostly in the evenings, discussing their lives and Kantaben tried to make Vijay understand that his life was there to be lived and he must take any and every opportunity he could, as memories are always better than dreams and that calculated risk-taking was always better than regrets.

She explained to him that success is achieved at many different levels and in many different areas of life, including material success, although that seemed to be the area that the majority of people think is the most important, and that a happy and fulfilling life is achievable if you are grateful and content with what you have, material and immaterial, whilst still having realistic goals and ambitions to aim for.

As an example, she quoted her own life, saying that she was grateful she was taken in by Jim and Doris to look after Florence, content with devoting herself to her, was never short of food and not having children of her own was compensated for by bringing up first Florence and then latterly him in his most important developing teenage years.

She told him that few people have everything, if indeed, anyone does. Vijay did not agree with everything she said but, respectfully, listened and only responded with comments that he knew would not cause her any distress.

Kantaben deteriorated faster than the doctor had predicted, so Vijay, after seeking and then receiving Kantaben's permission, sent for his mother, as they both realised that feminine care was going to be needed. This was the first time that the two women had met and although they were very polite with each other, Vijay sensed the tension, especially from his mother, who was meeting the woman who had been looking after her son for almost the past two and a half years.

His mother thanked Kantaben for all that she had done and Kantaben praised Sunila for bringing up such a well-balanced and industrious boy, especially considering that he had lost his father at such a young age followed by the tragic circumstances of his brother's death, although she did not know how his father had died as Vijay would not say.

Sunila did not enlighten her either.

They all agreed that Sunila was to have Florence's room, which was next door to Kantaben's and within earshot so that she could be attended to quickly. During the day, Kantaben would sit in the armchair in the drawing room and Sunila and Vijay pottered about doing work around the house, constantly taking turns to spend time with Kantaben. As she became weaker, Vijay would carry her up and down the stairs when she wanted to go to bed.

Kantaben died peacefully, during the early hours of Saturday 19 April 1941, in her room, twelve days after Sunila came to stay. Sunila returned home to her village two days after Kantaben's death, once all the preparations of the body had been completed.

Kantaben's funeral took place in the village of her birth with her younger brother, her only surviving relative, making all the arrangements. Sunila offered to go with Vijay but he told her that he preferred to be alone. Unlike the three funerals of his father, brother and grandfather, this time he would not be lighting the funeral pyre.

He also felt that one stranger at the funeral was more than enough. William Grundy had very graciously sent word to Florence through his office but, as they thought, it was impossible for her to make the journey in time for the funeral.

William did not go to the funeral either as he knew it would be inappropriate for him to attend; a single middle-aged white man at a single, admittedly old, Indian lady's funeral would cause unnecessary rumour and gossip and would be totally unfair to Kantaben and her family.

Vijay returned to Bombay on the same day as the funeral. The empty house was eerie and disconcerting. He made himself a light meal and then stayed up all night, sitting in the single armchair, the same one he had first been asked to sit in when he came on 10 February 1938, remembering as much as he could of all the times he had had with Kantaben, including the warning she had given him.

Although he loved his mother more than anyone else in his life, he knew that Kantaben would always hold a special place in his heart, because she had been more of an advisor on how to reach his goals, whilst his mother, although still wanting the best for him, was prejudiced because she also did not want to lose her son.

He reflected on all the talks they had, especially after Florence had left, discussing his future and his plans. On a number of occasions, because he would have liked to have known what her perspective would have been, he had almost told Kantaben about the circumstances of the death of his father and his desire for revenge but always desisted when the time came.

He now wondered what her advice would have been. He felt almost sure that it would probably have been for him to accept the incident as an accident and not to let the matter become an obsession. As he sat contemplating, he accepted that, because he was committed to achieving his goal of revenge, no matter how long it took, this was the most likely reason the subject was never broached by him.

He knew from discussions they had had on many diverse topics such as sport and war, where she had taken the view that sport could have winners and losers but war only had losers and the contest was about who lost the most or least, no favourable outcome would be possible. Vijay did not agree with her view about war because she did not take into account the reasons for the conflicts, whatever they were, but accepted her premise.

He was sure that, for the same reasons, she would have seen his desire for revenge as an act of malfeasance and would have tried to dissuade him from his actions. The morning light started to shine through the window, bringing Vijay back to the present, so, realising that there was a lot to do, he got up out of the armchair and set about packing up Kantaben's belongings, ready for her brother to collect the following day.

Chapter 15

Florence's letter to Vijay, which arrived about two weeks after Kantaben's funeral, completely took him by surprise. After expressing her sympathies and sadness at the death of Kantaben, and her regrets at not being able to attend her funeral, she went on to say that she wanted Vijay to send his application to Birmingham University as soon as he could in order to secure a place to start his course at the earliest opportunity, and that he was to make arrangements to travel to England, to then get a job and live there until he could start his studies.

He could continue to live in the house until then, after which she would ask Mr Grundy to sell the house once he had left. She also told him that she would send regular funds to him until he arrived in England.

Clutching the letter tightly in his hand, he ran across the street to Mr Grundy's house and knocked on the door hoping that he was at home. The door opened and Vijay almost fell over the threshold in his excitement.

"Whatever is the matter?" Mr Grundy asked.

Vijay handed him the letter without saying anything. After he had finished reading it, William Grundy handed back the letter, rubbed his chin with his left hand and quietly stood there. After about a minute he said,

"I know someone in Birmingham who might be able to help you to find some work. You get on with your application and I will try to find you a job." With that he ushered him out, giving Vijay the impression that time was pressing and was not to be wasted.

Chapter 16

Communication between England and India, because of the war, was taking much longer than normal, so by the time Birmingham University agreed to offer Vijay a place to study Electrical Engineering, following all the form filling and the verification of his academic achievements, providing proof of his date of birth in the form of an affidavit, as he did not have a birth certificate, and the documentation for his travel arrangements, it was mid-October 1941.

After completion of all the administrative work, an agreement was reached between Vijay and Birmingham University stating that he would start his studies in September 1942. Funding for his course was in the form of a scholarship given by GEC [General Electric Company] in return for a five-year commitment by Vijay to work for them as an electrical engineer after qualification.

He also had to make a legal agreement that should he fail to qualify or not complete his studies, the money would have to be repaid to the company. The negotiation of this contract was carried out on Vijay's behalf by Jim, who had graduated from Birmingham University in civil engineering many years ago and who also agreed to be his guarantor, an act of trust that Vijay was very thankful for.

In the meantime, William Grundy had managed to secure Vijay a job in a factory, HP Sauce, which made ketchup and sauces. He would be employed as a general labourer sweeping up the glass and debris as his main duties but also to help out in other jobs if necessary. The factory was in Aston, a suburb of Birmingham and William, through his contacts, had also found him accommodation in a house only a few hundred yards away from the factory.

The job was to start on the first Monday of January 1942. He told Vijay that the General Manager was the cousin of one of his fellow students at Cambridge and although he had not personally met him, he believed him to be an honourable man. Vijay made his travel plans to arrive in England on 27 December 1941.

He went to visit his family in Untdi a couple of weeks before his departure, provisionally hoping to sail on December 6th. This was a very emotional affair and Sunila could not stop crying. Vijay promised that he would write to her on a regular basis and also told Bhupendra that if all went well and he did make a success of his life, he would arrange for Bhupendra and his family to come to England, if they wanted to.

Back in Bombay after his visit home, Vijay went to see William Grundy.

They chatted for a while about life in England with Vijay asking many questions and William trying to answer them before Vijay finally changed the conversation and profusely thanked him for all his help and then politely asked him why first Florence and then himself had been so kind and generous to a complete stranger, especially as Florence had actually only spent nine months with him, although it was sixteen months in total between when she first met him and her leaving for England. He also asked if there had been any other boys who had asked for similar help and why, if there had been, Florence had chosen him.

William told him that as far as he was aware, there had been no other boys and that he had no idea why Florence had been so financially supportive to him, except that he knew her to be a wonderful, caring and generous person. As for himself, he had realised since their first encounter when he had thought him to be a 'street youth up to no good', that he had been totally wrong and that, in fact, he was a 'very nice young man who was seizing an opportunity that he was fortunate enough to have been given.'

This realisation had made him want to do as much as he could to support him in achieving his goals. After this explanation, he ended the conversation by arising from his chair and leaving the room, returning a few seconds later with a warm wool overcoat, which he handed to Vijay.

"Florence asked me to give this coat to you because the weather in England will be very cold when you arrive in December. It belonged to Clive, her husband but it has never been worn as they bought it in Kashmir when they were there on holiday and as you know, he died on the way home from that trip. She gave it to me the day before she left, knowing you would have refused to accept it if she had given it to you herself and I have bought you these gloves, a scarf and a hat," he said, pulling them out the paper bag which he had also brought in.

Grateful as he was, Vijay struggled to understand all this generosity, already knowing that Florence had paid for all his travel costs. He did not know anyone else who had been so well treated. Was this God's way of redressing the traumas he had suffered? Did God even exist? Why him as opposed to someone else? What about all those people he had seen at the rubbish site?

All questions he could not answer along with many more. He resigned himself to accepting the way things were happening and resolved to make the most of the opportunities he had already been given or any more that came his way.

Two days before he was due to travel, Vijay went to visit Gurwinder Singh. They met in his office and chatted for some time about a number of topics, including Ramesh and his tragic death, cricket, Ravi and his death and finally Florence. Vijay wanted to know how Gurwinder had found her and why he thought she had been so generous and accommodating. Gurwinder explained that, after Vijay's visit, he had approached his English superior, who had mentioned the situation at the British Club, which resulted in Florence indicating that she would be willing to help if possible.

As to her financial generosity, he had no explanation except that, seeing how well Kantaben had been treated as well as himself, she must just be a generous person and obviously could afford to be so. With no more meaningful information forthcoming, Vijay thanked Gurwinder for all his help and then left the office and went home.

December 6th arrived and Vijay gathered his belongings together, somewhat more substantial than the day he had arrived, packed them into his suitcase and carried them out of the house. He turned around and had a final look at what had been his home for the last three years, three months and twenty-one days and reflected that his time there had been a happy time for him, with the exception of the sad loss of Kantaben.

He saw William Grundy coming over followed by the carriage he had organised to take them to the docks. He was carrying an envelope in his hand. "There is £5 in this envelope," said William, "It is your twentieth birthday in two days time, and you will need some money until you start being paid. I hope it will help you to start your new life in England, so this is a joint birthday present and a leaving present."

"I can't accept so much money and I do have some money that Kantaben gave me before she died," Vijay said.

His remonstrations were to no avail so Vijay assured William that if he made a success of his life, both he and Florence would be reimbursed with interest. William smiled and then picked up Vijay's suitcase and loaded it onto the back of the carriage, after which they both climbed onto the passenger seat and the driver then flicked his reins, which livened the horse into motion and they set off for the docks.

Vijay looked back down the street and again reflected on the happy time he had experienced whilst he had lived there and then wondered if he would ever see the house again. A mixture of thoughts; worry, anxiety, fear and excitement filled his head as the carriage turned the corner and trundled away.

On the journey to the docks, Vijay and William chatted about what he could expect when he arrived in England, which worried Vijay even more, resulting in him not being able to make up his mind whether the conversation had been helpful or not as it brought up as many concerns and worries as comforts and reassurances.

On arrival at the docks, Vijay collected his one piece of luggage from the carriage and then shook William's hand. They said their goodbyes and wished each other well and Vijay thanked William for all his help, saying he looked forward to meeting him again either in England, if William decided to visit home or in India, if he returned.

Chapter 17

The ship sailed out of port and as Vijay watched from the promenade deck, the buildings of Bombay became smaller and smaller and the expanse of the Indian Ocean became larger and larger until all that Vijay could see was water. He walked along the deck towards the bow of the ship as far as he could and then looked over the rail and watched as it furrowed through the sea towards the Arabian Peninsula where the first port of call would be and stayed there until dark after which he went down to his room on the passenger deck.

As this was a cargo ship, his accommodation was very basic. There were only about twenty passengers on the ship and they had to share the same amenities as the crew. Florence had offered to pay for his travel on a passenger ship but Vijay had insisted on the cheapest passage. Gurwinder Singh had used his influence to secure him as best a cabin as possible, so he was only sharing with one other passenger, but as far as the other facilities were concerned, they were the same for everyone except the captain and his two officers, who had their own cabins and separate dining arrangements.

The journey took three weeks and was boring, with little to do for the passengers.

Vijay did talk to a middle-aged man who was with his wife and daughter; they were travelling to London to live with his brother and his family, who had moved to England five years ago.

However, they did not really make any meaningful friendship as the man was much older and had no ambition other than to give his wife and daughter a better life, which was a noble one to have, especially as he had no education or money but for Vijay who had grander visions, he wanted to meet people with motivation and a desire to be as successful as they could be.

They did politely agree that they would keep in touch and the man gave Vijay his brother's address, although Vijay explained to him that he did not see any point in giving his address as he was not sure how long he would be at that location.

The ship docked in Southampton during the early hours of Saturday, 27 December 1941 after an uneventful journey considering that there was a war going on in Europe. As Vijay disembarked the intense cold hit him, and his face, the only exposed part of his body, felt as if it was being attacked by thousands of needles.

He had never felt cold like this before. He wrapped his coat tighter around himself, silently thanking both Florence and William for their generous gifts of warm outdoor clothing and also now pleased with himself that he had accepted them.

After completing the administration and immigration process, he was directed to make his way to the passenger pick-up room and to take a seat there while he waited for his friends or relatives to arrive, which he duly did. He noticed the middle-aged man and his family come in a few minutes later, struggling to manage the four large suitcases and a number of smaller bags that they had with them.

He wistfully looked down at his single case. A few more people followed them in and settled down, all assuming or knowing that it would be some time before they would be met.

Gradually as friends and relatives arrived to pick up their companions, the numbers dwindled down again until only Vijay was left. He was thirsty and hungry but did not want to spend the money he had as he was unsure about his future income and wanted to remain cautious. At around midday, Florence and Jim walked in and Florence ran to him and gave him a huge hug, almost squeezing the breath out of him. She then introduced him to her father, who gave him a firm handshake and warm greetings.

Jim told Vijay that the journey from Bromsgrove had taken over seven hours and knowing that he would be exhausted, he had made arrangements for them all to stay overnight in a lodging house in Southampton, planning to set off home after breakfast the following day.

Vijay picked up his suitcase and followed Jim and Florence to Jim's car. After placing his bag in the boot of the car alongside their overnight cases, he then climbed into the back seat and they all set off for the boarding house. To Vijay's immense joy, Florence then opened up the small hamper which she had taken from the back seat and placed on her lap and took out of it a plate on which there was a cheese sandwich and a piece of cake and passed it to Vijay and then poured him a hot mug of tea from a thermos flask.

Vijay placed the plate on the seat next to him as he was sat in the back and having taken his gloves off, nursed the cup of tea in his hands, feeling the warmth spread through his fingers and palms. After a few seconds, he sipped the tea, enjoying the heat as much as the taste as it travelled down from his mouth to his stomach.

The journey to the boarding house took about half an hour and by then Vijay had consumed his food and drink. As they drove, Vijay saw the devastation that the bombing by the Luftwaffe had caused, Southampton being one of their major targets. He began to appreciate and understand how great an impact the war was having on civilian life in England, especially in the more important and strategic locations, such as ports, cities and industrial sites and hoped the war would end soon so that the people could again lead more normal lives.

On arrival at the boarding house, they checked in and then decided to go to their respective rooms to unpack, with Jim adding that he was going to have a lie down as he was tired and would meet them at seven o'clock for dinner, which, he grumbled, would, by his reckoning, undoubtedly be a meagre affair and after the blackout.

Florence and Vijay arranged to meet in the sitting room in about ten minutes to have a chat, which they duly did.

Having caught up on Vijay's time back in India, Florence congratulated him on his achievements and then went on to tell him about England and how hard it was to manage with all the rationing and the bombing. She told him how her father had spent weeks begging and borrowing from friends to collect enough fuel to make the journey to come and collect him.

As he listened to her, Vijay began to worry even more about his future, wondering how he would manage with all that was happening in England. He had been aware of the impact on India of the war and how millions of Indian soldiers had taken up arms to help the British and how the supply chain of goods and munitions to England from India had been a vital component of the war effort in Europe, but he had not fully understood the enormous toll the war was having on the indigenous population.

According to Florence, the constant bombing was not only causing physical destruction but was also demoralising the people. Air raid warnings were common every night, with the wholesale evacuation of homes to underground shelters, followed by the fear of whether their home had been destroyed or not, had led to a drop in their spirits, though she did add that the feeling of unity and togetherness was probably at the highest level in the history of the country.

After a while, Florence asked Vijay if he wanted to go for a walk to stretch his legs but he politely refused as he was only just beginning to warm up, so they continued chatting for a little while longer. Florence talked about her job as a primary school teacher, which she felt was as much about caring for the children as teaching them because of the war and the loss of life or injury to people close to them, be it family or friends.

She explained to him the difference between the adults, who worried about the war and its implications, and the children, who only saw the excitement and the danger. On many occasions, the parents, especially the mothers, would forego their own meals in order to feed the children, a story not alien to Vijay as his grandmother and mother had done the same in difficult times. He marvelled at the resilience of mankind and how it faced up to adversity so well.

After an hour or so, Florence rose from her armchair and said she would now retire and they should all meet at seven o'clock for dinner, as arranged by her father. Vijay sat for a while longer thinking about their conversation before doing the same.

Sitting at the small table in his bedroom, he wrote a letter in Gujarati to his mother, informing her that he had arrived safely and would be in Birmingham by the time she received it. He did not go into any details about the intense cold or the war's devastation, knowing she would only worry.

He then wrapped himself up, went downstairs, asked the landlady where the nearest post office was and set off into the cold afternoon. The trip should take no more than an hour he estimated, from the information and directions he had been given.

Vijay had always been aware of racism but had never really experienced it as personally as he did that day. When he was growing up in India, his experience had been that most of the British residents behaved with superiority, arrogance and aloofness, treating the indigenous population as servants with only a small minority of them being violent, aggressive or abusive. The British knew that they held power in India but also that this authority was being challenged and that their position was weakening.

Walking down the street towards him on his first day in England was a young woman pushing a pram who as she passed him, gave him a glaring stare and said in a loud voice, so that people in the immediate vicinity could hear, "Go home you wog, you don't belong here, go back to where you came from."

Then she raised her head and smiled, looking right to left, showing the pedestrians in the street that she was proud of her actions and then walked on jauntily down the street. Those people who felt uncomfortable about the situation turned away from looking at him and continued about their business, the remaining others smiled to show that they were in agreement with the young lady, except for one middle-aged man who shouted, "Well done, Mrs! You tell him."

Vijay felt humiliated.

Knowing that there was nothing he could do in response to this abuse, Vijay lowered his head and gritted his teeth, trying not to show his anger and quickened his step to get to the post office as soon as possible, post his letter and return to the relative safety of the bed and breakfast house. His steely determination to succeed in life was now further strengthened by this humiliating episode.

He felt certain that this racist behaviour towards him would happen again and maybe on future occasions, with more serious and violent consequences, so he told himself he needed to be better prepared to deal with it, although at this moment in time, he did not know how he would do this.

The post office, with its red pillar box outside and a sign attached to the wall, was now visible and Vijay sighed with relief, ran the remaining distance and entered the building. Inside was a small area for stationary and cards on one side of the room and a counter on the opposite side where people were queuing for the postal services.

Vijay joined the queue and stood with his letter in one of his hands and some money in the other in order to pay for his stamps. The plump middle-aged woman in front of him shuffled forward to create a larger gap between them, not unnoticed by Vijay, who now started to feel very uncomfortable.

Thankfully, the queue moved quickly and Vijay conducted his business and left the post office in a matter of minutes, put his head down and returned to the boarding house as fast as he could, keeping well away from any other people, crossing the street on one occasion to avoid walking past a man.

He went to his room, took off his coat, scarf, hat and gloves and lay down on the bed, his mind agitated, digesting the events of the last hour and struggling to come to terms with the prejudice that was blatantly being exercised towards him, exactly opposite to the way Florence and Jim were behaving.

This was a situation he was going to have to learn how to combat because he, following this experience, felt like this was going to be only the first incident in probably a lifetime of racial prejudice and abuse in his newly adopted country.

He lay there thinking, his thoughts moving on to the political battle between India and England with regard to the fight for independence and also Gandhi's attempt to delay the process so that England could concentrate on the international war taking place throughout the world, an action which did not suit the agendas of the Sikh's and Muslim's.

He could see no favourable solution for any party but as a 20-year-old, he told himself that he was not really knowledgeable enough to fathom all the intricacies of the discussions and be able to untangle the situation when greater minds than his were tackling the problem without much success.

Time moved on and with only an hour before they were to meet for dinner, he sat up and then got off his bed in order to start getting ready to go down for the evening meal. His room was only lit by an unshaded single pendant light fitting and with no street lighting due to the government's curfew, Vijay's gloominess was equally matched by the room.

He went to the bathroom and had a quick wash before getting changed. He decided not to tell Jim and Florence about his recent experience as he knew it would only upset them, especially Florence.

This was his burden, not theirs, he told himself.

He went downstairs to find Jim standing waiting in the front room. They exchanged the usual greetings and then sat down to wait for Florence with Jim asking him how his afternoon had been and Vijay telling him about his trip to the post office, only omitting the racial abuse.

Florence soon arrived, looking elegant in a dark blue wool dress, which reached just below the knee, with a white stripe down each sleeve, white cuffs, white trim on the round neckline and a similar white band around the lower border of the skirt section. A black belt and black high-heeled shoes finished off the outfit Looking at her so elegantly dressed, Jim said,

"People would think you are going to the theatre followed by dinner in an exclusive restaurant. You look very smart and sophisticated."

Vijay also complimented her on her appearance, for which she thanked them both, adding that just because there was a war does not mean that one should drop their standards.

They went through to the dining room and ate the meagre meal that the landlady had mustered up from her rations, just as Jim had predicted, feeling very lonely as they were the only guests, which also made the room feel eerie and uninviting, especially due to the curfew. Their conversation took many different directions as they tried to each put their own slant and views on the situation in the world.

As part of their conversation, they talked about what plans Vijay had made with regard to his future. He told them about William and his enormous help and generosity in finding him both a job in a factory and accommodation in Aston and the very generous gift of £5.

After about two hours, they all retired to bed, knowing they had a long journey ahead of them the following day. Vijay did not sleep very well as he was now more worried about his life in England following the day's events, which without doubt had dented his hopes and plans.

Chapter 18

Vijay came downstairs to the hall at the arranged time of nine in the morning to find that both Jim and Florence were already waiting for him, so Vijay gave them a polite apology even though he had been on time. Jim explained that he had been up and about since seven ensuring all was well with regards to fuel and provisions for the journey and had already put his bag in the car.

He had decided that they would make one stop on the way to Bromsgrove that being at Cirencester, which he had been reliably informed was an interesting and historical town where they would spend approximately an hour and a half including time for lunch, which had been packed for them by the landlady, at an exorbitant price for what they were getting, she knowing that they had little choice.

Vijay offered to pay for his lunch but Jim insistently declined the offer.

The car having been loaded up with Florence's and Vijay's bags, they set off on their long journey after a small breakfast of tea and toast. Florence sat in the front passenger seat and Vijay sat behind Jim so that he and Florence could diagonally see each other when they chatted.

The drive to Cirencester took just less than three hours with little conversation except for the occasional comment about how beautiful the countryside was or how pretty some of the villages were as they passed through. When they arrived in Cirencester, Jim parked the car and they collected their packed lunches from the boot and set off to walk around the town, all three of them glad to be able to stretch their legs.

Part of the walk took them past the beautiful ruins of the famous monastery and Jim told Vijay about its history and the monks who had lived there, although, he told him, sadly they would not have time to visit, which secretly gladdened Vijay as he was already feeling the cold.

Although it was cold it was also dry, so Jim decided to find a park where they could sit on a bench to eat their lunch, which turned out to be a bad decision as once they stopped walking they became very cold, especially Vijay. Lunch was hastily eaten, as Vijay had started shivering and then they quickly made their way back to the car. Jim started the car, switched on the heating and set off for Bromsgrove.

Vijay soon warmed up and then fell asleep, as he had had a very fitful sleep the night before and remained so until they arrived at Jim's house when he had to be woken up by Jim giving him a nudge. He blearily opened his eyes and looked out of the window, saw the pretty house and felt relieved that the journey was over.

They all got out of the car and Vijay helped Jim to carry all the luggage into the house. Doris stood just inside the hall and after hugging Jim and Florence, she stepped forward and introduced herself to Vijay. Unlike Florence, Doris was quite a plump lady with a jolly-looking face, who had her brown hair tied back in a bun and was wearing a floral cotton apron, which partially covered the dark green dress she had on. It was obvious by the specks of flour on her apron that she had been baking. A pair of brown winged glasses hung from her neck on a little cord.

Jim picked up Vijay's suitcase and took it upstairs, beckoning Vijay to follow him and showed him to a small room, compared to the one he had in Bombay, which was at the rear of the house, next to the bathroom and overlooking the back garden. It was evident from this view that Jim and Doris had spent a lot of time tending the garden as it was neat and tidy, even though it was winter. Jim left him to unpack and said that tea and cakes would be ready in about fifteen minutes, in the front room downstairs.

Vijay unpacked his clothes and toiletries and then carefully unwrapped the ornamental Taj Mahal he had bought in Bombay as a present for Jim and Doris, as a token of his gratitude for accommodating him for the eight days he would be staying with them. He had told Florence and Jim on the journey that he would be going to Birmingham on January the 4th, to his lodgings, so that he could start work on Monday, 5 January 1942.

His gift was much appreciated by Jim and Doris and took pride of place on the mantelpiece in their front room, replacing a photograph of Florence as a child, which was relocated to the hall table, much to a mild, jovial display of indignation on Florence's part.

The next few days were spent relaxing at the house or spending some social time with the neighbours with everyone trying to behave as normal as possible, considering a war was going on. Most evenings, they played bridge whilst listening to the radio, which was always kept on in the background as they did not want to miss any important news or announcements.

New Year's Eve was the hardest day as nobody felt like celebrating but in order to maintain tradition they did all, however, stay up till after midnight to welcome in the New Year.

Sunday, 4 January 1942 soon came and Vijay packed up his belongings and took his suitcase downstairs. Jim had checked the train timetables and they decided that he should catch the train that was leaving Worcester at 11 a.m. and arriving in Birmingham at 11.50 a.m. Jim would be driving Vijay to the station.

The journey from Jim's house to the station would take about 25 minutes so they decided, Florence said she wanted to go as well, to leave at 10.15 a.m. to allow more than enough time for them to reach the station well before the train was due to arrive. When the time came for them to leave, Doris gave Vijay a big hug and wished him all the best for the future and also gave him the packed lunch she had made for him to eat whilst he was on the train.

They arrived at the station just before a quarter to eleven and went to the waiting room after Vijay had bought his single ticket. This was the first time that he had to use some of the £5 he had been given by William Grundy, managing all his previous expenditure by using his own money and the money bequeathed to him by Kantaben. He felt a small rush of panic and started, for the umpteenth time, to worry about his future.

How would he manage? For the last three years and four months, he had experienced no financial worries but now that security was gone he knew that he was going to have to fend for himself. He took solace and comfort in the knowledge that he had a job to go to and that, hopefully, he would be able to continue working at the factory whilst he was studying.

Whilst he was having this contemplation, Jim had been talking to a young couple who were also waiting for the train and had managed to secure a favour from them that they would make sure that Vijay was taken by them to the Number seven bus stop outside New Street Train Station from where he would be able to catch a bus, which would take him to the Sutton Street bus stop from where he could walk the short distance to Upper Thomas Street, where his lodgings were.

The train chugged into the station at 11.07 and Vijay boarded after saying goodbye to Jim and Florence, promising to visit them as and when he could. He sat down opposite the young couple who then struck up a conversation with him, although it seemed that he was doing all the talking as they quizzed him about his life. The little he did learn about them was that they had been married for three years and lived in a terraced house in Selly Oak, an area near Birmingham University.

The man worked in the maintenance department for the university and his wife did some tailoring and clothing alterations from home. They explained that the best way for him to go from Aston to the university would be to go back into the city centre on the Number 7 bus and then catch one of the buses that went along Bristol Road, getting off at the bus stop opposite the Gun Barrels, the name of a large public house.

The road adjacent to the pub would lead him to the university campus. He thanked them for that information and as their conversation continued in a friendly manner, he began to appreciate that not all white people in England were racist and of those who were, only some expressed their feelings publicly, such as the lady pushing the pram, thereby trying to rouse anger and hatred in the indigenous population. Some others, he was sure, hid their feelings. He thoughtfully hoped that the majority of people were like this couple who were friendly and helpful.

The train arrived in Birmingham at 12.00 noon and they all disembarked and walked down the platform towards the exit, handing their tickets to the waiting ticket collector as they crossed the barrier. The couple did as Jim had requested and walked with him to the No.7 bus stop, even though it was easy to find, and offered to wait with him until the bus arrived but Vijay declined the offer and thanked them again for their help and they, in turn, wished him every success in his future career as an electrical engineer, after which they went off to wherever they were going, which he assumed was home to Selly Oak.

As he waited, he again noticed how cold the air was as it bit into the exposed parts of his face and he was very appreciative that he was wearing Clive's overcoat and William's hat, scarf and gloves and also glad that he had accepted them, not only because he was nice and warm but also because he felt accepted in the queue as everyone else was wearing similar outdoor clothing.

The bus arrived after a few minutes and Vijay embarked on it, sitting down on the nearest seat he could, so that he would be able to disembark quickly, not wanting to risk missing his stop. Jim had already explained that the bus conductor would come and charge him for his journey and give him a ticket.

"Make sure you keep the ticket handy because if an inspector comes aboard, he will want to see it," he had emphasised to him.

The bus set off and soon afterwards the conductor came to issue him with his ticket and charge him for it. The relatively short journey only cost one half of a penny and a ticket was issued from the small metal machine hanging from the conductor's neck and shoulder.

He asked the conductor to let him know when the bus would reach his stop, to which the conductor pointed to the red buttons placed at regular intervals along the bus, which had writing around the rim, saying 'press to stop' and said,

"You are only three stops away. Press one of those buttons after the second stop and it will let the driver know that you want to get off at the next one. If I am downstairs, I will remind you."

A few minutes later, Vijay got up from his seat and pressed the nearest red button knowing his stop was next. He picked up his suitcase and stood on the small square platform at the back of the bus onto which the stairs from the upper deck also came down. A man and a young child came down the stairs and they all exited together when the bus stopped.

Vijay looked around as the bus moved on. The crossroads a few yards ahead of him had two shops, one a greengrocers and the other a butchers, one pub, The Aston Arms and a church, St James, on its four corners. The first street on the left was marked with a street sign on the wall above the greengrocer's shop which was on its corner, with the butcher's shop opposite. Sutton Street. Being a Sunday the shops were closed. The pub was open but Vijay had been told by many people that it would not be wise for him to go into a pub until he had made friends with someone he could go with as he might get into trouble, although they were vague as to what kind of trouble that might be. As he stood there getting his bearings, a group of young boys, all dressed in matching khaki-coloured uniforms and wearing caps that had badges on them, came out of the church, accompanied by two men also in khaki uniforms but not wearing caps.

Vijay watched as they all marched in a procession down the street at the side of the church. Could these be the cubs and scouts that William had talked about when he had been chatting to Vijay about life in England? he mentally asked himself. He walked the few yards to Sutton Street, turned left and started up the gentle slope. A red post box stood on the pavement just past the butcher's shop and further up the street, he could see a telephone box.

The shop was adjoined to a row of terraced houses and then about halfway up they ended to reveal a large detached stone-built house with grounds that extended behind the dwelling. The whole plot, he guessed, was probably about the same size as one of his grandfather's fields. A sign on the wooden five-bar gate informed any passer-by and visitors that this was 'The Vicarage.'

He continued on and another row of terraced houses began and then finished at the next crossroads and the sign on the street crossing read Upper Thomas Street.' He turned right and walked along the street noticing that the numbers on his side of the street were odd numbers and those on the other side were even. The first house he came to on his side was numbered 173 and the numbers progressed in descending order.

He wanted number 27. As he walked along, he could see into the front rooms of the terraced houses, as they did not have a front garden. He noted that these houses were not as nice or as large as those on Sutton Street and were only two storeys whereas those on Sutton Street were three storeys and had front gardens.

At the next crossroads, he saw the HP Sauce factory on the opposite right-hand corner, which had high windowless brick walls with two large wooden gates set into the wall facing him, presumably to allow the lorries to come and go. No doubt he would find out all the workings of the factory over the next few weeks, he assumed. He continued along Upper Thomas Street, passing Upper Thomas Street Junior School after the factory and then the senior school.

He crossed the next street and saw that the first house was numbered 57 but also that the houses now had three storeys and front gardens, similar to those on Sutton Street. A few minutes later, he was outside number 27 where his lodgings were. He paused and looked the house up and down. There was a tessellated block paving path that led from the street to stone steps that ascended to the front door and there was a small garden to the left-hand side of the path and steps.

The front door was made of timber with two oblong glass panels in the upper half and was painted dark green with its surrounding framework being painted white. All the paintwork was of poor quality and was peeling. The ground-floor and first-floor front rooms, which overlooked the small front garden, had bay windows which were similarly painted like the front door with the windows of both these rooms having faded net curtains.

The second-floor window was a flat sash window and also had a faded net curtain and was painted only white as were the first and second-floor windows above the door. Vijay walked along the path and climbed up the steps and then he put his suitcase down and knocked on the door. A few seconds later, the door opened and a smaller version of the landlady in Southampton emerged.

"You must be Vijay," she said, expectantly. Vijay nodded his head.

"Come in and sit by the fire, you must be freezing," she continued and then turned around and went back into the house. Vijay picked up his suitcase and followed her, closing the door behind him. He found himself in a hallway that had a tiled, parquet floor, from which, to his left, was a door that he assumed led to the front bay windowed room and straight ahead was a staircase with a balustrade rail.

The hallway continued to the left of the staircase and a second door on his left was halfway down. He followed the woman past this door and then into the room at the end of the hallway. He had noticed a door on his right at the end of the staircase, which was set into the wood panelling and presumed, rightly, that this led to the cellar. He entered the end room behind the landlady and was greeted with a blast of warm air, which reminded him how cold it was outside.

The landlady's husband was sat on an armchair in front of the fire and Vijay could hear a radio in the background playing music he did not recognise. The man stood up and held out his right hand. Vijay took the hand and gave a firm shake.

"I'm Vijay," he said.

"I'm Ken Grimshaw and this is my wife Mary," he said, pointing to the lady who had just brought Vijay in, "come and sit by the fire and warm yourself while she makes us a cup of tea and some biscuits."

Vijay eyed them up; Mary was a well-rounded but not fat, lady, not very tall and was wearing a floral apron over a patterned dress and plain cardigan, thick woollen socks and furry slippers. She appeared to be in her early to mid-forties.

Ken, on the other hand, was tall and wiry with black hair and was wearing navy blue corduroy trousers held up with braces and a plain light blue cotton shirt and appeared to be younger than his wife. On the dresser stood a photograph of a young man dressed in a naval uniform, who Vijay surmised was, most probably, their son.

Vijay sat down on one of the armchairs by the fire as Mary went to a door at the right-hand side of the fireplace and disappeared into the kitchen. Soon, he heard the instantly recognisable sounds of tea being made, as it is made in the same way in most British households in the world, irrespective of class. He turned his attention back to Ken who was explaining to him the geography of the house and the people who lived in it.

His room was on the top floor and had a window looking out onto the back garden. The floor plan of the house was shaped like the letter 'd'. Following this explanation Vijay assumed, having looked at the houses on either side whilst he was waiting outside, that Nos. 25 and 29 would be mirror images and therefore shaped like a 'b'.

There were four lodging rooms, two on the ground floor and two on the top floor, the back top floor one being his. The shared bathroom, basically a sink where one could wash and brush their teeth, was on the first floor, directly above their kitchen. The first-floor front room, the largest in the house, was their bedroom. The first-floor backroom was the joint kitchen for the lodgers and was below his room.

The cupboards in the kitchen were equally shared between the lodgers and had locks on them. The ground-floor front and back rooms and the second-floor front room were the other three lodging rooms. The cellar was accessed by the door under the stairs and was the coal store. All the rooms had coal fires and were the responsibility of the individual tenants to be cleaned and maintained. Coal was delivered once a week.

At present, all the rooms were occupied and he would introduce Vijay to the other lodgers as and when the time arose. Public baths were available, halfpenny for just hot water and a towel or three farthings for hot water, soap and a towel, two streets away. The washer room was outside, next to the toilet, where he would be able to wash his clothes. The garden was for the use of everyone. Mary would explain the rent and charges. Vijay felt bombarded with all this information, which had been delivered in very fast, short staccato statements.

He had just about mentally visualised the layout of the house when Mary came in with the tea and biscuits. She placed them on the coffee table (it should be called a tea table, he thought to himself, as very few British people drank coffee in his experience) and they all sat down around it, facing the fire. Mary served the tea and handed around the biscuits, homemade of course.

They talked about Vijay for a while and then Mary told him that the rent would be twelve shillings and sixpence a week, payable every Friday and was all-inclusive, except for food. No hoarding of coal was allowed. She would clean his room once a week and his bedding would also be washed once a week; any extra washing, ironing or cleaning would be chargeable, assuming that she had the provisions.

Ken then stood up, gave Vijay three keys on a key ring and said,

"This one is for the front door," holding out the longest key, "the brass one is for your room and the little silver one is for your cupboard in the kitchen."

He took this to mean that he should now take his leave and go to his room, so he stood up, picked up his suitcase, took the keys off Ken and said,

"Thank you very much for taking me in as your lodger and for your hospitality today," and then left their sitting room and went upstairs.

When he opened his room, he was pleased to see that the fire had been lit and the room was nice and clean. He put his suitcase down, lay down on the bed and gazed around the room, taking in the layout. The room housed a double bed, a dressing table with a mirror, a free-standing double wardrobe against the wall opposite the bed and an armchair. There was a chair tucked into the space in the dressing table.

The window had a set of floral curtains as well as a faded net curtain and a picture of a vase full of flowers hung on the wall over the fireplace. He noticed that the smoke from the fire had, over the years, yellowed both the picture and the frame, which had been white when it was new. The grey and white diamond patterned wallpaper was ready for replacement, he also noticed. He closed his eyes and rested.

After a short while, having not managed to sleep, he got up and went to the window and looked out onto the back garden. It was a long lawned area with a high wall at the end, fences along the sides separating it from its neighbours and a large oak tree in the right-hand corner as he looked out.

He turned around, placed his suitcase on the bed and unpacked his belongings, hanging his clothes in the wardrobe and his underwear and socks in the drawers underneath and then tucked his suitcase under the bed. He picked up one of the three books Jim had given him to read and lay down on the bed again and started to read it. After a couple of hours, there was a knock on the door and then it opened and Ken walked in.

"Mary knew that with it being a Sunday, you probably had no food so she sent me with this plate of cheese and onion pie," he said. "Just wash the plate when you have finished and bring it downstairs, tomorrow you are on your own."

"Thank you," said Vijay. He had gone without meals many times before and had been prepared for another one of his 'starvation' nights, as he called them, so was very pleased that, after all, this was not going to be another one. He sat down on the armchair after moving it nearer to the window and ate the pie, more onion than cheese but warm and filling.

When he had finished, he did what had been asked of him and washed the plate and returned it to the room he had left earlier. The room was empty, so he left the plate on the coffee table.

He went back to his room and settled down for the night.

Chapter 19

Vijay woke up and looked at his watch. His father's watch, which had been given to him following his father's death, was a Rotary and had been purchased by his father, as a present to himself, when he had succeeded in becoming a senior manager with the Bombay City and Gujarat Textile Company. It showed 6.17 a.m.

He got out of bed, dressed, picked up his toothbrush [he was introduced to tooth brushing when he lived with Florence] and soap and went to the bathroom. The fire in his room had gone out during the early part of the night and the cold had woken him up, so he made a mental note to himself not to allow that to happen again, telling himself that from now on he would make sure there was enough coal on the fire to keep it burning until the morning. Five minutes later, he was back in his room.

He cleaned the old ashes of the fire and then laid out some paper and wood in the fireplace, went to the cellar brought up some coal and made up the fire so that it would be ready to be lit when he came home that evening. He then went to the kitchen, opened his cupboard and was pleased to see that tea was available, so he made himself a cup and went back to his room and read a little more of his book until it was 7.30 a.m., then he put on his coat, gloves, hat and scarf and set off for the HP Sauce factory.

He had been told to report to the factory at 8:00 a.m., however, he wanted to make sure he was there early, so he allowed himself plenty of time, even though he knew that the factory was only approximately ten minutes away.

He arrived at the factory at 7.41 a.m. and very politely asked the first man he saw to direct him to the manager's office and, following those directions, arrived at and then duly knocked on the door of Mr Hargreaves, General Manager.

"Come in," shouted a voice from within the room. He opened the door and entered the room, walked to the desk and stood there.

Mr Hargreaves was a small rotund man, probably in his late forties or early fifties, dressed in a suit and tie and was stood side-on rummaging in the top drawer of a filing cabinet. He turned his head round and looked at him, his hands still in the filing cabinet.

"You are Vijay, I assume," he said. "My cousin's and your mutual friend Mr Grundy has told me all I need to know about you in the letter that he sent." Before Vijay could respond in acknowledgement, he continued, "You will make sure any broken bottles and any spillages are quickly cleaned up, especially in the loading area, and also help with any chores given to you by the foreman, Mr Williams. You will be paid three pounds and ten shillings a week. When you start your university course in September you will work every evening, from six till nine, and Saturday mornings and your pay will be adjusted accordingly. Now off you go, I have my own work to do."

With that, he sat down at his desk and opened the file he had just taken out from the drawer of the filing cabinet and started to read the documents.

Vijay left the room, closed the door behind him and went to find Mr Williams.

The next nine months are not going to be easy, he thought to himself, following his first encounter with Mr Hargreaves. He made his way back into the factory and went to the foreman's office where he found Mr Williams who was busy allocating jobs to the men and women waiting for their instructions. The women were given the machine work, that is the conveyor belt, and the men did the more arduous work of loading the crates onto the lorries.

Mr Williams finally turned to Vijay and told him that his job was to make sure that all glass and sauce following a breakage was cleaned up as soon as possible to ensure maximum safety for the workers.

"Your tools are a big brush and a mop and bucket. The method of cleaning the mess is to throw water onto the spillage to thin out the sauce, when sweep out the glass and deposit it into the waste glass bin and then mop up the watery sauce. Always in that order," he said emphasising the last sentence. "When there is no cleaning to do, you are to help with the loading."

Vijay immediately knew that he was not going to be able to do this job for the duration of his university course but at this moment, he was grateful to have a job. He went off and collected his equipment and placed it near the end of the conveyor belt and then joined the loading team.

Barely ten minutes had passed before he heard a female voice shout 'Breakage' and off he ran to collect his brush, mop and bucket (already filled with water in preparation) to clean up the mess. During that day, there were eleven broken bottles. Lunchtime was from one o'clock till half past one. Vijay had no lunch that day.

Work on this shift finished at six o'clock and Vijay went straight to the corner shop to buy as many provisions as he could, bearing in mind that there was rationing. He then went back to his lodgings, made himself a meal and went to his room, lit his fire, wrapped his blanket around himself, sat down in the armchair and consumed his meal whilst waiting for the room to warm up, pleased that he was on the top floor because this meant that he benefitted from the heat rising up from the rooms below.

After a few minutes, he stood up, unwrapped the blanket, went to the bed plumped up his pillows, stretched out on the bed and continued reading his book. He could hear movement in other parts of the house and wondered when he would meet his fellow lodgers and what they would be like. As if in answer to his thoughts, there was a knock on his door, so he clambered off his bed, went to the door and opened it.

Outside stood a young man, over six feet tall, of West Indian descent, probably in his mid to late twenties, wearing grey flannel trousers, a white shirt, a navy blue V-neck jumper and carrying a heavy wool coat over his right arm. His tight curly hair was cut short and looked like a skullcap on his head. His jet-black eyes matched the colour of his hair.

"Hello," he said, "I'm Eulet Redmond and I am in the room next door. Would you like to go for a cup of tea in the cafe down the road? It's cheap and they sometimes have some leftovers. The Grimshaw's told me last week that you were moving in yesterday."

Vijay did some quick thinking and said, "Yes, that would be nice but I will probably just chat with you if you don't mind, as I don't get paid till the end of the week and I want to make sure I don't run out of money as I will have to pay Mrs Grimshaw her rent on Friday. I am not sure whether she will want paying in the morning or the evening."

"We all pay in the evening after we have been paid at work. Anyway, don't worry, I will buy you a cup of tea," said Eulet.

Vijay went back into his room and grabbed his coat, followed Eulet, who had now put on his coat and was in the process of wrapping a scarf around his neck, out onto the hallway, down the stairs and then out into the cold evening air. As he walked along the road, he could feel the freezing wind biting into his ears and he wished he had brought his hat. He noticed that his neighbour, Eulet, had moved his scarf up to cover his ears.

Ten minutes later, they reached the cafe and went in, glad to escape from the cold. They looked around the room and searched for a table as far away from the door as they could and sat down. The cafe was empty except for a middle-aged man who was nursing a cup of hot tea or coffee, holding it up so that the steam warmed his face, whilst reading a book.

"He's a regular here," said Eulet. "I think he is a widower."

A young waitress came over and asked what they would like.

"Two teas and anything that's going cheap," he said with a twinkle in his eye and a broad grin.

"I'll see what I can do," she said, smiling back.

Eulet then asked Vijay about himself and listened with interest to a brief recount of Vijay's life, all twenty years told in less than ten minutes, with great omissions by Vijay, as Vijay was more interested in finding out about life in England in order to plan his future rather than talk about his past. He asked Eulet about his life, what his job was where he worked and how well-paid it was.

Eulet told him that he had travelled from Barbados with his parents and younger sister seven years ago, sailing to Bristol because that was where his father, who had secured a job working on the docks before they had left, had decided to settle. When the war started, he left his family and moved to Birmingham to work for the munitions factory BSA (Birmingham Small Arms) which is in Small Heath, about three miles from Aston and along the inner circle No.8 bus route and had lodged at the Grimshaw's since he had arrived in Birmingham.

He was being well paid compared to other factory workers in non-armaments companies, partly due to the fact that the arms and ammunition were so desperately needed, so long hours had to be worked and also because the factory was under constant threat of being bombed, the workers were given extra money for their risk-taking; 'danger money' they called it.

While he was talking about his job, he also made the passing comments to Vijay that a large problem the factory had at the moment was finding competent people to work in both the administrative offices and on the factory floor, due to the fact that so many young men had joined up to serve in the forces. Also because of this shortage of young men, the company now employs a lot of women as well.

During their conversation, the young waitress had served them with their tea and a slice of toast each, apologising that there was no butter but told them she had managed to find a little homemade jam. They thanked her for her efforts.

Also as part of their conversation, Eulet told Vijay that the two rooms on the ground floor were being rented by a family, the man of which worked for an insurance company in the centre of Birmingham. He walks with a limp which possibly explains why he was not serving in the forces, although no one has asked him. He and his wife share the front room and their two daughters sleep in the back room. They have only lived here for a few months and he thought they were looking to buy their own house. The daughters attend the school down the road.

They had now finished their tea and toast, so Eulet pushed his chair back, stood up, collected the crockery and walked over to the counter putting the dirty cups and plates down on the worktop and paid the bill, and then came back to the table.

After a few more minutes of chatting they both stood up, wrapped themselves up again and set off back to the house. The middle-aged man was still reading his book when they left. Once home, they shook hands, thanked each other for their company and agreed to meet up again soon.

Vijay snuggled up under his blanket and started to formulate new ideas for his future having listened to Eulet. He realised that there was more money to be made by working for BSA than HP Sauce and also more to be made by buying and renting property than by working for a company and being paid a salary. A different future filled his thoughts as he slowly drifted off to sleep.

Chapter 20

The alarm on his clock, a present from Florence, sprung to life and woke Vijay from his deep sleep. He swung his feet out from under his blanket, pulled the rest of it from his body and stood up, gathered his toothbrush, toothpaste, towel, soap and comb and went to the bathroom. Ten minutes later he was ready for work.

He sat down at the dressing table and started writing a letter to BSA, asking for a job in the accounts office, detailing his academic achievements, especially his excellent grades in mathematics, but specifically did not mention his place at Birmingham University to study engineering. He set off for work, posting the letter on his way.

Tuesday, Wednesday, Thursday and Friday were no different at work than Monday. Although the factory was open on Saturday mornings, the staff numbers were greatly reduced, so the other men worked in a rota to do the sweeping and cleaning of breakages which meant Vijay did not have to go in; that pleased him as he was not enjoying his job at all.

Saturday morning Vijay stayed in bed a little later, even though he woke up at the usual time. He saw the pile of coins on his bedside table and remembered that he had been paid the evening before and also that he had paid Mary as soon as he had arrived back at his lodgings.

He also remembered knocking on Eulet's door, hoping to go out for a cup of tea with him again, only to be told by him that Friday nights were when he met up with some fellow West Indian friends and they would play music and drink beer. There was no invitation extended for him to join them.

He got up, washed and dressed, had some breakfast and went downstairs and knocked on the Grimshaw's living room door.

"Come in," came Ken's voice. Vijay went in and saw a roaring fire with Ken and Mary sitting in front of it, Mary knitting and Ken reading, and his ears heard the sound of music coming from the radio on the dresser, again playing a tune he did not recognise.

"What do people do at the weekend?" asked Vijay.

"Before the war, people would go into town, shop, perhaps have some lunch, go to football matches, go to parks, visit museums, go to the cinema, and play football in winter or cricket in summer, in fact, lots of different activities. Nowadays, very little. Family gatherings are more common these days," replied Ken.

"Thank you," said Vijay and left the room.

He decided to go out for a walk and explore the area.

He went to his room to collect his coat, scarf, hat and gloves. As he was putting on his coat he, out of the corner of his eye, noticed two young children, also wearing warm clothing, playing in the back garden. The bigger girl and therefore, presumably the older one, was climbing the oak tree and the other girl was watching her, clutching a doll. They must be the children from the family downstairs, he thought to himself as he finished putting on his coat.

Having wrapped himself up, Vijay exited his room, locked his door and went downstairs and out onto the street, turned right and went towards the cafe, glancing through the window as he walked past to see if he recognised anyone inside. Only the middle-aged man was in the cafe, in his usual place reading a book, with a cup of tea or coffee on the table.

A short distance further on past the cafe brought him to a crossroads. He stood still for a moment contemplating which way to go and then decided to walk straight across leaving the left and right directions for another time and followed the road as it took a curve to the right and discovered that it led to the gates of a park.

He passed through the gates and carried on along the path looking around as he walked. To his right, he saw a play area with some swings, which had some girls on them; a slide, which was empty, an octagonal roundabout made of steel tubing which had three boys playing on it, one pushing it and the other two sat on a bar each, and a small climbing frame which was also unoccupied like the slide.

To the left of the path was a grassed area where some boys were kicking a football around. He continued along, heading away from his lodgings. A few hundred yards on, a line of trees at right angles to the path that he was walking along, came into view, with his path dissecting its way through the middle of them.

Beyond he could see the shape of a large building. He meandered along until he came nearer and then stopped. He could now read the name on the building, written in big capital letters, ASTON VILLA FOOTBALL CLUB.

William had talked about football being a popular sport in England, more so than cricket, and Aston Villa was mentioned to him as one of the teams in Birmingham. He also knew that Saturday afternoons were when the matches were played, but because of the war the schedules were much reduced, although for morale, the government encouraged as much normality as possible. Coming to a wooden bench, he decided to sit down for a while and watch people as they went about their activities.

A few people walked past him, most just acknowledging him with a little nod of the head in his direction or a warm smile to which he responded in a similar fashion, the remainder behaving in a more private way and walking past without any form of acknowledgement at all. He checked his watch, 11.23 a.m. and decided to set off back, secretly hoping that Eulet might be in the cafe so he could join him for a chat and a drink, perhaps even a little lunch.

Good and bad luck met his eyes as he peered through the window of the cafe. The good was that Eulet was in the cafe, the bad was that he had company. He decided to enter the cafe and, at least, initially, sit at a table on his own, hoping to be invited to join them.

Luck was in his favour, as on seeing Vijay enter the cafe, Eulet beckoned him over and pointed to an empty chair at his table. Vijay walked over and sat down and was introduced to Eulet's companion, Caprice, a young lady also of West Indian descent.

"Caprice works at BSA with me. She is part of the group that meets on Friday evenings," he said.

Vijay looked at Caprice and offered his hand which she took and shook, whilst also giving him a broad smile that made him notice the brilliant whiteness of her teeth, which was accentuated by the contrast between them and the darkness of her skin.

Vijay sat down and started the conversation by telling them about his walk that morning. Eulet interjected occasionally to give more information and explanations as and when he felt it would be relevant, such as:

"When Aston Villa play Birmingham City, it would be advisable to stay well away as local derby matches could become violent between the rival fans, although the last few games had been reasonably quiet as most young men were away fighting for their country."

After about half an hour and a cup of tea, Vijay, not wanting to overstay his welcome, stood up, said his goodbyes, left the café and walked back to his lodgings and went to his room. His eyes lit up when he saw that a letter had been pushed through under his door. He eagerly opened it and was absolutely delighted to read that he had been invited to attend BSA for an interview, for the position of Accounts Clerk, which had been arranged for Wednesday 21st January at 9.30 am, and that he was to contact them if this was not convenient.

He sat down at the dressing table and started scribbling some notes to prepare for his interview, after which he made himself some lunch, then finished off his interview preparations in a neater version after which he then settled down on his bed and continued reading his book.

Sometime later, having nodded off, he woke up suddenly when there was a knock on his door. He quickly got up and put away his letter and notes before answering the door wondering who it could be. On opening it, he saw Eulet standing there smiling.

"Come on, get your coat on, we are going out. You can't stop in otherwise you will go mad with boredom; you haven't even got a radio," he said.

"Where are we going?" asked Vijay, grabbing his coat, scarf, gloves and hat. "We are going to take this beer that I have bought and go to Caprice's house. Her parents have gone to some friends, so we are going to listen to some music and have a dance. Her sister, brother and some other friends will be there too. We should be home about eleven o'clock," replied Eulet, pointing to a bag full of beer bottles which he was carrying. Vijay locked his room and followed Eulet, pleased that he now had a friend.

They walked past the cafe, now closed, which triggered rumblings in Vijay's stomach as it reminded him that he had not eaten since his lunch, until they reached the crossroads Vijay had been to earlier that day.

Eulet turned left at the crossroads and Vijay followed him, noticing as they walked that this road was very different to Upper Thomas Street with the houses on it having no front gardens, were two storey in height and smaller in width. As they walked along the road, the sound of music could be heard emanating from one of the houses, which became louder and louder the more they progressed towards it.

On reaching it, they found that the door had been left unlocked and slightly open, so they went straight in without knocking. The house had no hallway which meant the door into the property opened directly into the front room, from which there was another door to access the back room and it was from there that the sound of the music could be heard. As they went through the second doorway, Vijay saw a flight of stairs leading from the back room to the upper floor.

"These are council houses," explained Eulet. "If people can't afford to buy their own house and also can't afford to rent in the private sector, the council will help by providing cheaper accommodation. Caprice and her family waited a long time for this house and were lucky because most times the houses are split into two and you have two families living together in the house, usually the front two rooms for one family and the back two for the other.

"Because they are a family of five, two parents and three children, two girls and a boy, they were given the whole of this house. This hasn't gone down well with some of the residents as you can imagine. This type of housing all started following the Industrial Revolution and was accelerated after the First World War."

Caprice came over as she saw them come into the room and, as Eulet gave her the beer, she welcomed them both to the party and then went off to chat with her friends, putting the beer on the table as she went past. Eulet moved swiftly and grabbed a couple of the bottles, keeping one for himself and giving the other to Vijay. Vijay, having not imbibed alcohol before, was wary but decided to have a taste.

"It's an acquired taste," laughed Eulet, as he watched the definite look of 'why do people drink this' on Vijay's face. "Two weeks from now, you will look forward to a drink of beer, I promise."

Vijay looked around the room counting the number of people as he gazed round. There were seven people in the room; himself, Eulet, Caprice, two other boys and two other girls. He assumed that one of the boys was Caprice's brother and one of the girls was Caprice's sister.

Eulet told him the names of all the people there as he pointed them out, but with the loud music he couldn't hear him properly, after which he moved on to dance with Caprice. As he stood there on his own, he noticed that they were all of West Indian origin.

Safety in similarity, he thought to himself.

Perhaps he should also search out fellow Indian families so that he could have social friends who had similar backgrounds to himself, was his next thought.

The evening was pleasant enough for Vijay, as he would otherwise have been on his own but the music was not to his taste and he was not and had never been a dancer of any note, so he did not join in even when invited to do so by Caprice, politely refusing.

He did chat to some of the others during the evening but the conversation was disjointed as they were, quite rightly he told himself, enjoying themselves getting up and down with dancing, only sitting down to rest or drink. He was also pleased that Caprice had put out some snacks for them all, which appeased some of his hunger.

During the evening, he did notice that Eulet and Caprice disappeared outside for a short time and assumed they must be together as a couple and had gone out for a kiss and a cuddle, this having been described to him by Florence as common behaviour in England when a young man and a young woman like each other.

He and Eulet left shortly before eleven o'clock and when outside Vijay remarked to Eulet that the streets were dark and quiet with a dangerous feel about them.

"Maybe it is the fear of being bombed, the uneasiness of the war or just the fact that we are two non-white men walking home in a country where racial abuse and violence against coloured people is not uncommon, that are the reasons for your worries," Eulet replied.

Whether it was one or more of those factors that was causing his anxiety he was not sure but he was relieved when they were back safe and secure in their lodgings. Eulet was a little unsteady on his feet, having drunk a number of beers and was quite noisy climbing the stairs, unlike Vijay, who over the course of the evening had just about managed to finish his first beer; although, as Eulet had predicted, he did think that he could get to like beer after all.

They said their farewells and went into their rooms.

Vijay undressed, climbed into bed and fell asleep almost instantaneously. The next day, apart from carrying out some more preparations for his interview, he had a quiet and relaxing time.

Chapter 21

Monday morning, Vijay was outside Mr Hargreaves's office by 7.45 a.m. and because he could hear noises from inside, he knocked on the door.

"Come in," boomed a voice which he recognised as that of his General Manager. Vijay entered the office.

"What do you want?" he shouted at Vijay and then continued with, "I hope that whatever it is has importance as I am busy and don't need any trivial or unnecessary interruptions."

"Would it be possible for me to have the morning off on Wednesday 21st, please?" asked Vijay.

"Why would that be?" enquired Mr Hargreaves with a quizzical look.

"I have only just arrived in Birmingham and I need to buy some things. I couldn't do this before as I did not have enough money but I will by then," said Vijay, having thought that it would be a plausible reason.

"Why does it have to be that date?"

"I don't know my way around, so a friend is going to come with me but that is the only time he has free, as he works shifts," lied Vijay.

"Only this once, so don't make a habit of it and of course, you won't be paid," Mr Hargreaves said in a condescending manner. "Now go off and do some work, otherwise I will be docking your wages."

Vijay left the room, wondering whether William knew that his friend had such a horrible and arrogant cousin. Perhaps he had become like this because of the war, he thought to himself, trying to give Mr Hargreaves the benefit of the doubt.

Anyway, the important outcome was that he had managed to get Wednesday morning off for his interview, which was what he wanted. All that he needed now was to, hopefully, borrow a tie from Mr Grimshaw (he had been wearing a tie on Sunday, so he knew that he wore them) to wear for his interview.

That evening he was delighted to not only be lent a tie but to be given a choice. He chose a plain blue one, thinking that it would be the best match for his jacket. He went up to his room, sat down and mentally assessed all that he had done in preparation for his interview and concluded that he had done all that he could think of and was now as well prepared as he could be.

He also rationalised to himself that if he were to be offered the job he would not be so worried, especially after the way he had been spoken to that morning, which he felt had been terse and rude, about having to tell Mr Hargreaves.

He reasoned that if the job worked out well, then life could become a lot better and he might be able to go back to India sooner than he had originally thought, thereby seeing his mother again, perhaps even having an arranged marriage and then bringing both mother and wife back with him to England.

He went to bed that evening feeling happy and positive.

Tuesday evening, 20th January, Vijay went to the public baths and, having paid his three farthings, was taken by the attendant to a small cubicle, one of many, in which there was a cast iron bath and a chair, on which was a threadbare towel. The attendant then ran him a bath of hot water, approximately one-third full.

The hot water tap was then locked off ensuring that the bath could not be topped up. Once the attendant had left the cubicle, Vijay locked the door, undressed and then gently climbed into the bath, not wanting to add cold water, as that would cool down the bath water and thereby shorten his bathing time. He enjoyed the bath, the first he had had since leaving Jim and Doris's house, although he had washed at his lodgings every day.

Thirty minutes later, he succumbed to the coolness of the water and grudgingly, slowly extricated himself from the bathtub. After drying and dressing, he pulled out the bath plug and left the cubicle, leaving the towel over the chair.

Thanking the attendant on his way out, he went back to his lodgings, made himself a meal and then retired to his room to plan for his interview. He also decided, should he be offered the job, to buy himself a radio as soon as he could afford one. He went to bed early but fell asleep late due to the turmoil of thoughts circulating through his mind.

His sleep was broken by the sound of the alarm on his clock going off. He turned it off and then stayed in the warm bed for a few more minutes, eventually slowly shaking off his covers and then climbing out.

Grimacing against the cold, even though the fire still had hot embers, he went to the bathroom, brushed his teeth, washed his face and then went back to his room and dressed in his best shirt and trousers, struggled to knot the blue tie he had borrowed, taking him four attempts before he was happy, cleaned his shoes, put on his jacket and then went downstairs warmly wrapped in his coat, hat, scarf and gloves.

Turning left outside the house, he retraced the route he had taken on the day of his arrival. However, this time he turned left at the crossroads when he reached the end of Sutton Street, thereby going away from the city centre. After about three hundred yards, he reached another set of crossroads which were controlled by traffic lights.

Turning right at this junction, he saw the bus stop he was looking for, No.8 Inner Circle. The No.8 bus travelled a circular route around the city approximately one and a half to two miles from the centre. He also now knew that the No.11 bus route, known as the outer circle, took a similar circumferential route approximately three to four miles from the centre and all other routes ran out from the central bus station like spokes on a wheel crossing the inner and outer circle bus routes on their way, which allowed people to traverse the city by changing buses to choose the shortest journey.

Fortunately for Vijay, a segment of the No.8 bus route ran from Aston to Small Heath, passing through Nechells, Saltley and Ward End, which meant he would not need to change buses.

A few minutes later Vijay was on the bus. The journey took about thirty minutes passing through residential areas, factory areas, under and over railway lines, past the Saltley Gas Works and then on to Small Heath.

Alighting from the bus, Vijay followed the instructions he had been given by Eulet to find his way to the factory. He need not have worried as it was well signposted.

Eulet had also given him some background information about the factory to help with his interview, which he had memorised as best as he could. He went through it in his mind as he walked.

"Built in 1861, with encouragement from the War Office, the site occupied twenty five acres in Small Heath. However, due to erratic demand and false promises from the War Office, the company was forced to shut down for a year, 1879, and then in 1880 started manufacturing bicycles, finding that the gun-making machinery was remarkably adaptable for this purpose.

"The company had sold its ammunition business but had shown its patriotism by returning to firearms production during the First World War and then again for the duration of this war, however long that it might last."

Vijay walked down Armoury Road towards the main entrance of the factory. Once in, he followed the signs for the main office, knocked on the door and waited. The door opened to reveal a young lady dressed in a dark blue suit with her brown hair tied in a bun.

"Can I help you?" she asked in a sweet voice. Vijay noticed that she had a very pretty face, red lipstick and eye make-up. Her nails were painted to match her lipstick.

"I am here for an interview. My name is Vijay Patel," he said.

"You are a little early, so please come in and take a seat. You can hang your coat on the stand over there," she said, pointing towards a corner of the room where a mahogany coat stand stood.

Vijay followed her into the office, took off his gloves and put them in his coat pockets, took off his coat and hung it up with his scarf and hat and then turned around and sat down on one of the chairs against the wall. The young lady, a secretary, he assumed, went back behind her desk, sat down, picked up the telephone and informed the person on the other end that Mr Patel had arrived for his interview and then continued her work, which appeared to be the typing of a letter or document.

The pedestal mahogany desk she sat at had a design that consisted of drawers on either side and an opening in the middle and because of this Vijay could see her shapely legs extending out from under her below-the-knee length skirt and disappearing into her black stiletto-heeled shoes. Her legs were crossed over at the ankles. He thought the secretary was a very attractive lady.

He looked at his watch, 9.21 a.m.; only nine more minutes to wait. He became a little nervous and his hands started trembling, so he sat on them to stop them shaking and tried to focus his mind on what he had prepared to say to his interviewers. As he sat waiting, two more young men arrived and told the young secretary that they were there for interviews also.

They took off their coats and hung them up. He became even more unsettled when he noticed that they both had suits on. At 9.28 a.m., according to the clock on the wall, the door opened and a middle-aged lady came in, again dressed in a suit, this being grey with white trimming, and black Cuban heeled shoes.

"I am Mrs Oakenshaw, please come with me, Mr Patel, Mr Adams and Mr Smith," she said.

The three young men followed her out of the office to another room further down the corridor.

"Please take a seat at a desk each. You will find a paper which has some mathematical questions on it. You have thirty minutes to complete as much as you can. There is a separate sheet of paper for you to use for any working out that you may need to do. I will come back in half an hour." With that, she left the room and shut the door behind her.

Vijay walked to a desk as quickly as he could and started on the examination, as did the others.

He was pleased to find that the questions were not too difficult and he finished in twenty-three minutes. He was good at mental arithmetic, so did not need to do much working out. The last seven minutes he spent checking the more challenging of the questions but felt sure he had correctly answered all of them.

The middle-aged lady reappeared exactly thirty minutes after she had left. She collected the papers and then told them to take a seat back in the main office.

Vijay went back to the office, knocked on the door, waited a few seconds and then walked in, followed by Mr Adams and Mr Smith.

The attractive young lady looked up, gave them a smile and then continued her typing. Vijay, Mr Adams and Mr Smith sat down in the same chairs that they had occupied previously.

Forty-five minutes later, the middle-aged lady came in and beckoned Vijay to follow her. Going past the room where he had just taken his test, she led him to a set of heavy polished double doors with a large brass plate on each door, one of them inscribed with the word BOARD and the other with the word ROOM. She knocked on the door and walked in.

Vijay followed her into the room. The large room was dominated by an enormous table made of oak with a green leather top that had been fitted and studded into the wood. It was surrounded by leather-bound chairs, the leather matching that of the table. A quick mental count told Vijay there were twenty chairs, nine along the length on both sides and one each at the ends.

The frames and the legs of the table and chairs were highly polished and glistened in the light from the overhead electric bulbs, which had goldfish bowl-style lamp shades. The floor felt soft to his feet as they sunk into a thick, plush, diamond-patterned green and brown carpet. Three of the walls had large portraits on them of men he did not recognise; he could not see if there were any on the wall behind him. There was a single oak door in the wall to his left. He knew that someone had spent a great deal of time designing this room.

"This is Mr Patel," said the middle-aged lady to the three men, all smartly dressed in suits, shirts and ties, who sat behind the table.

"Thank you, Mrs Oakenshaw," said the man in the middle. "Please take a seat, Mr Patel," he continued, pointing to the chair opposite him.

"I am Mr Robinson and I am head of the accounts department. I am pleased to tell you that you scored full marks on your test. We are now going to ask you a few questions to find out what sort of person you are and whether you would fit into our department."

He was asked a number of questions by all three men about himself and his interests and hobbies and also what he knew of the company. Vijay recited the facts and figures he had learnt and gave a silent prayer of thanks to Eulet.

When he mentioned his cricketing skills, the man facing him diagonally to his right looked pleased and told him that the company had a cricket team that played in the city league and he could be an asset, provided he was good enough to make the team.

Vijay acknowledged that his skills could be high, low or similar relative to those of the rest of the team, but that should he become an employee of the company, he would certainly try out for a place in the team. As the questions were now more about him, Vijay assumed the interview was coming to an end and was slightly taken aback at the next question.

The man diagonally to his left, who had been the quietest of the men, suddenly interjected and said, "Shut your eyes and tell me about this room."

Vijay did as he was asked and was glad that he had taken the time to peruse the room and described the room in as much detail as he could remember.

"Very impressive," said the man.

Mr Robinson looked at his two colleagues and said, "Any more questions?"

Both men gave a sideways nod.

"Please take a seat back in the front office. We will deliberate on you and then give you our decision."

Vijay went back to the office. The clock on the wall told him it was 11.17 a.m. The other two candidates then went through the same process.

12.39 clicked on the clock as the door opened. Mrs Oakenshaw came through.

"They are ready for you, Mr Patel," she said.

Vijay stood up, glanced at the secretary, who gave him an encouraging smile and wished him good luck and then exited the room, nodding to the other men as he left, turned right and followed Mrs Oakenshaw down the corridor.

This time she did not knock on the door, just opened it and gestured to Vijay to walk through.

"Take a seat," said Mr Robinson, pointing to the same chair he had sat on previously.

"After considering your interview, we have decided to offer you the position of Accounts Clerk. Your salary will be £6 a week and your hours will be from 9 a.m. to 5 p.m. with a 15-minute tea break at 11 a.m. and a 45-minute lunch break at 1 p.m. We expect you to finish any work you have started, so in that respect, we have a flexible fifteen minute extension on your working day, which means that on some days you may need to work late and on others, you may finish early.

"We trust that you will be fair with this arrangement. A two week holiday is part of your contract. Mr Goddard will be your immediate superior. Have you any questions?"

The man who had asked him to describe the room gave him a nod to acknowledge that he was Mr Goddard.

"When can I start?" asked Vijay enthusiastically.

"Shall we say Monday, 2nd February?" said Mr Robinson.

"That will be fine and thank you very much," said Vijay.

Mr Robinson picked up the phone in front of him and dialled a three-digit number.

"Miss Cutler, you can ask Mr Adams and Mr Smith to leave as the vacancy has now been filled," he said into the telephone.

All three men then stood up and left the room by the door he had noticed earlier. Simultaneously, the double doors opened and Mrs Oakenshaw appeared. How did she know to come in, he wondered, as he followed her. She led him to the main office, bade him goodbye, turned on her heels and went back down the corridor.

He found out later that there was a buzzer system with a button under the desk, which Mr Robinson had pressed as he stood up. He went into the office to collect his coat, hat and scarf and noticed the other two men had already left, per Mr Robinson's instructions.

Vijay made his way back to the HP Sauce factory, thinking over how to tell Mr Hargreaves about his new job, deciding that bluntness would be the best approach. He arrived at his office and knocked on the open door.

Mr Hargreaves looked up from his desk as he closed the ledger he was working in.

"Yes," he said in an exasperated voice, beckoning Vijay to come in.

"I will be finishing working here on Friday 30th January as I have secured another job working in the accounts department at BSA," said Vijay, in a strong and assured voice. There was a short silence, as Mr Hargreaves glared at him.

"No, you can finish this Friday by which time I will have re-organised the staff to cover your work. You can't behave like this. You should have more loyalty. Why I listened to my cousin, I'll never know. I don't think he or William will be very happy when they find out about your disgraceful behaviour. Now, get out and do some work," he shouted.

Vijay walked out with mixed emotions. He was angry about the way he had been shouted at, worried because he had lost a week's wages and thoughtful as he appreciated that there was some truth in what Mr Hargreaves had said. He had created managerial problems.

This was a lesson learnt for when or if he ever became a manager or employer.

Chapter 22

Friday morning Vijay set off to work his last day at HP Sauce. It was snowing and must have been during the night as well, as there were at least two inches of snow on the ground, so he was relieved that the factory was within walking distance and that he did not need to catch a bus, as he definitely did not want to be subjected to another tirade of shouting off Mr Hargreaves if he had been late. He told himself to always set off early when he went to work for BSA.

His last day at HP Sauce was uneventful and as he had made no friends, there were no goodbyes to be said, so he collected his wages and left.

He had never known boredom as much as he did for the next nine days.

Worried about his financial situation because he would be losing a week's income, he refused invitations from Eulet for coffee trips on both weekends, making up excuses for not being able to go.

He walked into the city on two of the days and went 'window shopping.'

He wrote a letter to his mother saying all was well and gave her details of all he was doing, which extended to almost six pages, and also to William in order to prepare him for his next meeting or communication with Mr Hargreaves's cousin, informing him about his changed job situation but did not mention his thoughts of not going to university.

Finally, Monday 2nd February came and Vijay arrived at the main door of BSA at 8.30 a.m. and went inside and waited. The noise he could hear out in the yard suggested that the factory workers had already started work but there was no evidence of any administrative staff in the office building. At 8:55 a.m., the pretty young secretary arrived and unlocked the door to her office.

"Come in and wait here," she said. "Mr Goddard will come and take you to your workplace after he has allocated work to the rest of his team. He usually gets here by 8:00 a.m." Vijay made a mental note to be at work by 8:00 a.m. in future.

The young lady introduced herself as Miss Mavis Cutler, sat down behind her desk, organised some papers and then started typing. Vijay sat down in the same chair that he had on his interview day and again admired Mavis's shapely legs.

A quarter of an hour later, Mr Goddard came in, said good morning to them both and asked Vijay to follow him. Going towards the board room, they turned left down a corridor just before it and then at the end of the corridor, went through a door which revealed a small room with six desks, two rows of three or three rows of two depending on your perspective. Men dressed in suits, shirts and ties sat behind all but one, busily pouring over papers. Mr Goddard took Vijay to the empty desk on which there was a folder.

"This is your desk. You will check all the invoices from Thawtin Engineering, which are in this folder, and cross-check them with the deliveries we have received. This company provides us with all the screws, nuts and bolts that we use to make our bicycles and motorbikes and all the rivets for the guns. Let me know when you have finished. My office is the first door on your right as you leave this room. By next Monday, I expect you to come to work in a suit and tie. C&A is a reasonably priced department store in the city centre." With that, he turned around and left the office.

The other five men, all white and middle-aged, looked at him and then went back to their work. At eleven o'clock, they all stopped working and left the office together without extending an invitation to Vijay to join them on their tea break. Feeling alienated, Vijay stood up and stretched and then made his way to the canteen. Groups of people, men and women, sat at tables drinking tea, eating biscuits and smoking and the whole canteen was noisy with multiple conversations.

Vijay sought out an empty table and sat down, deciding not to spend any money on tea or biscuits, then started looking around, hoping someone might acknowledge him or better still, invite him to join his or her table. On his second circumferential look around, he saw a slender hand protruding from a dark blue sleeve waving frantically at him, beckoning him over. It was Miss Cutler, sat with two other young ladies he had not seen before. He made his way over to them.

"Come and join us," said Mavis as he approached the table. "This is Veronica and that's Maureen, who both work in the typing room which is where you will have to go to collect any post that hasn't already been delivered to your office or if you need any letters typing." Vijay leant over the table and shook their hands, then sat down and said,

"Hello, nice to meet you."

They then all made polite conversation about the weather and the war, expressing their concerns for the soldiers, sailors and airmen until the factory whistle, sounding the end of the tea break, halted their chatting. The whole canteen emptied quickly as they all rushed off to restart their work.

Vijay went back to his desk, waited for a few minutes and then broke the silence by introducing himself to the other men.

"I am Vijay, I am twenty years old and come from India," he announced.

After a small pause, the men, in rotation as if they had rehearsed, introduced themselves and then resumed working. Vijay could not work out whether it was his age, colour, genuine disinterest in him or some other factor that was the cause of this unfriendliness but because of their behaviour, he resigned himself to the fact that he was not going to be a welcome member to the team.

He picked up his pen and continued his work deciding that he would continue through his lunch break to make sure he completed the accounts on that day. By four o'clock, he had finished his tasks, so he gathered his papers, left the office and knocked on Mr Goddard's door.

"Come in," came a voice from within the room.

Vijay walked in and placed the papers on the leather-top desk.

"There are three orders that do not tally with the invoices," he said. "I have left them on the top, the others are all correct."

"That was quick work, did you double-check them?"

"Yes," said Vijay, resisting the urge to tell Mr Goddard that he had worked through his lunch break and had triple-checked the figures.

"As this is your first assignment, I will re-check them. If your figures are correct, then it will be your job to make the corrections and then send both the invoices and the order forms back to Thawtin with the adjusted accounts.

"Also, inform the payments department of the order numbers and ask them not to make any payments for any invoices for those orders. I will give you your next task tomorrow morning. Now, as you have a little time, please take these letters to the typing room and ask for them to be typed and ready for posting by Wednesday."

Vijay left the office and found his way to the typing room, went in and looked around, spotting Veronica who was sat three desks along, so he went straight to her, knowing that a friendly and recognisable face was what he needed.

He explained Mr Goddard's requests to her as she took the pile of papers off him and then, smiling at him, she said,

"You can always join us in the canteen during the tea and lunch breaks if you want."

"That's very kind of you. It will be nice to have someone to talk to especially as the men in the office don't say much," he said in response to her offer.

"Vijay, what you don't know is that all five of them have sons who have been either killed or are missing, so they are, as you can imagine, feeling very low and tend to always stick together as a group and don't mix with the rest of us and because of the unfortunate circumstance of them all being in the same office, they have become a collective grieving group. There are others who work in the factory who have lost their sons but they seem to cope better as they are in a minority in their working environment and their colleagues try to lift up their spirits. The man you are taking over from had to be moved because he found it hard working in that office. Try to be kind and understanding with them."

"Thank you for telling me about them, I will do my best to understand their personal grief," said Vijay. "Now, I wonder if you could help me?" he then asked.

"I'll try," replied Veronica.

"Mr Goddard wants me to buy a suit for work. I am not any good at that sort of thing, so can you give me some advice?"

"If you are free on Saturday morning, why don't you meet Maureen, Mavis and me in the town centre and we will help you choose something as we always go shopping on Saturdays. Meet us outside New Street station at ten o'clock."

"Thank you. I'll meet you on Saturday," he said and then left the office.

Pleased and grateful that he had met some nice, friendly people, Vijay slowly meandered back through the corridors to Mr Goddard's office.

"All seems to be correct after a cursory glance. I will check them more thoroughly tomorrow," he said on seeing Vijay, "I am giving you another company to deal with, so you will now be responsible for both. You must always keep me informed and up to date with the accounts and if you have any problems, you tell me immediately. We will meet weekly to discuss your progress." He pointed to a small stack of files on his desk.

Vijay felt pleased with himself. He picked up the files for Scartel, a company making steel tubing and left the office. He locked the files into his desk and then, as it was almost time to go home, he wandered off to discover more of the factory.

The noise from a large building suggested to him that this was probably where Eulet and Caprice worked as he knew they both worked in the machine shed, as it was known by the blue-collar workers. His watch told him that the whistle was due to be blown in less than a minute, so he decided to wait outside for Eulet and then travel home with him.

Sure enough, the whistle blew at five o'clock, the noise subsided and the workers started to stream out of the factory building. Eulet saw him waiting and came over.

"Everything alright?" he inquired.

"Just thought we could go home together," replied Vijay.

"Caprice will be here soon, so we can all go home together," said Eulet.

As he was speaking, Caprice came out through the doors and made her way over towards them, greeting Eulet with a kiss. They held hands on the walk to the bus stop and sat next to each other on the bus whilst Vijay sat on the row behind, watching them behave typically like a young couple in love. Caprice said her goodbyes when they reached the Grimshaw's house and continued her walk home.

Saturday 7th February, Vijay met up with Mavis, Maureen and Veronica and ended up buying a suit, two shirts and two ties for work and decided to use the jacket, shirts and trousers that Florence had bought him as his casual wear when he was not working. Over the next few weeks, Vijay, Eulet and Caprice travelled home together on random occasions as Vijay did not always finish at five, whereas Eulet and Caprice always travelled home together.

Vijay also found out that they went to work together every morning as well but as they went in even earlier than he did, their paths did not meet. In the next months, Vijay concentrated on becoming as proficient as he could at his job and because of this effort, he was praised for his work; his colleagues in the office, although not engaging in conversation with him, had gradually started to acknowledge him by greeting him in the mornings with a 'hello' and leaving with a 'goodbye.'

Mavis, Veronica and Maureen kept him up to date with office gossip, including their own personal lives, with him finding out that Mavis had a boyfriend who was in the RAF, working as ground crew at a base in Suffolk and that at the moment both Veronica and Maureen were unattached.

He learnt more about BSA, including the terrible bombing in November 1940, when fifty-three people were killed; the extent and size of the company; that it employed more than thirty thousand people; had multiple sites; and how committed it was to the war effort. After work, since the beginning of April, he now went to cricket practice on two evenings, Mondays and Wednesdays, with the BSA team, and having secured a place on the team he became a regular member for their weekend games against other local teams.

It transpired that Mr Sinclair, the third member of the interviewing panel, was the team captain. The matches proved to be a pleasant distraction from the war for all the players, and the wives who had husbands in the team did their best to rustle up some sandwiches, cakes and tea for the interval, the 20-minute break between the innings of the teams, in order to try and keep the games as normal as they used to be before the war.

Vijay was soon recognised to be a very good batsman and the team admired his skills, especially his elegant stroke play. He was pleased that he had fitted into the team so well.

By July, Vijay had decided that working for BSA was enjoyable, fulfilling and, for him at this time, lucrative enough for him to forgo a university education. Having considered the cost (accommodation and living expenses) and the binding contract with GEC which could limit his choices in the future, he concluded that he would have more control over his options in his present employment, so he wrote to the engineering department at Birmingham University and to GEC notifying them of his decision.

Birmingham University was understanding in its reply and informed him that they would consider him again if he decided to re-apply, whereas GEC were not very pleased or accommodating, explaining that an earlier notification would have allowed them to offer the opportunity to somebody else.

Another lesson learnt, Vijay told himself.

Early September brought about an unexpected change to Vijay's job following one of the regular meetings he had with Mr Goddard when he was told that he was going to have a wider role.

"You are now to travel to some of our other factories with me and check random accounts to make sure they were correct, whilst I will be touring around the factory with the senior manager, discussing any problems and future planning," he said.

The first factory that was to be visited was in Castle Bromwich, which was about five and a half miles away, with the journey taking approximately twenty five minutes using Mr Goddard's car. On the way, Mr Goddard asked Vijay about his thoughts on the war to which Vijay openly admitted that he was not very knowledgeable about the politics but believed that the Germans should be defeated.

After Vijay had finished Mr Goddard said,

"I noticed that your observational skills were very good at your interview, so I was wondering if you could help me out. One of the problems we have is that some Nazi sympathisers could be passing information about our weapons and our scientific developments to German spies. We need someone to report on any unusual activity by any members of staff or the workers.

"You would only be expected to provide us with the information, not to act on it yourself. I work for MI5 as well as BSA and I have been discreetly monitoring you and your friends over the last six months. I think you could be of good service to us.

"You would spend a few weeks at a site doing your accounting job whilst also looking out for possible sympathisers. You could then tell us the names of any persons that you deem need further investigation. Your part in the investigation is then over and we would take any action we felt was necessary. Would you be interested?"

Vijay remained quiet for some time.

"How do I know you are genuine and not a German spy yourself?" He eventually asked.

"I will arrange for you to meet someone who can allay your fears and convince you that I am who I say am if you agree to work with me," replied Mr Goddard.

The remainder of the journey there and the whole journey back was then spent talking about cricket, football and work. Whilst at the factory, Vijay was introduced to the management as a junior clerk with great potential and they were also informed that he could possibly be back in the near future to carry out an accounting audit, the prospect of which, as they had both expected, did not receive an enthusiastic response from the Castle Bromwich staff.

Being checked on by a younger man, who was also a foreigner and coloured, was an affront to them, so much so that one of the more senior managers protested quite vehemently, being abusive and aggressive, to which Mr Goddard was unmoved and dismissive.

Once back at the Small Heath factory, they went to Mr Goddard's office.

"Thoughts please," he said in a curt, business-like voice. "Today's discussions and conversations are to be kept completely confidential, including this one."

Vijay had thought about nothing else since the moment he was approached. "I don't think the staff liked me and they won't be very cooperative," he said.

"I am fully aware of this and your accounting will not really matter. We already randomly check them without their knowledge. This is now all about the information you gather; your accounting job is the cover you need to be there. If you agree to join us, you will be of great service to this country and also remember to take into account that many of your fellow countrymen are fighting for us too, so you will be of great help to them as well. You have until tomorrow morning to make a decision. Now, off you go," replied Mr Goddard.

Vijay decided to walk home, the weather being dry and, for him, relatively warm, though hot for the native population as they were having an Indian summer (he didn't know why a warm September was described as such but was just glad of the high temperatures) so that he could think about the events of the day.

He had mixed feelings; pride that Mr Goddard thought he, at such a young age, was capable of carrying out this espionage work (it sounded better than being called an informant), fear that he could make mistakes (suspect and then identify an innocent person or, even worse, not discover a spy), worry that Mr Goddard is not who he said he is (which would then make him a German spy and the consequences that would cause) and excitement (he could never have imagined this in his life, as nine months ago, he had left India to embark on a career as an electrical engineer and should now be at Birmingham University, having a quiet time studying).

He also reflected on the letter he had received from William, asking him to reconsider his decision, explaining that a degree would give him lifelong security. His reply to William had been polite but firm and with this new development, he now felt even more vindicated in his choice.

He arrived back at his lodgings, made himself a meal and then walked to the cafe in the hope that there would be someone there whom he could talk to in order to take his mind off the decision he had to make. Looking in through the window, he saw that good fortune was on his side as Eulet and Caprice were sitting inside having a drink. He went into the cafe, bought himself a tea and then joined them.

They looked very happy and excited. No sooner had he sat down, then Caprice waved her left hand in front of him, pointing with the index finger of her right hand at the engagement ring on the third finger of her left hand.

"We are going to get married," she said exuberantly, "and you are invited." "Congratulations, I am very happy for you and thank you for the invitation," said Vijay in a joyful voice, delighted to be considered a close enough friend to be invited to their nuptials. "Will the wedding be soon?" he then asked.

"Next March, we hope," replied Caprice. The next twenty minutes were then filled with her excited voice describing her wedding plans. Eulet and Vijay patiently listened with only the occasional interjection. Vijay was pleased for them and was also glad for the respite the conversation gave him from thinking about the difficult decision he had to make.

After a while, not wanting to overstay his welcome, Vijay said goodbye and went back to his lodgings. He made his choice on the walk back.

The next morning, Vijay was outside Mr Goddard's office by 7.50 a.m. He slouched against the wall facing the door with his hands in his trouser pockets, gazing at the writing on the glass; MR T. GODDARD-ACCOUNTS MANAGER. He wondered what name the 'T' stood for.

He mused over the fact that everyone in a junior or middle-ranking administrative role was addressed by their surname or their job title or both and anyone senior was addressed as Mr. He had no idea where this had originated from but did know the same was the case in his private school in Bombay.

He stood up straight and brushed himself down as he heard footsteps approaching. As he turned his head towards the sound, Mr T Goddard turned left off the main corridor and walked towards him. Without saying a word, he unlocked his office and walked in, leaving the door open. By the time he had sat down behind his desk, Vijay was inside, shutting the door behind him.

"Well?" asked Mr Goddard with an inquisitive gaze.

"Yes, I'll do it but I will need answers to many questions before I agree," replied Vijay.

"Good, meet me after work here in my office and I will introduce you to someone who will verify me and also act as another contact if I am not available. Now, off you go and do some work."

Chapter 23

As the day progressed, Vijay's mind became a turmoil. Questions regarding the future consequences for those he exposed were paramount. What does happen to them? Are they tortured? Are they executed? Are they turned into double agents? Are they locked away? His young brain was finding it difficult to reconcile his decision with the possible outcomes.

He decided to go for a walk at lunchtime to try and clear his head, although it did mean him missing his daily catch-up on gossip with Mavis, Veronica and Maureen, who between them gave him factory information, interesting and unimportant, in a humorous and giggly way, as if they were giving away secrets that should really be taken to the grave. It was always an enjoyable and amusing interlude to his working day. The walk did not answer his questions but did condense them. He returned to work more settled.

Five o'clock was acknowledged with the factory whistle. Three of Vijay's office colleagues had left earlier and the other two now locked away their papers, said their mechanical goodbyes and departed. As soon as they had closed the door, Vijay also locked away his work and went to Mr Goddard's door and knocked gently and then went in. Surprise and astonishment at seeing Mrs Oakenshaw sitting in the office were just two of the emotions he experienced.

"Come and sit down. I believe you have already met," said Mr Goddard.

Mrs Oakenshaw stood up and offered her hand, which he shook, still with a look of disbelief on his face. He stepped back and sat down.

"She is my immediate superior and is responsible for passing information to London. She works directly with an MI5 officer called Eric Roberts, who in turn works for Victor Rothschild. This small department is responsible for finding possible Nazi sympathisers and then asking them to pass information to Mr Roberts, who poses as the Gestapo's man in London, which he will then forward to Berlin.

"This method is considered highly controversial, as some see it as entrapment, hence all the secrecy. Our work, assuming you join us, will never become public knowledge. Prior to working for this department, she worked on the Twenty Committee, so-called after the Roman numerals for 20, that is XX, standing for Double Cross, which targets enemy agents entering the country and then offers them a reprieve from the death penalty in exchange for transmitting bogus intelligence back to the German Secret Service, the Abwher," said Mr Goddard.

Vijay slumped further down in his chair and took a deep breath.

"We will of course deny all knowledge of this meeting and any future ones, should they occur," said Mrs Oakenshaw. "I moved up from London just over twelve months ago to take this job, which is a cover and because of this I am paid by the government not BSA, which allows me the freedom to come and go as I wish.

"I understand your dilemma but you have to make a decision. Thomas thinks you would be good at this and he has always made good choices before, so I have every confidence in this one. Now, I am sure you have many questions, so fire away."

Thomas, that's what the T stands for, thought Vijay.

He then took a deep breath, sat up straight, calmed his external appearance, knowing that internally the pressure in his vascular system was high and his grey matter was anything but calm and started methodically to ask all the questions he had rehearsed on his lunchtime walk.

He knew that he could never be sure whether the answers would be truthful or not but he rationalised the situation by telling himself that the nature of the course of action he was contemplating, by definition, was going to involve some deception.

The question-and-answer session finished and Vijay accepted that at face value his concerns had been dealt with and if the responses to his questions were true, those he exposed would not be harmed, mentally or physically.

The positive response to Mrs Oakenshaw's question about his decision, saw Thomas reach into a drawer of his desk and pull out a bottle of whisky. Three glass tumblers that were then taken off a shelf and placed on the table next to the bottle.

"This calls for a celebration," he said as he poured out the drinks and handed them out. Another first for me, thought Vijay as he had never drunk whisky before.

"It's an acquired taste," Thomas said, smiling when he saw Vijay's face after he had taken a small sip from his glass.

"Welcome to the team, Vijay," said Mrs Oakenshaw, raising her glass, "Just a couple of ground rules you need to observe," she continued, "firstly you are never to talk to me at work unless I approach you and secondly, I will never discuss this secret aspect of our relationship whilst we are here at BSA, so there will never be a need for you to contact me unless it is an absolute emergency. Do you understand?"

"Yes," replied Vijay.

"You do grasp that this is not a game and mistakes will, I emphasise, WILL, have serious consequences," she said in rather a chilling voice, bending towards him. Then straightening up, she lightened her tone and stated, "Now, I am off home. Thomas will start you off in a day or so, once I have cleared this with head office, which will be a formality as they are already aware of our interest in you." She put her empty glass down on the table, retrieved her coat from the door hook, folded it over her arm, picked up her handbag, opened the door and left the office without any further conversation.

Vijay took another small sip of his whisky and then politely asked if he could leave the rest, placing the tumbler on the desk.

"I hope I am making the right decision," he said aloud as more of a rhetorical statement than to Thomas in particular.

Thomas sat down on his chair and rested his feet on his desk, a resigned look on his face and a tired look in his eyes.

"When this damned war is over and you realise what you will have done for this country, you will be very proud of yourself. Unfortunately, only a handful of people will ever know of our efforts and the risks we take. Everyone else will, quite rightly, praise our army, navy and air force.

"In the fullness of time, others will be recognised for their services, such as spies, code breakers and senior members of the armed forces, maybe some politicians but people like us will have never existed and may even be despised as the perception will be that we have not played an active role in the war effort.

"A sobering thought, don't you think? Anyway, off you go home, I will see you tomorrow." With that, he took another mouthful of whisky. Vijay watched him slowly swirl it around in his mouth and then swallow, savouring the experience. Maybe I will acquire a taste for whisky if that is how you drink it, he thought to himself.

He left the office and went home.

Chapter 24

Three days later, Vijay found a note on his desk asking him to go to Mr Goddard's office on his arrival. He screwed up the note and threw it into the waste paper basket, then went out of the office. Mr Goddard's door was open so he gave a gentle knock to attract his attention and then walked in.

"Take a seat, Vijay," he said, "and close the door behind you." He closed the folder he had been perusing, pushed his chair backwards away from his desk, crossed his legs and leaned back.

"We have been concerned about leaks from the Castle Bromwich factory for a while. I want you to go there next Monday and see what you can find out. I have already contacted the senior manager and told him you will be coming and that he has to assist you in every way possible. He, obviously, has no idea why you are really there.

"You will bring back accounts from any two suppliers and I will allocate someone here to carry out the audits. Whilst you are there, I want you to explore the factory and look out for any unusual activity, then report back to me."

Vijay left the office and returned to his desk and continued his work until the lunch break. As he entered the canteen, he saw Mavis, Veronica and Maureen were already there sitting at a table, so he bought himself some lunch and then went and joined them.

News of Eulet and Caprice's wedding had filtered through, so that was their topic of conversation when he sat down and therefore, for the first time he became the questioned rather than the questioner as they asked him numerous questions about the wedding plans.

He told them the little information that he had including the fact that the best man and maid of honour were yet to be decided, which caused the three women to start making guesses as to who they might be. Vijay listened but did not join in as his mind was otherwise preoccupied.

The next few days Vijay concentrated on how he was going to carry out his investigations without arousing suspicion.

By Saturday, he had formulated a plan.

Chapter 25

Vijay arrived at the Castle Bromwich factory on Monday 14th September and sought out the senior manager, Mr Proctor, and told him that he wanted to wander around the site before he started on the audits. When challenged as to why he wanted to do this, Vijay simply told him that head office had concerns about the high overheads of the factory compared to others, so he wanted to make sure that the work being done was as efficient as it could be, as well as auditing the accounts for possible mistakes.

He went off and explored the site, walking around both the factory buildings and offices. He noticed that one of the office windows had a good view of the front gate and delivery yard, so he decided that this window would be an excellent vantage point from where to watch the coming and going of not only deliveries but also of the workers arriving and leaving, as the main gate was the only entrance to the site.

He counted out the windows so that he would know which one it was when he went to the office. The desk next to that window was going to be his workplace during his time at the site, he now also decided. Half an hour later, he went back into the office building, found Mr Proctor and requested the desk by the window he had spotted.

After a short, heated discussion, Mr Proctor still refused to allow Vijay to have the desk, as it was already occupied by a long-standing member of the staff, resulting in Vijay reluctantly but forcibly asking him to telephone Mr Goddard.

Two minutes later, with a scowl on his face, the senior manager led Vijay to his requested desk and the man using it was moved, despite his protestations which contained both racist and abusive language.

Vijay placed his briefcase next to the desk and then went to the accounts department, randomly chose two files and returned to the office.

The atmosphere in the office was hostile towards him. Glares, mutterings and blatantly racist comments greeted him when he returned, especially from some of the male staff. The behaviour of the other staff was passive and indifferent, as if by ignoring the situation they could absolve themselves from any responsibility.

Within half an hour, he had been verbally abused twice, foul language being used to complement those comments, one man deliberately bumped his desk causing his files and pens to be strewn over the floor and one woman walked past him, holding her head up high and pinching her nose, intimating that he had an awful smell.

This last action was just too much for Vijay.

He sat in his chair, contemplating his situation and how to deal with the problem. Outwardly, by keeping his clenched fists hidden under his desk and slightly bowing his head to hide the bulging jaw muscles caused by clamping his teeth together and to also hide the tension in his face, the other occupants of the room were unaware of his anger. Inwardly, he was seething.

After a few minutes, having recovered a small amount of composure, he slowly stood up and left the office, sought out Mr Proctor and told him what was happening. Mr Proctor was unimpressed by Vijay's situation and shrugged his shoulders, saying:

"What did you expect?"

"I expect you to tell your staff that I am here to do a job demanded of me by their employers and all I want is to be allowed to do that. I am not asking them to cooperate with me. If they are aggrieved by this situation, then they should seek employment elsewhere. Please put together a memo saying all this and send it out. A copy for me as well, please. Thank you." He forcibly made sure that he was as polite as he could be.

With that, he turned around and walked off, his heart racing and his hands trembling. He went straight to the reception desk and asked to use the telephone and rang Mr Goddard and told him of the dreadful treatment he was receiving and the action he had taken. Thankfully, Mr Goddard was very supportive of Vijay's actions and promised him that he would immediately speak to Mr Proctor to reinforce his position.

As it was almost lunchtime, Vijay decided to have a walk to find a cafe for something to eat and drink. His heart was slowing down and he felt calmer.

An hour later, he returned to the office. The glares and the mutterings still continued as he walked to his desk. He noticed that the papers and pens had been picked up and scattered on his desk and a copy of the memo he had requested was on the top.

He gathered the papers together and stuffed them into the two folders, not bothering to sort them out and then placed them into the briefcase that Florence had given him before checking that the pen Mr Grundy had given him was amongst his collection and was relieved to find it was. He knew that Mr Goddard would allocate someone at head office to sort out and check the files.

Collecting all his belongings, he left the office. He had decided that the day had been stressful and he wasn't in a frame of mind to do any productive investigating.

Tomorrow will be different, he told himself. He couldn't have been more wrong. The staff behaved the same except that there was no physical action, such as knocking into his desk.

Chapter 26

Peter Foley, a thin man in his early thirties with strands of grey hair, had been delivering steel tubing from Scartel to BSA at Castle Bromwich for over ten years. Well known to the security staff, he was always waved through without any checks. Not that any checks would have revealed anything.

His delivery day to the factory was every Tuesday. 15 September 1942 was just another delivery day for him.

He backed his truck into the yard and up to the unloading bay. Jumping down from his cab, he shouted his customary greetings to the unloaders and said he would be back in one hour and then sauntered off towards the canteen. Twenty minutes later he had finished his two slices of toast and mug of tea and left the canteen.

Keeping close to the wall, he stealthily sneaked to the back of the building, keeping a watchful eye as he went. The camera was hidden in its usual place under the tarpaulin covering the pile of waste tubing, which was always collected on Fridays. He took off his coat hung the camera over his right shoulder and then replaced his coat.

After looking around to make sure no one had seen him, he nonchalantly made his way back to the loading area, then climbed into his cab and waited for the unloaders to finish. He saw the thumbs up in his wing mirror, started his engine and drove off, waving his arm out of the window in acknowledgement. He hooted his horn as he passed through the gates.

Vijay had watched the delivery from his window.

Three weeks passed and Vijay was getting bored and impatient, having found no evidence of any suspicious behaviour by any of the staff and was still feeling very unwelcome. However, Mr Goddard insisted that information was being leaked, so he needed to be more observant and would have to continue for some time.

Tuesday, October 6th Peter Foley drove in as usual. Vijay watched him with passing interest from the office window. Just another driver doing his job. Same routine. Vijay continued checking some accounts.

Forty minutes later, he saw Peter Foley returning to his truck. He turned his head back to continue his work. He suddenly stopped and looked out again. Yes, he said to himself, there is definitely a bulge under his right arm. The poor man had such a deformity, he thought. He continued his work.

On Tuesday, October 13th, Peter Foley arrived at the factory as usual. Vijay saw him descend from his cab. His bulge has gone, he mentally exclaimed to himself. His suspicion was aroused enough for him to at least investigate the man. After all, he wasn't doing anything else and this was the first time since he had started that anything remotely worth investigating had come to his attention.

He left his desk and made his way to the canteen. Finding a table from where he could watch both Peter Foley and the door he placed a folder on it, went to the counter and bought himself a cup of tea, then settled down and pretended to be studying a page from the folder. Twenty minutes later, Peter Foley stubbed out his cigarette, rose from his chair and made his way to the door, glancing at Vijay as he passed his table.

Vijay continued looking at the paper from his folder, whilst sipping his tea. As soon as Peter Foley had left the canteen, Vijay gathered the papers, stuffed them into their folder and quickly went to the door. Gazing down the corridor, he waited until his target reached the stairs before himself leaving the canteen and following. He stealthily stalked the driver and watched his every move.

Peter Foley walked around the building and made his way to the back of the factory where the waste tubing was stored. Seeing him collect the camera from under the tarpaulin made Vijay's heart beat faster and excitement took hold of him. This was surely what he was here for. The bulge appeared under Peter Foley's right arm as he buttoned up his coat.

Vijay went back to the office, collected his coat and briefcase and left. He walked out of the factory gates just before Peter Foley drove out, tooting his horn.

An hour later Vijay was in Mr Goddard's office. Surprised to see him, he asked why Vijay hadn't telephoned.

"There is nowhere private to telephone from," explained Vijay.

Mr Goddard decided that Mrs Oakenshaw should be present, so telephoned her office and invited her to the meeting.

The story having been told, the plan of action had to be considered.

Mrs Oakenshaw, being in charge, made the initial plan which was then modified with input from Thomas and Vijay. As agreed beforehand, Vijay was not going to take any further part in the surveillance and arrest of Peter Foley, and was therefore asked to leave the room whilst that discussion took place. He waited next door at his desk, pretending, again, to be doing some accounting. His fellow workers, thankfully, carried on in their usual manner. Ten minutes later, Mr Goddard called him back.

The plan turned out to be very simple. Vijay was to continue as usual for the time being. Once Mrs Oakenshaw and Mr Goddard had confirmed for themselves Peter Foley's actions and found out who he was passing the camera to, arrests would be made. If no further leaks were found after another two weeks, Vijay would be moved to another factory, as evidence suggested there were a number of leaks of information from other workplaces.

3 November 1942, Vijay watched the Scartel lorry drive into the yard. He did not recognise the chubby, slightly balding driver who was probably in his fifties. The man climbed down from his cab and made his way to the canteen building. Vijay left his desk and also made his way to the canteen, a folder under his arm. The lorry driver was at the counter ordering his cup of tea and a piece of cake.

He collected his beverage and food, sat down at a table, removed a book from a pocket in his coat and relaxed. The next forty minutes Vijay, from a convenient table, watched him consume his food and drink, smoke a cigarette and read. The man then collected his cup and plate, returned them to the waitress, went back to the table, put his book back into his coat and left the canteen.

Vijay discreetly followed him back to his lorry.

An uneventful hour, he reflected as he made his way back to the office.

Vijay found a note on his desk on his return asking him to telephone Mr Goddard as soon as was convenient. He went to the reception desk, made the call and received three items of good news from his superior; one, that Peter Foley had been apprehended and was now in custody awaiting interrogation regarding his activities; two, that his accomplice, unknown to Vijay and therefore no information would be disclosed to him, had also been apprehended and was being questioned and three, that he could wind up his work at the Castle Bromwich depot and return to Small Heath as soon as he wished.

Again, as at the HP Sauce factory, having no goodbyes to make, Vijay had cleared his desk and was on the bus to Small Heath within less than an hour of the end of the phone call.

Chapter 27

Between September 1942 and the end of the war, Vijay became involved in the detection, apprehension and exposure of five 'Nazi sympathisers' and an unknown number of their associates. The five consisted of four men and one woman. He never found out what became of them all and he never asked either and just hoped that they had all seen 'the error of their ways' and had 'turned', thereby helping the British and their allies, rather than being resistant and therefore suffering torture or possible death. His ignorance of their outcomes made his life much easier.

13 March 1943 had seen Eulet and Caprice tie the knot and in December of that year, they announced that she was pregnant and that the baby was due at the end of June the following year. He saw less and less of them as time moved on, with them both being busy making plans for their future, even though Caprice had moved into the house with Eulet. They had relocated to the front ground floor room as it was larger, when the family living there had left.

Vijay was moved to a number of different factories during his espionage work, the furthest away being near Coventry and also one at Tipton in the West Midlands and one at Kidderminster. He visited Florence, Jim and Doris whilst he was at Kidderminster as Bromsgrove was not too far away and on that visit, Florence told him how much she was enjoying her teaching job and was now also a volunteer at a local hospital.

BSA had over sixty sites, so Vijay assumed that there were other men and women carrying out similar espionage work at other factories. He also discovered, through his conversations with Thomas, that the government had seconded some car manufacturing sites to set up 'shadow factories.'

These were not secret places but were adjoined to the factories and were easily adaptable to make guns, rifles, ammunition or other equipment should the major factories, such as those belonging to BSA, be bombed.

He realised that he had been lucky in the speed with which he had exposed Peter Foley as his subsequent detections took much longer and proved to be more difficult.

The most difficult turned out to be the woman. She worked at the Radford Works near Coventry and her job was to type up and keep an inventory of the parts for tanks, guns, rockets and other munitions, their storage location and their delivery dates and destinations.

There had been four air raids at the Radford Works in 1940 and then two more well-targeted and seriously devastating attacks in 1941 which had caused much concern and worry, especially as the raids in 1941 destroyed almost half of the factory. It was widely believed that inside information had been provided for all the raids but no evidence had been found.

Vijay was despatched to the Radford Works in May 1943, after having spent months at Tipton during which time he had discovered and exposed a man who was 'letter dropping' information. His drop was to tape his letters to the underside of the bottom step of a children's slide in a local park, always after dark and when the park was closed.

Once he had disappeared out of sight, a man appeared from the shadows behind the bowling green clubhouse, which was next to the children's play area and retrieved the letter. Again Vijay reported his findings and, as far as knew, they were caught and detained.

His suspicions had been aroused when he had spotted the man going back into the factory on a regular basis during his lunch break, to the office section, which had no relevance to his job as a machine operator. Unfortunately for Vijay, he also spent many an hour following and investigating a number of persons who turned out to be 'persons of no interest.'

His lodgings at Coventry were booked for six months, with the option of two weeks' notice to cancel should they not be needed for all that time. He could return to Birmingham every weekend if he wanted to, knowing that all expenses would be covered.

The woman at Radford Works, Mrs Susan Chaney, an attractive woman in her late twenties, had worked there for over ten years, starting soon after leaving school and had worked her way up from being the office runner to her present position. She was well-liked by her colleagues and was always cheerful and bubbly.

She welcomed Vijay and befriended him as a work colleague, offering him any assistance she could, often collecting files for him, inviting him to join her and her friends at lunchtime in the canteen and after about three months, asked him if he would like to come for Sunday lunch at her home and meet her husband and children, two boys aged seven and five. As he was free that Sunday, because there was no cricket match arranged back in Birmingham that weekend, he accepted.

On Saturday, he bought some flowers as a present for Susan and some toys for her sons and then spent the day walking around Coventry, surveying the damage caused by the bombings. A warm summer's day meant many people were out and about. Apart from the occasional 'look' and one racist comment about his colour, he had a pleasant day.

Sunday afternoon, he set off with his flowers and toys and followed the directions given to him by Susan Chaney and made his way to her house. He had to change buses once and arrived fifteen minutes early due to the bus timetables, which he knew was definitely better than being late, so he decided to walk a little and view some of the area.

A middle-class area with a mixture of detached and semi-detached houses, all with nicely kept gardens, he thought to himself that this would be the sort of area he could aspire to live in when he was in a position to buy a house and settle down. Many years off, he knew, but no harm in thinking and planning for the future, he thought to himself.

Arriving at the house two minutes before his invitational time, he knocked on the door and waited. The door was opened by a man who appeared to be in his early thirties, wearing smart trousers, belted and pleated, a white, collared, shirt and a patterned tie. Vijay was glad that he had decided to put his suit, shirt and tie on.

"Come in, you must be Vijay," he said. "I'm Richard and these two little urchins peering from behind are Jonathan and Julian." The blonde-haired boys definitely had their mother's looks, thought Vijay.

The house was semi-detached, similar to Jim and Doris's but the decorating was more modern. Richard worked as the manager of the main branch of Coventry Building Society, which was in the centre of Coventry and also volunteered as a fireman, which meant he had seen some very horrific and devastating sights during the bombings, although he never talked in any great detail about them.

During their meal, they talked about many topics, some involving the children and others not, but the war, because of the children, was not mentioned at all.

The conversation was kept light, until Richard, making a seemingly innocuous comment, alerted and intrigued Vijay, which, had he not been doing the job he had been asked to do, he would not have taken as much notice of it as he did.

Talking about his job, Richard made the comment that a disproportionately high number of his savings customers were Jewish and that they, he believed, did not integrate with the British as much as he thought they should and also hoarded their money. Susan, as if supporting her husband, said that the Jewish members of staff in her office tended to stick together and not mix and then flippantly, made light of it by saying that they were middle-aged men and would probably be boring anyway.

The conversation was interrupted by the boys who wanted to play outside, so they all went out into the back garden and played a few games; football, hide and seek and cricket. A pleasant afternoon was had by them all.

The time to go came, so Vijay gave his thanks and left. The usual 'you must come again' offer was extended to him to which he gave the standard reply "That's very kind."

The journey home was spent thinking about whether he was being overly suspicious or not.

He decided that discreet observation would do no harm.

The following morning he was more watchful and started keeping a log of Susan's activities. All day she was either at her desk or taking papers to and from other offices. All week he could not find anything suspicious and decided that he had been wrong. Friday afternoon, he telephoned Mr Goddard and said he had found nothing out of the ordinary and asked if he should wind down the operation, as it was now over three months.

"Not yet," came the reply.

"We know there is a leak because one of our other agents has apprehended someone with information on his person that could only have come from that office," he was informed by his superior.

Three months became six months, and Vijay repeatedly requested to be recalled and repeatedly, his request was denied. Other individuals he had carried out surveillance on proved also to be 'persons of no interest.' Thankfully, he did have enough accounting work to keep him busy, so that became his 'day job' again. In the meantime, he had spent more very pleasant and innocuous Sunday afternoons with the Chaney family.

Late November brought a change of luck for Vijay. He was at his desk and Susan was walking from her desk towards the door, which meant that she would walk past him. She was carrying a small pile of papers in her arms and was so busy being her cheerful self, nodding at and acknowledging others in the office as she went past them, that she did not notice that the man at the desk behind Vijay had dropped his pen and had bent down to pick it up.

She walked straight into him, went sprawling over him and her papers scattered onto the floor alongside Vijay's desk. Whilst apologies were being exchanged, Vijay started to collect the papers on the floor. He noticed that some but not all, had been duplicated. Before he could have a good look at them, Susan knelt down and quickly gathered the papers together and told Vijay that she would sort them out and returned to her desk.

Minutes later, she had sorted them out and left the office. Vijay discreetly followed. Susan went to the ladies' bathroom, spent about five minutes in there and then emerged. She continued her deliveries. Vijay mentally told himself off for being suspicious.

However, in order to be thorough, he visited the three offices where Susan had been and asked to see the documents that had been delivered under the pretext that he had been asked to check them for any mistakes. None of the documents were duplicates.

Now he felt justified in his actions. The next ten days he carried on monitoring her and discovered that on certain, though random, days her routine was the same. He concluded that on days she had sensitive information, she must be going to the bathroom and secreting the copies on her person. He reported his findings to Thomas Goddard.

Two days later, he was informed of the plan. A false but authentic-looking report containing seemingly sensitive information would be given to her to type. If she undertook the same routine as previously, he was to inform Thomas, who would then put in place a surveillance team to follow her.

A week later, Thomas contacted him to say that the surveillance team had followed Susan but nothing happened. She had gone straight home and never left. However, through other sources, they discovered that the false information had been passed on. It was decided to try again, so another false document was generated.

The result was the same. After some deliberation, the obvious conclusion was considered. She was giving the information to her husband, who, in turn, was taking it to work and then passing it on. Surveillance was placed on Mr Chaney and his place of work and more false documents were passed to Susan Chaney. Sure enough, regular visits, coinciding with the false reports, were made to Robert Chaney's office by the same man.

Three weeks later both Mr and Mrs Chaney were detained and the children were placed into care on a farm somewhere in the Lake District. The other man was also detained. This was the only time that Vijay had any feelings about his detainees.

He concluded that this was because he had been drawn in by Susan and her husband, especially the Sunday meals with their children and the thought crossed his mind that, perhaps, they had been trying to recruit him. He would never find out.

He was recalled to Small Heath days after the detentions.

Chapter 28

On 8 May 1945, the allies accepted the unconditional surrender of Germany. The war was still raging in the East but some celebrations were organised around the country. At the end of May, Vijay was called into Thomas Goddard's office and told that his services for the sub-department within M15, for which he had been working, were no longer required.

He was also informed that Mrs Oakenshaw would be leaving to return to London, to be with her husband and presumably, continue her work in another role or department for M15. He would now revert back to working in the accounts office.

Mr Goddard then thanked him on behalf of the country and himself for the sterling work that he had done and that his efforts, although they would never become public knowledge, would be recognised.

Sure enough, a short letter of thanks, notable for its lack of specifics, and a cheque for £250 arrived mid-June.

To Vijay's surprise, July saw an unexpected and monumental shift in British politics. In the general election, the people voted for a labour government which promised to change the country for the benefit of all, by introducing a huge spending programme, including a health plan to look after everyone irrespective of their place in society and nationalisation of many institutions such as public transport would also be undertaken.

The rebuilding of Britain was the vision and Vijay could see the potential, for some people, especially those in the building trade, to make substantial amounts of money with the right plans, because the war had left much destruction and devastation. He knew that the country needed to believe that winning the war had a beneficial outcome and this investment in public services was the answer according to the new government.

Vijay hoped they were right.

Chapter 29

Vijay decided that he would buy a house with his money. After some research, he bought a three-bedroom semidetached house in Handsworth Wood for £450. Not all the neighbours were pleased with his arrival but like his father at a similar age, he wanted to be successful and achieve, so buying a house in a middle-class area seemed the right thing to do.

Being able to buy the house with a mortgage of £150 (he used £50 from his savings to add to the £250 from the government) helped the purchase, as his borrowing was only a third of the value of the house. Although he could have bought a more expensive house as his salary was now £7.50 a week which meant, in theory, that he could have borrowed in excess of £500, he decided to be cautious.

Vijay moved into his home in September 1945. He was pleased with his purchase and walked around his little castle with pride. Although nowhere near as grand as Florence's house in India (he knew that it actually belonged to Jim but he had only lived there when Florence was making all the decisions, so regarded it as Florence's) he felt that he was on the ladder to higher achievements. This, he hoped, would be the start of a future of success and prosperity.

The front door of the house was between the single garage, which was on the right as he faced the house, and the bay window of the lounge and opened into a hallway. From the hallway, a door to his left led into the lounge. Straight ahead was a door leading into a kitchen and to his right was a staircase. From the lounge, a set of French, glass panelled, double doors led into another reception room, which he planned to use as a dining room.

A view of the back garden could be had from this room. The bay window of the lounge had a view of the front garden. An archway in the right-hand wall of the planned dining room accessed the kitchen. Upstairs were three bedrooms, a bathroom and a toilet. One bedroom was over the lounge, one over the dining room and the third over the hallway.

The bathroom and toilet were over the kitchen. The previous owners had taken everything they could, including the carpets and curtains, light fittings and furniture. Vijay, having not taken much advice about purchasing a house, realised afterwards that he could have negotiated the deal better, finding out subsequently that he should have included the fixtures and fittings as part of the purchase price.

He would not make the same mistake again, he reassured himself. Thinking more positively, he told himself that he could now make the home as he wanted. His next-door neighbour, to whom he had introduced himself by knocking on his door whilst bearing gifts of chocolates and flowers, owned a small factory making ornamental metal moulded decorative figures, which, during the war had been seconded and used for the manufacture of small metal objects such as buckles for belts and toe caps for boots.

He had a wife and two children, both boys. They were a Jewish family and were very friendly and helpful, especially with sorting out his house, and in order to show his appreciation for the help he had been given and was still receiving, he regularly bought the wife and children small gifts.

The previous month had seen the war in the Far East end with the surrender of Japan.

He was thankful that the war was over but was also saddened by the terrible devastation caused by the nuclear bombs and was glad his decisions did not have such consequences.

His new house was now a few miles away from Aston, so contact with Eulet, Caprice and their baby son was even more sporadic. Caprice adored her son and, having given up her job, she was enjoying her domestic life. They were on the waiting list for a council house.

The new government kept their promise and announced the implementation of large building and infrastructure projects to restore the country and generally, the people were happy and optimistic, even though rationing and food shortages had yet to be abolished and overcome respectively.

Vijay applied for and was successful in obtaining a second job as a bus conductor on the late shifts, which started at seven o'clock in the evening and finished at two o'clock in the early hours of the following day. He was usually home by 2:30. Friday and Saturday night shifts paid double because they were considered to be antisocial evenings, so he always volunteered for those.

Although the job provided extra income which was extremely welcome, he did not like it. Many nights he was verbally abused, mostly for his colour but sometimes because of his job. The passengers at that time of the day were usually young men who had been drinking. On one occasion, because of the aggressive behaviour of a group, he had cause to ring the bell in quick succession, indicating to the driver that he needed help.

The bus stopped, and the driver, who was always white, came round from his cabin and asked the group to leave. Fortunately, they disembarked peacefully, due to one of the more sober of the group apologising to the driver but not to him and encouraging his friends to do as they had been asked, rather than risk the police becoming involved.

These incidents frightened Vijay but as he had plans for his future, he needed to earn as much money as he could, so even though he did not like his bus conductor's job, he continued with it. Generally speaking, Vijay was enjoying his life. The job at BSA was secure and paid well. He was now playing cricket on a regular basis in the summer and through Mr Robinson, head of accounts, he learnt to play the game of squash.

Mr Robinson was an ex-pupil of Harrow, one of the most exclusive private schools in England and it was there that squash was started over one hundred years previously and was played mostly by members of the upper classes. Vijay felt honoured and privileged that he had been asked to learn the game and join their group.

Although no match for Arnold Robinson, after two years he managed to give him a competitive game, especially towards the end of the match, when his youth and fitness gave him an advantage. Another advantage was that the squash courts were part of the sports facilities of a school, the headmaster of which was Mr Robinson's brother, so they played for free. Another example of wealth and power having additional benefits, he noted to himself.

They were a group of six men who met every Wednesday evening and played their own small league. After about eighteen months, Vijay was able to compete equally with two of the lesser able players.

He subsequently found out that space in the group had become available because one of the members had injured his back and could no longer play, which made him feel even better about Mr Robinson because he knew that Arnold could have asked others but he chose to ask him.

Not all people are racist, he reminded himself.

Chapter 30

15 August 1947 brought about, after many political and violent exchanges, the independence of India and the partition of the sub-continent into two dominions, but three areas, namely India, West Pakistan and East Pakistan. The partition and the subsequent movement of the people caused some of the worst violence ever seen between the Muslims and the Hindus and hundreds of thousands of deaths occurred, with communities destroyed and the worst kind of ethnic cleansing taking place.

Young men, on both sides, fresh from the Second World War and trained in combat, were largely responsible for this, although the politicians had their part to play, as they could not agree on how to achieve peaceful independence. Gandhi, who had constantly spoken out against partition, had been overruled during the talks by Mountbatten, Nehru and Jinnah.

Vijay, hearing all this news, was deeply concerned for his family but took comfort in the fact that the area of Gujarat that they lived in was not in the direct line of the movement of people.

This worry prompted Vijay to start thinking about visiting his mother and grandmother, especially now that he had some money and could afford to do so.

Also, as he was now approaching his 26th birthday, had a house, jobs and lived in England, finding a bride and having a family was the next logical step in his plans, especially as both his cousins were now married and had a child each.

He knew that he would be considered a good prospect for anyone looking to find a husband for their daughter. He also knew only too well that once his mother was told of his return, she would expect him to marry and the local grapevine would grow and expand to try and find him a wife. His biggest problem, he thought, would be securing the six weeks leave he would need.

Surprisingly to him, this turned out to be his smallest problem. Mr Robinson, now a friend as well as his head of department, acquiesced without hesitation and Mr Goddard offered him longer should he need the time, saying he deserved a favour for his efforts during the war. As he would find out, choosing his future bride was the biggest problem, thankfully not for him but certainly for his mother.

On informing his mother of his intentions, he expected, as had happened to his parents, he would turn up on the day and marry the young lady his mother had chosen, with all the arrangements already in place. The reality was far different. Upon his mother sharing the information with the local communities of her son's return to India and his desire to marry, more than two dozen interested sets of parents contacted her for an audience to discuss the possibility of their daughters marrying Vijay.

They were all from the same caste and all had the surname Patel. After discussing the matter with her brother-in-law Bhupendra and her sister Nalini, they managed to shrink the list down to three. One was Hemant's sister-in-law and was two years younger than Vijay and the others were from neighbouring villages.

They decided on Anshula, Hemant's sister-in-law, on the basis that her older sister, Rupal, had worked out well for Hemant. Vijay was informed of the decision that had been made for him and to his surprise, a photograph of his intended bride was included in the letter he had received. He was also told that there had been a number of other interested parties but no other information was given to him.

He was very pleased with their choice, not only with Anshula's looks but also that she was well-educated and had trained to become a teacher. A first, as far as he knew, he was also encouraged to write to Anshula so that they could make plans for the wedding and their future. This daunted him more than he thought it would.

Making shared decisions was not very easy as he was used to either being told what to do or making his own decisions unilaterally. He decided to write back saying he had full confidence in all parties to arrange everything for the wedding.

The wedding was arranged for Friday 16 April 1948.

Vijay telephoned Florence to tell her of his impending wedding. After a little giggle about the fact that he was having an arranged marriage, she congratulated him and wished him well. He invited her to the wedding but she politely declined.

However, she did invite him for dinner on his birthday. As it fell on a Monday, they agreed for him to come on Sunday 7th December for lunch. The four of them would go to the venue where she had married Clive. At the meal, Vijay also agreed to spend Christmas with them, so they decided that, with Christmas day falling on a Thursday, Vijay should arrive on Christmas Eve and leave on the following Sunday.

December became an exciting and busy month for Vijay with all that was happening and by New Year, all his arrangements were in place and Anshula had also completed all the necessary paperwork for her to travel back with him after the wedding. Vijay's plans were for him to finish work on Friday 19th March and leave for India on Sunday 21st March and then to return to England to restart work on Monday 10th May.

When he arrived in Bombay, he would spend two days and one night with William Grundy at his home and then travel to Untdi. Both William and Gurwinder would travel together, for the day, to attend his wedding.

30 January 1948 sent shock waves around the world. Since the partition of India, Mahatma Gandhi had resigned himself to preaching for peace. A frail man of seventy eight years, weakened by his many hunger strikes, he spent most of his time at his home, Birla House, in New Delhi, holding daily prayers in the grounds every afternoon. About a thousand people usually attended.

That day, physically supported by two of his grandnieces, he was walking to the prayer meeting when Nathuram Godse, a militant Hindu, shot him three times in the chest at point-blank range. He died where he had wished; at daily prayer. Vijay was very upset by this news, especially as he knew his father had met Gandhi during the mid-twenties and had extolled his virtues and described him as a great man.

This brought back memories of his father and also a reminder, not that he needed reminding, that, unlike Godse, who was now in custody and would, no doubt, be executed, his father's murderer was still at large.

This event refreshed his promise to himself to seek revenge for his father's murder and acted as a renewed aide-memoire that this was yet to be fulfilled.

Chapter 31

Saturday 20th March, Vijay left home for Southampton with his neighbour, Yosef Goldstein, who was driving him to New Street station early in the morning, knowing that his train journey would take at least seven hours with one change at Reading. This time, he had a large suitcase full of clothes for himself and another full of presents to take back for his relatives, unlike his arrival in England when he had only one small suitcase.

At the station, he thanked Yosef for the lift and then gave him a small paper bag, which contained a bar of chocolate for his wife and a comic magazine for each of the boys. Yosef had previously asked him why he had this way of thanking him and his family and the only answer Vijay could give was that when he was a child he remembered the same being done by his father's friends when they had visited so he assumed that is how things are done, that is, no present for the man, only presents for the wife and children. They shook hands and then Yosef got into his car and drove away. Vijay watched him leave and appreciated the convenience of having a car.

Buying a car had not been important to Vijay because as a bus conductor he, unofficially but the same as all the other employees of the bus company, enjoyed free travel, so he had not seriously thought about it but now that he would be bringing a wife home, he knew that he would have to consider purchasing one for them to go shopping or visiting and because a small number of the residents of his road already had cars, he wanted one as well.

He walked into the station, bought himself a newspaper and a car magazine and then made his way to his platform and waited until it was time to board the train and find his seat for the seven hour journey to Southampton, via Reading. He had read both his newspaper and car magazine, from front to back, had had a little sleep and had also chatted to the passenger opposite by the time the train arrived in Southampton. Another reason to buy a car he told himself, thinking that he could have had more flexibility in his travel arrangements.

He had decided to stay at the same boarding house that Jim had booked for the night of 27 December 1941. Mavis had telephoned for him a few weeks earlier and made the booking. Arriving in a taxi from the station, he saw that the property had been renovated since his last visit. Politely greeted by the same landlady, who still owned the property, he mentioned that he had been a previous guest some years ago but she had no memory of him until he described Florence and her elegant attire, after which she recalled his stay.

She told him dinner was in three-quarters of an hour as she guided him to the same room he had stayed in on his previous visit. After settling in, he quickly bathed and changed, then went back downstairs for dinner. The boarding house was full and most of the residents, the property could accommodate up to ten people in five bedrooms, were already seated at their tables waiting for their meals.

He sat down at one of the two empty tables and surveyed the room. Three couples were already sat at tables laid out for two people and the other two tables were laid out for single persons. He chose the table nearest to the window and sat down. The other residents gave him varying stares ranging from a cursory glance from one young man, curious looks from the women, to another man who glared at him in such a way that he felt that if looks could kill, he would be dead.

Over six years of these situations had toughened up Vijay, so unless there was a risk of any physical threat, he had taught himself to stare back vacuously and unemotionally, rather than look away. This usually, but not always, resulted in a short awkward moment before the other party looked away and resumed his or her meal.

The moment moved on as the door opened and the final resident, a young lady probably in her mid-twenties, entered the room. She immediately greeted everyone with a cheerful, 'Good evening' and gracefully walked to the empty table and sat down. A very sociable person, she had engaged in conversation with all the other guests within the first few minutes and after about ten minutes, the room was buzzing with conversations between all the tables.

Even the man with the deadly looks had a brief conversation with Vijay, as it became obvious that Vijay was fluent in English, albeit with a West Midlands accent, picked up during his time with Florence, who had picked hers up from her parents. The conversations varied from sport to politics for the men and hair, make-up and fashion for the women, as well as the usual polite inquisitive questions about each other.

It transpired that one couple had arrived from Barbados and were going to London the next day, another couple had arrived from America and were going to Leeds via Manchester and the third couple [the man with the deadly glare and his wife] were going out to Aden to join the troops stationed there. The young lady was sailing to Brazil to join her husband who worked for the Foreign Office and had been posted there.

He mused over the fact that the evening had changed from a quiet and insular group of persons to a happier and friendlier group of eight all due to the actions of one woman. Slowly, the guests left the dining room and retired to their rooms.

Vijay went to his bedroom shortly after the first couple had left and was fast asleep within minutes of his head resting down on his pillow.

The next morning, he was up early and went for a walk. He retraced his steps to the same post office he had visited some years ago. This early in the morning on a Sunday, there was hardly anyone on the streets, so there was very little possibility of a repeat of the encounter he had experienced the last time he had walked this route. In fact, the only people he saw were the milkman and the paperboy.

Arriving at the post office, which now also doubled as newsagents, he went in and bought a newspaper, The Sunday Times and then walked back. The dining room was laid out for breakfast, so Vijay sat down at the same table as the night before and started reading his newspaper. The rest of the residents trickled in over the next ten minutes and conversation resumed between them without needing the young lady's initiation.

After breakfast, they said their goodbyes, collected their suitcases and left for their various destinations. Vijay and the young lady, Mrs Constance Sayers, had agreed during breakfast to share a taxi and so left for the port together.

Chapter 32

Vijay arrived back in India early on the morning of Tuesday, 13 April 1948. This time he travelled on a passenger ship and had his own cabin. The majority of passengers were British, mostly people returning to their jobs supporting the Indian government and helping the country to progress during the transition phase, which was expected to last three to four years.

William met him at the docks, shook his hand firmly and carried one of the suitcases to the taxi. A step up from the horse and cart they had used when he had left, he jokingly commented to William.

They talked about their lives, Vijay telling William about his progress in England, leaving out his espionage work and William again expressed his disappointment that Vijay had not taken the opportunity to go to university and get himself a degree, but did show his admiration for him, commenting that Vijay had worked hard by holding down two jobs and thereby being able to buy his own home.

His future plans were discussed more in terms of his family; wife and children; rather than his career because Vijay was not sure where he wanted to be in terms of his ambitions. He did know that working for himself and being independent was definitely his goal.

William was still working for the Times and was very busy. The army had virtually pulled out, just leaving a few advisors, so he spent more time at the British Club, which was still very active. He had turned down a move to New Delhi, even though it would have meant promotion and an increase in salary, as he planned to retire in about five years' time and did not want change in his life at present.

They arrived at William's house and as he climbed out of the taxi, Vijay looked across the street at his previous home of some years ago. One of the more noticeable differences was the children's toys in the garden, which reminded him that Florence and Kantaben had both been childless. A little boy was playing with another boy of a similar age whilst two ladies sat on chairs, drinking tea and chatting

Both were dressed in saris.

That was the other notable difference.

India is taking over its own destiny, he thought to himself, pleased that this was the case. Not that he wished the British any harm as he had been helped by many of them but being ruled by a foreign power is not right for any country was his firm belief. William had noticed his gaze and explained that the house had first been sold to a British civil servant and his family after Vijay had left and then had been sold to an Indian government minister and his family after independence. This man held a very high office in the Indian government and was still the present occupant. The other houses had also changed hands and William was now the only person left who had lived on the street when Vijay was there.

He was also the only British person now.

Entering William's house was like going back in time. Nothing had changed in almost ten years, from his first visit a few weeks after he had arrived at Florence's house, to now. Same carpets, curtains and furniture. He surmised that they were probably the originals from when the house was first bought and furnished by William. He carried his suitcases up to the guest bedroom and unpacked just enough to last him the two days he was staying.

After a quick wash and brush up, he went downstairs and joined William in the kitchen where he was busy preparing lunch. Over lunch, Vijay discussed his plans for his time in India, all of six days. He had decided that he wanted to spend that afternoon on his own to collect his thoughts and relax. William then told him that he had arranged dinner at the British Club that evening and, yes, before Vijay could interject, Indians could now be members or be taken as guests.

Vijay continued by saying that he would be catching the ten o'clock train to Surat the following morning. After the wedding, he and Anshula would travel back to Bombay on Saturday, 17 April and stay in a hotel, which Gurwinder Singh had already booked for them. The ship taking them back to England was sailing at two o'clock on Sunday, 18 April.

They agreed that as Vijay could manage with taking only one suitcase to Untdi, William would meet them at the docks with the other one. Vijay had already, politely but firmly, instructed Anshula that she could only take two suitcases for all her belongings. He did explain to her that his suitcase would be almost empty once he had given out his presents, so she could use that one as well.

After helping William to clean up after lunch, Vijay went off for a walk. He knew exactly where he was heading. Walking up the street for only the fourth time in his life, he lost himself in the memory of that first day; however, this time he did not weaken at the knees.

He reached the end of the street and turned right and saw the grand house with its protective wall and gated entrance, which was guarded by two soldiers, one on each side, rifles on their shoulders, who were from a Sikh regiment, he guessed, looking at their uniforms and head dresses.

He walked past them. No movement apart from the eyes, which followed him all the way, he noticed admiringly. He then visited the street where he was born, stopping to chat with one of the residents who still remembered him from all those years ago.

He resisted the temptation to call on the occupants of his birthplace and just stood outside for a few moments, reflecting on his time there and how different his life might have been had his father not been murdered. He gave a big sigh and then retraced his steps back to William's house.

He dressed for dinner in the grey suit he had bought for his job at BSA, pairing it with a white shirt and a diamond-patterned black and white tie and went downstairs. William was already waiting for him dressed in a navy blue jacket, beige corduroy trousers, pale blue shirt and a blue, red and white paisley patterned tie.

Arriving at the British Club in a taxi, they entered and were escorted to their table, which Vijay noticed was set for three people.

"Is someone joining us?" he asked.

"Yes," replied William, giving no indication who the third person was.

They sat down at the table and were served with glasses of water. William picked up and started reading the club newsletter, which had been left on the table for members to peruse whilst they waited to be served.

Vijay was seated with his back to the door and had a view of the grounds through the French doors behind William and saw a few members enjoying a game of bowls on the crown green bowling area, which did not surprise him as evenings were probably the most comfortable time of the day in terms of the weather. The players all looked very smart in their whites, shirts and trousers for the men and long dresses for the ladies.

A tap on his shoulder and the booming voice of Gurwinder Singh broke his thoughts. He immediately stood up, turned around, saw Gurwinder and held out his hand in greeting, perusing him as they shook hands. Smartly dressed in a black suit, white shirt and a black tie and a white turban, he looked the successful man he was.

"This is so good," Vijay enthused, as they shook hands. "Thank you so much for inviting him," he said, turning to William.

Gurwinder Singh sat down in the empty chair after shaking William's hand.

They all chatted to each other. By the end of the evening, the past six years of all their lives had been discussed and dissected. Gurwinder was now one of the directors for The Bombay City and Gujarat Textile Company and had an office on the fifth floor. He jokingly said his next move upwards would be to heaven.

He had recently had his fiftieth birthday and his eldest child, a son, was getting married in three months time. His three other children, all daughters, were already married and he had one grandchild, a girl. He acknowledged that independence had allowed him to become a director as, until then, only British men had occupied such high positions.

He listened intently to Vijay as he described his time in England.

Gurwinder also expressed disappointment that the opportunity to study at Birmingham University had not been taken and hoped the decision would not be regretted. The food was excellent and Vijay, who through his friendships with Arnold Robinson and Thomas Goddard had been introduced to fine wines accompanying good food, wished that both William and Gurwinder were not teetotal, as he would have really enjoyed a glass or two of wine with the meal.

He never mentioned to his present companions that he drank alcohol as he did not want his family to find out. After about three hours, Gurwinder rose up and said it was time for him to leave as he was meeting with his future daughter-in-law's parents the following day. William and Vijay said their goodbyes to him and then stayed for another half an hour or so before going home.

Chapter 33

Vijay had set his alarm clock for seven o'clock but woke up well before then, so got up and was washed, dressed and packed before seven. Not that there was much packing to do. The one suitcase he was taking was mostly full of presents for his mother, grandmother, uncle, auntie, his two cousins, their spouses and their sons.

His wedding clothes had been chosen by his mother and were ready for him at his home in Untdi. On the day of the wedding, his family would travel to Anshula's village, Chichli, in a car that Bhupendra had organised. All five of them would be in the same car.

Both Hemant and Gita were now married and had a child each. Gita's husband, Arun, was a pharmacist and had a pharmacy in Surat, next door to the doctor's surgery and the family lived in a house on the outskirts of the town.

Hemant, on the other hand, was not very academic and had struggled at school but was, however, very hard working and entrepreneurial, and having bought himself a lorry, he drove around to the surrounding villages selling goods, food, hardware or anything else he thought the villagers might buy.

He would order in bulk from warehouses in Bombay and then, with the help of his wife, Rupal, they would repackage the goods into smaller parcels and then sell them for a profit. He also very shrewdly lived a frugal life, well within his means, for two reasons.

Firstly, he did not want to create a degree of envy amongst his family and friends and, secondly, he thought that he could deter competitors if they believed that all his hard work provided little reward. For these reasons, they lived in a small house in Untdi, a few hundred yards away from his parents, auntie and grandmother.

Vijay had struggled to choose presents for the family. Eventually, he decided to buy three transistor radios, one each for Bhupendra, Hemant and Arun, a necklace each for Sunila and Nalini, earrings for Gita and Rupal and clothes for his two cousins once removed, both boys. Gita's son was called Bhaskar and Hemant's son was called Vinod. He bought a pair of leather sandals for his grandmother.

He had been greatly helped by Mrs Mavis Woodford, nee Cutler, his first contact at BSA and now a good friend. She had taken him shopping with her husband and son. Her husband, Robert, had left the RAF at the end of the war and now worked for an engineering company in Hockley, another industrial area in Birmingham. Their son Andrew, just one-year-old, was pushed along in his pram by Robert while they did the shopping.

The only presents she did not help him with were his wedding ring present for Anshula, the perfume he had bought for her, after Robert's recommendation and the toy for Andrew. He also bought historical books for William in recognition of his help and kindness. He felt that William would appreciate them and the thought that would have gone into choosing them, more than material goods.

Placing his suitcase in the hall, Vijay went out of the front door and into the garden. He walked to the gate and looked down the street. His gaze lingered on the spot where he had stood over ten years ago, 10 February 1938, another date imprinted in his mind. He remembered William marching towards him with menace. How times have changed, he thought to himself.

Moving his eyes further round, he saw the toys were still in the garden opposite. After a short time spent in contemplation and reminiscence, he turned around and went back into the house. He heard noises emanating from the kitchen and surmised that William was now up and in the kitchen, making some breakfast. He picked up the parcel, containing the books he had bought, off the hall table where he had placed it earlier and went into the kitchen.

"Good morning, can I help?" he enquired. "By the way, this present is for you," he added, placing the parcel on the table. "I hope you like it."

Vijay then started to lay the table. He reflected that William had always been self-sufficient and had never had servants. By the time breakfast was over and everything had been cleaned and tidied away, it was time for Vijay to go to the station. William had arranged for a taxi to pick him up at nine o'clock, allowing ample time for him to catch his train at ten.

"Just enough time for me to open my present," he said and began unwrapping his parcel. His face beamed when he saw the books and Vijay knew his choice had been right.

They shook hands and then Vijay walked into the hall, picked up his suitcase and exited the house. A taxi was already waiting for him.

Arriving at the station, he bought his ticket to Surat, boarded the train and settled down for the journey.

Hemant met him at the station, greeting him with a hug, then picking up Vijay's suitcase for him, they walked to his lorry. After gently placing the suitcase into the back of the lorry, they climbed into the cab and drove to Untdi, with Hemant spending the entire journey quizzing Vijay about England and asking what his own chances were of making a better life for himself and his family if he was to go there.

Vijay told him that hard work and endeavour would give him a good chance of success but there was no guarantee, as racial prejudice was prevalent in many places and industries, and in his opinion, the higher up the social scale you went, the more difficult it was to break into that circle; however, in his experience he felt that earning money was relatively easy as there was a shortage of labour, but fitting into society was much more difficult; however if he wanted to come to England, he promised to help in any way he could.

Arriving at the family home, Vijay saw all his family excitedly waiting outside but was upset to notice that his mother had become much frailer since he had left and consequently looked very old. Both his mother and grandmother were dressed in white saris and white blouses, the traditional colour for widows. He climbed down from the cab as soon as the lorry came to a standstill and ran to his mother.

They hugged each other without saying a word.

Eventually, after all the greetings had been exchanged, they went into the house, which had not changed over the years. Hemant had already taken in Vijay's suitcase, so presents were handed out with everyone pleased with his choices.

After a while, Hemant left, taking his radio, Rupal's earrings and Vinod's clothes with him, saying his son would be the next best-dressed male at the wedding, second only to Vijay and that his wife would wear her earrings but he laughingly promised that he would not play his radio during the ceremony.

Vijay chatted for a while with the family and then decided to go for a walk on his own, choosing to go along the same route as he had done on the day of his brother's death, stopping and sitting on the same rock he had sat on that day. However, on this day he was more reflective and less angry.

He was still contemplating his past life when his thoughts were disturbed by the sound of footsteps, causing him to look up to see who was approaching. His mother came and sat down beside him and started the long overdue conversation she knew they needed to have, just between them, openly and emotionally.

She began by telling him how proud she was of him and his achievements and then went on to say how pleased she was that he had returned home to marry an Indian girl of the same caste and thereby uphold his tradition and also maintain the honour of the family.

She explained that she had been worried that he would meet and marry an English girl and thereby bring dishonour and disgrace to the family. They then discussed and imagined how different their lives might have been had both Ramesh and Ravi not died at such young ages and what influences they might have had on them.

Sunila did most of the talking with Vijay only interjecting now and then, happy that she was releasing all her years of pent-up feelings. He agreed with his mother most of the time but also emphasised that he would probably never have gone to England if his life had been as it would have been planned by his father, as it was most likely that he would have ended up working in Bombay in a well-paid job, behind a desk, either for The Bombay City and Gujarat Textile Company or some other similar enterprise.

Although he could not tell her everything, he did try to explain to her that his life had been more challenging and exciting because of all that had happened and his life experiences would make for interesting stories to be told to his children and grandchildren in years to come.

He thanked her for all she had done for him, especially when she had taken him for the day trip to Bombay, which became the turning point in his life, changing him from an angry, disgruntled and petulant teenager, who had become so obsessed with his own misfortunes that he could not envisage how to make his life better, into the person he was now. He had needed that reminder that there were people less fortunate than him and that life is only improved by a sustained hard-working ethic.

Wallowing in the misery and circumstances of your life, believing them to be injustices or bad luck, rather than tackling them by discovering and then implementing ways of improving them, is of no benefit to yourself or anyone else, he now believed.

As the sun had started to set and the air was cooling, they stood up and walked home. On the way, Vijay asked his mother what she would like to do with regard to her future life. She told him she was happy living with her mother, sister and brother-in-law and did not want that to change. However, if in the future, an opportunity arose for her to visit England, she would like to do so.

Vijay promised that he would arrange that for her as soon as he could. The rest of the family were on the porch when they arrived home enjoying a late evening drink, so they joined them for a short chat before they all retired to bed.

The following day was busy for everyone except Vijay and his grandmother. His mother, auntie and Rupal were rushing around preparing food, which Bhupendra and Hemant then transported to Anshula's village and Vinod was getting under everyone's feet, so to help out, Vijay offered to take Vinod for a walk in his baby stroller, another of Hemant's purchases through his business.

The second-hand stroller had been bought in Bombay off a British family, leaving India after independence and no longer having the need for it. He asked his grandmother to join them but she told him that she was very happy resting on the porch and declined his invitation.

He decided to walk to the train station and back, a trip that would probably take just over an hour. Memories came back as he walked and he was pleased for this time to himself. Arriving at the station, he went into the waiting room which was empty and sat there for a while as Vinod had fallen asleep, contemplating his situation and the wedding, staying there until Vinod awoke, after which they set off again back to Untdi.

The priest had arrived earlier than the arranged time and was waiting for him when he arrived back at the village, so his grandmother took charge of Vinod whilst the priest and Vijay discussed the ritualistic elements of the wedding ceremony that would be taking place the following day and also a few preliminary prayers were chanted by the priest, as was the custom.

He had already been to do the same for Anshula that morning. By late afternoon, all the hurrying and scurrying had finished and an exhausted family settled down for the evening, glad that everything was going to plan. After they had all eaten their meal, Hemant, Rupal and Vinod went home, the beds were made and an early night was decided upon by them all.

Vijay again slept in his bed on the rafters. He had a fitful night's sleep as he had much on his mind. His mother was also restless, so they whispered to each other to get up and sit on the porch for a while. Wrapped in their blankets, they continued their earlier conversation.

Eventually, in the early hours of the morning, they went back to bed with Ramesh and Ravi having been their only topics of dialogue, as Sunila and Vijay both, from different viewpoints, wished that they were both still alive to be part of the wedding that was to take place later that day.

Chapter 34

Vijay was awake before the rest of the family, so he quietly dressed and then went out onto the porch and sat in the chair his grandmother had sat in the day before. He saw one of the other villagers walk by and recognised him as one of the schoolboys he had fought with years ago during his wayward days. They acknowledged each other with a polite nod of the head.

From his home country of India, apart from family, he had only invited William and Gurwinder to his wedding as he did not have any other close friends there. Realistically, he knew that his ties with India would diminish as time went on and his only contact would be present family and even that contact would lessen over time.

Back in England, he had invited Eulet and Caprice as well as Florence but all of them had declined. They had sent him presents, which he had left at his home in Handsworth Wood so that he and Anshula could open them together.

His mother came out and sat down in one of the other chairs. They exchanged morning greetings and asked each other how they were and then his mother went back indoors and emerged a few minutes later with two cups of tea, one of which she gave to Vijay.

They drank their tea silently, each having their own private thoughts, until noises from inside the house told them that the others were awake, so Sunila quickly finished her tea and went back into the house to take charge of the proceedings of the morning, knowing that organised chaos would ensue as it does at all weddings.

Bhupendra and Vijay were told to wash and dress first and then to go to Bhupendra's friend's house, three doors away until it was time to leave, which would be 9.00 a.m. Vijay's wedding clothes, white tunic and pantaloons type trousers trimmed with silver braiding, had been hung up ready for him by his mother.

Both men dutifully did as they were asked and by 7.30 a.m., they were ready and had left the house. The car, which had been borrowed from a doctor in Surat who was a close friend of Bhupendra's son-in-law Arun, that they were using had already been dropped off sometime earlier and was parked outside the house, ready for Bhupendra, who had been taught to drive by his son Hemant.

Bhupendra, his friend and Vijay sat on the porch and chatted until two minutes to nine. Everything from politics, sport, the past and the future were discussed by all three, with both Bhupendra and his friend being adamant that Vijay was lucky to be in the position he was in.

Vijay tried to tell them that seizing opportunities and working at them was the actual reality and that taking the gamble and its associated risks was the difficult decision that had to be taken when any venture was embarked upon.

Luck, in his opinion, was at which level in society you were born, because being born into the higher echelons of society and having wealth gives a person great advantages over other members of society and no matter how much a wealthy person believes that he understands poverty, he has to experience it for some considerable time to fully appreciate it, adding that the latter applied to all kinds of prejudices as well.

They finished their conversation, agreeing to disagree, when it was time to leave and shook hands. Bhupendra's friend and his family were setting off to attend the wedding later on in the morning.

As the women were all ready and waiting when they returned home, they all climbed into the car, men in the front and women in the back and set off on the journey to Anshula's village.

Arriving at the school hall fifteen minutes later, Bhupendra parked outside to let his passengers alight from the car, then drove the car to a shady place further down the dusty street. Walking back to the school, he passed groups of men, Anshula's side of the wedding guests and stopped to chat with them as he knew most of them from when Hemant had married Rupal, Anshula's older sister, and as Ramesh was dead and had no brothers, he was the father of the groom, in effect, and was greeted and treated as such by them.

Once in the hall, he sought out Vijay and escorted him to the ceremonial altar, which was set out on the raised stage at the front, consisting of two cushions next to each other on which Vijay and Anshula would sit and one cushion opposite on which the priest would sit.

Between where the couple and priest would sit were a number of steel bowls containing different coloured flower petals, one bowl half full of a red dye, sindoor, and a small jar that held some incense sticks.

Bhupendra explained to Vijay that once Anshula was seated and some prayers had been said, the priest would beckon him to come and sit down next to his future wife. There would then be some more prayers for them both, followed by some incantations, in which the assembled women would join in, with the whole ceremony taking about four to five hours, during which the men would have their meals and mingle about, the children would have their meals and play and the women would chat and eat whilst also watching the ceremony. Arun would be in charge of collecting and documenting the gifts, mostly always money.

A noisy, happy-sounding commotion, which announced the arrival of the bride halted their conversation. They turned to look. Vijay could not see Anshula as her parents and sister were with her as they shepherded her into the building. He followed the group with his gaze and saw her once she reached the stage and her entourage had moved away.

A bright red sari with gold braiding and a matching red blouse was her wedding outfit, with her head being covered with part of her sari. He noticed henna on her hands and sandals on her feet and watched as she, keeping her head bowed, made her way to the ceremonial altar and sat down.

Vijay wondered if she was as nervous as he was. The priest, who had quietly come in through another door and was already seated, started his prayers and the noise level in the hall dropped.

Half an hour later, Vijay was beckoned by the priest. Three hours later, the ceremony had reached the part where Anshula could uncover her face and head, which she slowly did. Vijay turned his head and looked at her. She had her eyes closed.

The priest rose from his cushion and gestured to one of the men to get him a drink, moving away a little distance from the altar. A hush fell over the hall as the women stopped chatting and turned their attention towards the couple. The majority of the men and children were still outside, the men smoking and talking, the children playing.

Anshula turned her head towards Vijay and quickly opened and closed her eyes, taking only a furtive glance before returning back to her former position. Vijay hoped she liked what she had seen because he certainly was very pleased with what he had seen. She was much prettier in person than in the black and white photograph he had been sent.

The priest returned and the ceremony continued. An hour and a quarter later, the ceremony concluded and the respective mothers of the bride and groom brought over drinks and food for the newly married couple. An awkward silence followed as they ate their meals, still seated on their cushions, with neither of them daring to lift their heads to look at each other.

Once the meals were over, Vijay was escorted outside to talk with the men and Anshula sat with her mother, sister and mother-in-law. Outside, Vijay saw William and Gurwinder chatting to each other, so he went over to join them and thanked them for coming, appreciating that they had both taken the day off from work.

A few minutes later, Hemant came over to say it was time for William and Gurwinder to leave if they were to catch the last train back to Bombay, having already offered to drive them to the station. Hasty goodbyes and a 'see you on Sunday' shout to William, were exchanged as they climbed into the car. Once the car was out of sight, Vijay went back to the other guests to continue with the festivities.

The guests started to leave at about seven o'clock and by eight o'clock, only immediate family remained, many of whom would return the day after to help with the cleaning and tidying.

An agreement had already been made that Anshula would return home with her parents that evening and Vijay would go back to his home. With this in mind, the newly married couple were allowed a few minutes to talk privately a short distance from everyone else but still in full view.

Vijay spoke first, in a 'matter of fact' way, by reminding her of the plans for the following day and the time for her to be ready and all the practical arrangements that had been made up to boarding the ship.

Anshula listened and nodded her head, indicating that she understood. When he had finished, the only words she spoke were,

"I promise to do my best to be a good wife."

Vijay felt embarrassed and stupid, realising that he should have made a similar comment and also that he should have told her that he would look after her. After all, as of today, she was his responsibility, because her parents had given her to him in the hope and belief that he would give her a good life and had entrusted her to him with the conviction that their research had been as extensive and full enough as was possible in order to give their daughter a caring husband.

Whilst he stood there mentally admonishing himself for his unthoughtful and inconsiderate behaviour, Anshula walked back to her waiting family and they all left the school hall.

Vijay joined his family a few seconds later and they also left.

Chapter 35

The following morning, Vijay and Bhupendra drove to Chichli to pick up Anshula and her three suitcases, Hemant having dropped off Vijay's empty case the day before the wedding. On the journey, Bhupendra gave Vijay a large envelope full of money, telling him it contained the dowry and the wedding gifts and also that he had kept a record of who had given what so that reciprocal amounts could be gifted when the time arose for their children's weddings and that he would contact Vijay when that became necessary.

Vijay took out the dowry money and gave the rest back to Bhupendra, asking him to keep it safe and then to use it as and when he had to for those future weddings, knowing that it would be very unlikely that he and Anshula would be attending.

When they arrived in Chichli, Anshula was waiting outside her home with her parents standing on either side of her. Vijay and Bhupendra loaded the suitcases into the car and then Vijay, trying to make amends for yesterday evening, assured Anshula's parents that he would look after her and treat her with respect. A tearful Anshula climbed into the back seat and waved to her parents as the car drove away.

Arriving back in Untdi, they were met by Hemant, Rupal and Vinod who had come to bid their farewells. Whilst Bhupendra collected Vijay's small bag from the house, Sunila, Nalini and their mother, in turn, hugged Vijay, all three of them in tears and then, as he was getting into the car, Hemant reminded Vijay that he had promised to search out any opportunities for him in England.

Anshula remained in the car and spoke to her sister through the window, whilst trying to stop Vinod from getting into the car. A few minutes later, the car was on its way to the station. Once there, Bhupendra and Vijay carried the cases to the platform and Anshula carried the small bag and then they waited for the train to arrive, which it duly did ten minutes later.

After helping to load on the cases Bhupendra left, whilst Vijay and Anshula boarded the train, found two seats and sat down. Nervously, they started to talk and began the lifelong journey of getting to know each other as a married couple, and not just as relatives through a marriage, who had never met. Anshula told him that after Rupal's wedding, murmurings had begun about this possible alliance but her parents were concerned that he might have become a man of ill-repute in England.

Asking her what she meant by ill-repute, she told him that they worried about him eating meat, drinking alcohol and having girlfriends. He admitted that he ate meat and that it was very tasty, drank alcohol but had never been drunk and categorically denied having had any girlfriends in a romantic sense but informed her that he had friends who were ladies, some married and others not, explaining to her that this type of socialising was normal in England.

They also discussed becoming parents, agreeing on having children but disagreeing on the number, with Vijay wanting to stop once they had a son, whereas Anshula wanted to stop after two, irrespective of gender. Anshula closed that topic of conversation by saying she would pray for a daughter and son in that order.

Another topic discussed was life in England and how they would be welcomed. Vijay explained that racism was prevalent in the society and prejudice was openly displayed but, as the coloured population increased because immigrant labour was needed for the economy, he firmly believed that the situation would improve as time went on and he was convinced that by the turn of the century, everyone would be treated equally.

He also thought that great opportunities were available to become successful.

He told her that he had decided to buy a car, a four door Ford Prefect, when they had settled into their life in Handsworth Wood, which would make travelling around much easier for them, especially with regard to shopping and visiting.

Small Indian communities were springing up in areas all over the country, particularly in the small towns north west of Birmingham, such as Walsall, Wolverhampton, Bilston and West Bromwich, which meant that if they made friends in these areas, they could travel more easily to visit.

The train pulled into the station in Bombay, so the conversation stopped as they collected their belongings and alighted onto the platform. A porter came and helped with the cases leading them to where a number of taxis were waiting.

Gurwinder had booked them into the Taj Mahal Palace Hotel, one of the finest hotels in Bombay. Vijay remembered the hotel from before when he had been there with his father, as a visitor, to meet one of his father's company superiors who was visiting from England. At that time it was one of the few places that had electricity and Vijay had marvelled at the lights.

The one-night stay was a joint wedding present given by William and Gurwinder. Opened forty five years ago, the rumour was that Mr Tata, a prominent industrialist, had built the hotel after being refused entry into the Watson Hotel, which had been built by Mr J H Watson, owner of a large textile business, and had a 'whites only' policy.

They settled into their room and then washed and changed before going to dinner, taking turns to use the bathroom. No intimacy, not even the holding of hands, had yet taken place between them. Vijay expressed that he was pleased with her looks and praised her attire and Anshula reciprocated.

Both found the situation difficult, neither knowing how to broach the subject of intimacy, even though both had received advice and guidance, from her mother and sister in the case of Anshula and from his cousin in the case of Vijay. They went downstairs for their meal during which Vijay gave Anshula the envelope containing the dowry money and told her she could do whatever she wanted to do with it, including returning it to her parents.

Anshula thanked him for his gesture but said she would not give it back to her parents because they would be offended but thought that perhaps they could use it to help pay for her parents to visit England once their first grandchild was born. Vijay said that it was a very nice idea and an excellent use of the money.

After the meal, during which they learned more about each other, they retired to their room. Once they had changed, again separately in the privacy of the bathroom, they got into bed. Vijay had already decided that he would not make the first move, so lay on his side in the bed, facing towards her and said, "Goodnight."

Anshula, who was lying on her back, replied but remained motionless and continued looking up at the ceiling. Eventually, with no more verbal exchanges occurring, Vijay rolled over and turned onto his other side so that his back was towards her, settled down and went to sleep. Anshula did not sleep that night.

The next morning, Anshula apologised and explained that she was nervous. Vijay said that no apology was necessary and there was no rush on his part. However, he was pleased to notice that when she went to the bathroom to wash and change, she left the bathroom door very slightly open, not enough for him to see anything but enough to suggest that she felt a little more at ease and relaxed with their relationship.

After breakfast they went back to their room, packed their suitcases, called for a porter and made their way to the lobby. A taxi was waiting outside to take them to the port, which was only a few minutes' drive away. Vijay tipped the porter and also gave some money to one of the many beggars on the street outside the hotel before climbing into the taxi.

They saw William waiting for them as the taxi pulled into the port with Vijay's other suitcase at his feet. He greeted them with a wave and then, once they had alighted from the taxi, he said,

"I hope you had a lovely meal last night and your room was nice and comfortable."

"Yes, all was fine," replied Vijay.

"Well, I wish you both a safe and pleasant journey and please keep in touch. I am off now." With that, he shook their hands and then turned and walked off.

A couple of porters from the ship came over and carried their luggage on board and they followed them up the gangway. Tears filled Anshula's eyes as she stood by the ship's rail on the promenade deck; a mixture of happiness, sorrow, excitement and fear would have best described her disposition and she felt very lonely as she stood there, especially as there was no one to wave to. She knew that she was now totally dependent on the man next to her on her right and hoped her parents had made a good choice.

Vijay, seeing her tears understood only too well how she must be feeling, so he put his left arm around her and placed it on her left shoulder gently pulled her towards him and whispered.

"You are now the most important person in my life. I will always put you and your needs before anyone and anything, including myself. I will love you unconditionally."

She looked at him and smiled, then returned her tearful gaze to the dock area. As the ship sailed away, they stood there silently watching the city of Bombay disappear over the horizon.

Vijay had booked a second-class cabin, which allowed them to dine in the restaurant with their food being prepared and cooked by the crew. Although the cost had been three times that of steerage, the level he had travelled at six years and four months ago in the cargo ship, he knew he could afford the upgrade in both cabin and ship. He also hoped that Anshula would appreciate the luxury, even though she had no previous experience to compare to, having never been on a ship before.

They docked in Southampton on Saturday 8 May 1948, the third anniversary of VE day, and were pleased to see a party atmosphere at the docks with everyone going about their business in a jovial mood, with flags flying on the buildings. They had met and engaged in conversation with a few other passengers, mostly at meal times, but generally, they had shied away from them in order to try and develop their own relationship.

They had talked about their future and also about their past, Anshula allowing Vijay to talk openly about his father, noting the change in his voice and temperament when he talked about the day and circumstances of his murder. She admired him for his endeavours and perseverance, his courage to take on challenges and his strength of character to make difficult decisions, when he told her about his life.

The weather had been dry and sunny for the whole journey with the temperatures only dropping significantly in the last few days as they made their way northwards in the Atlantic from Gibraltar to Southampton. Anshula felt the cold the further north they travelled and was glad of the warm clothes she had brought with her. Vijay told her that the Bay of Biscay had been notably calm compared to December 1941, when he had been seasick.

The marriage had still not been consummated during their journey but their intimacy levels had greatly increased. A mutual agreement had been reached by them that they would consummate the marriage on their first night together in the privacy of their home, which alleviated the situation during the voyage.

Because Vijay would be back at work on Monday, he had booked the train to Birmingham, again via Reading, for the day they docked, which would allow him to spend Sunday orientating Anshula with the house and the local area. By the time they reached their house it was early evening.

Vijay gave Anshula a quick tour of the house, after which they unpacked their suitcases and put everything in one of the empty bedrooms for Anshula to organise where it would all be stored or kept. They found a note in the kitchen from the Goldstein's welcoming them and saying that they had left some basic provisions for them, namely tea, milk, sugar and cake, for that evening and that they were invited to join them for lunch on Sunday.

Vijay and Anshula enjoyed their tea and cake and after clearing up, went to bed. Sunday morning was spent hanging up their clothes and generally deciding on how to share the cupboard space. A giggly Anshula and a grinning Vijay confirmed that the consummation of the marriage had taken place and both were happy.

A knock on the front door interrupted their work. Vijay went downstairs to see who their visitors were.

Outside stood Sarah Goldstein and her two sons, Jacob, ten and James, eight, who invited themselves in and went straight into the lounge and sat down. Vijay called to Anshula who came downstairs and he introduced them all to each other, after which he then thanked Sarah for her generosity and thoughtfulness for the food, commenting that it was much appreciated as there were no shops open on a Sunday.

Sarah and Anshula chatted to each other and made arrangements to go shopping the day after whilst the boys asked Vijay all about his trip and the ship. After a short while, the Goldsteins' left with Sarah asking them to come to lunch at one o'clock. Vijay and Anshula continued their work until it was time to go next door, at which moment Vijay carefully carried the ornamental Taj Mahal, similar to the one he had given to Jim and Doris, that he had bought as a gift for Yosef and Sarah for looking after his house whilst he had been away.

Yosef answered the door and introduced himself to Anshula, then took the present off Vijay, asked them to follow him in and gave the present to Sarah, who, having carefully unwrapped it, was delighted and gave it pride of place on the middle shelf of their oak display cabinet.

They all sat in the lounge and chatted, discussing life in England as well as Vijay and Anshula's wedding, whilst enjoying a drink; Yosef and Vijay consuming beer, Sarah, Anshula and the boys having orange juice. After a while, Sarah went to the kitchen to continue with her cooking and Anshula followed her, eager to watch and learn about cooking in a modern kitchen and excitedly thinking about her chance to do the same from tomorrow.

They were having chicken, vegetables and gravy, except for Anshula who, being vegetarian, only had the vegetables with a dash of gravy. No one told her that the gravy contained meat products.

After helping Sarah wash up the dishes, Anshula and Sarah both went back into the lounge, settled down on the settee and talked about life in England. The boys had disappeared to their bedrooms to play with their toys and Vijay and

Yosef had started a game of chess. Vijay and Anshula took their leave at about five o'clock.

Once back home Anshula confided that, apart from the tasteless meal, she had enjoyed the visit and hoped that a friendship would develop with Sarah. She had, however, greatly missed the spicy taste of Indian food. Vijay said he hoped she could adjust as he had done and start eating English food such as fish and chips, pies, roast dinners and so on but Anshula was not so sure.

Vijay also told her that since he had come to England, when the Indian population of Birmingham was about one hundred and fifty, the increase had been rapid, especially after the end of the war, with a present population of over one thousand. In London, especially in the areas of Southall and Wembley, there was an even larger number.

"Perhaps," he said to her: "We should try and meet up with some of them, especially any Gujaratis." July 1948 proved to be a turning point in that respect. The British Nationality Act was passed in parliament leading to a large influx of immigrants from many British colonies and territories, mostly to London but also to many other parts including Birmingham, Manchester, Leeds and Glasgow. By 1950, there were over one hundred thousand Indians in the United Kingdom.

Chapter 36

Vijay and Anshula settled down in their home and Vijay continued to work for BSA and was now an established member of the department and earned a comfortable income. Anshula had given birth to a baby girl on 5 August 1949 and was also becoming more accustomed to her way of life in England.

She regularly met up with Mavis, usually at each other's homes, more so because Mavis was conscious of possible racial abuse and wanted to protect Anshula and Meena.

However, the lack of Indian food and spices was a constant source of annoyance to Anshula, especially during her pregnancy, when she yearned for home-cooked Indian food. After many weeks of expressing her feelings to Vijay, Anshula came up with a solution, which she discussed with her husband.

"I want you to agree for Hemant, Rupal and Vinod to come to England and then Rupal and me will open a shop to sell Indian food and spices to the growing Indian population," she said.

"Hemant will be responsible for travelling to London to collect the food and spices, where the imported food is stored in warehouses, from which local shop owners in London are already buying them to sell in their shops. At weekends Hemant could, with your help, drive around the Black Country towns, so-called because of the nineteenth-century iron and coal industry, selling the food from the back of a lorry. I am confident that the shop and weekend trips will bring great profits," she continued.

"Haven't you enough to do with Meena being only a week old? Don't you think that you won't have the time to run a shop?" asked Vijay.

"It will take a few months to set up the venture by which time I will have finished breast feeding, so with Rupal, we can manage the shop and the children," replied Anshula.

In mid-September 1949, Vijay wrote to Hemant with their plan, outlining to him what his and Rupal's involvement in the venture would be and also gave him some information with regard to Vinod's schooling opportunities. An immediate, enthusiastic and positive response from Hemant gave Vijay and Anshula all the encouragement and reassurance they needed to proceed.

Following this encouraging response, Vijay and Anshula searched for suitable premises in Handsworth, the location which they had decided on for the shop on account of two main reasons, which were, firstly that this was the area with the fastest growing Indian and Pakistani population in Birmingham and secondly, that it was only a ten minute drive from their home.

They also needed to make sure that the property would be large enough to have space to house Hemant and his family. After approximately two weeks of searching, they found a corner house, with good-sized accommodation, on Soho Road.

Vijay, with advice and guidance from Yosef, negotiated with his bank for a loan and with the local council for planning permission respectively, to buy the property and convert it into a shop on the ground floor and living quarters on the first floor.

It was decided that one of the three bedrooms on the first floor would be used as a living room. Downstairs, the kitchen was reduced in size and the front room was extended into the second room to increase the shop size and the remainder of the second room was used to store stock. They decided that two bedrooms, a lounge and a bathroom would be adequate living space for a small family. If all went according to plan, they anticipated that the shop would be ready to open by March 1950.

Hemant sold his business to a friend in the village and made arrangements to arrive in England in late February 1950. However, after some thought, discussion and deliberation, he and Rupal decided that he should go on his own initially, in order to be sure that the project worked, as they did not want to risk any more money than they needed to.

Then if all went well, Rupal and Vinod could follow and in the meantime, they would manage on money already saved and the additional amount received from the sale of the business with Hemant sending over extra money if needed.

A second-hand army lorry had been purchased by Vijay and then alterations internally made it suitable for transporting fresh food using ice boxes. Initially, Hemant would make two journeys a week to London, Tuesdays and Fridays to keep the shop stocked. Because of the change of plan with only Hemant coming over, a decision by Vijay was made that he and Anshula would own the business outright and bear all the costs of setting it up, paying Hemant as an employee.

The rationale behind this plan was that if the business failed, Hemant would be able to return to India without debt and if the business was successful, he could buy a share if he wanted to, at a price that reflected the success. Hemant was happy with this arrangement and duly arrived on Saturday, 25 February 1950, much the same as Vijay in 1941, with few belongings.

He stayed with Vijay and Anshula for the first two days, then moved into the shop to prepare it and his rooms ready to start business on Monday 6th March. He planned to make his first journey to Southall, London, on the Friday before, March 3rd, accompanied by Vijay.

An order had already been placed by Vijay the week before, much to Anshula's dismay as she had wanted to do it, but, after some persuasion and knowing how business was conducted in India, she reluctantly accepted that a man making the arrangements would be better received and was more likely to be successful.

Anshula wanted to be cautious and had decided that the first order should be small so that if some stock did not sell she could use it for herself, but she had worried unnecessarily because as soon as news of the shop spread around the Indian community, they came in large numbers. The population of Asian and West Indian nationals in the Midlands was increasing exponentially.

By September 1951, the business was a great success. A few rules were bent, such as customers coming to the back door on Sundays as shops were not supposed to be open, because there were always some people who ran out of ingredients or had forgotten to buy an item.

Also, some of the cash was 'put in the back pocket', making it tax-free, which they had found out was a common practice by many businesses, along with other practices, such as buying as many of their personal goods as they could, such as cleaning products, stationary, stamps and so on and paying for them out of the business account thereby making them tax deductible, as they would be declared as expenses for the business.

The lorry trips taking the goods around the towns also boomed, so a second lorry was purchased and a driver was employed to pick up the goods from London, now three times a week, with Hemant driving to the local towns every day, having increased the number of towns he supplied. He sold in two towns every weekday, one in the morning and another in the afternoon but on Saturdays he only went to one town in the morning.

Saturday afternoons and Sundays were his days off from driving, although he continued to help in the shop. Vijay would manage the shop on Saturdays allowing Anshula to have the weekends off to spend time with Meena. All meals were eaten at the shop meaning that all the food and the power used was tax efficient.

With the business becoming a successful enterprise, Hemant felt confident enough now to bring his wife and son to England and they duly arrived in December 1951.

Vijay was pleased with the progress of the shop and the sales of the goods from the lorries, and, with his job at BSA, he felt he was now in a strong financial position, and also relieved as he had already given up his job as a bus conductor once the shop had opened. His mind now turned to how to build on this.

He knew he was constrained very much by his customer base being limited to Indians and West Indians, with very few white people coming to his shop, even though the shop also stocked some English produce. Also, he was aware that London was the place where the majority of immigrants were settling, especially in Southall and Wembley.

After discussing the matter with Anshula, they decided that they should sell the shop and the lorries to Hemant if he wanted to buy the business, or look for another buyer if he did not, and move to London, buy a large house and convert it into a bed and breakfast for immigrants, providing evening meals as well if required.

Initially, he thought he could work for an accountancy firm to maintain income, feeling sure that Mr Robinson would help to find him a suitable position. They agreed a price and sold the business to Hemant, who was delighted with the purchase, knowing that this gave him a degree of security. The plans were instigated and by January 1953, a large three-storey, six-bedroom house had been found, bought and converted.

The ground floor was reserved for them, consisting of a lounge, kitchen, bathroom and two bedrooms, which also meant that the garden was easy access for Meena to play in. The first floor had four bedrooms and one bathroom and the second floor had two further bedrooms and a bathroom. His customer target was men such as Hemant, coming over to test the water, so to speak, or married couples with no children.

He had tendered his resignation to Arnold Robinson in early October 1952 to finish on 31 December 1952 and afterwards told Thomas Goddard and all his colleagues at BSA of his plans.

Arnold Robinson was very helpful, putting him in touch with an old Harrovian school friend, Mr Christopher Kingham, who was the managing director of an insurance company in the city. Christopher Kingham, having interviewed Vijay and then offered him a position in his company, told him that, with his trilingual skills, he would be very well placed to sell life insurance to the growing immigrant population.

His remuneration would be commission-based, with a regular amount paid to him for the duration of each policy that he sold, plus an initial setting up fee. This target-based job suited Vijay as he could work as many hours as he wanted and flexibly. He also discussed with Hemant the possibility of him setting up potential clients in Birmingham for him to visit at the weekends. In return, Hemant would receive a fee for everyone who bought a policy.

Mavis, who was now secretary to the managing director of BSA, was in charge of organising the staff Christmas party, so with the MD's permission, she combined it with a leaving party for Vijay. She also organised a collection for him, the proceeds of which she used to buy him a set of cufflinks and a matching tie pin.

Knowing that Vijay did not celebrate Christmas, she used the remaining small amount of the collection, adding a little money of her own, to buy a doll for Meena. Both Vijay and Anshula appreciated the gesture.

Chapter 37

The house in Handsworth Wood had sold for a small profit of £70. However, with the large mortgage on the house in Wembley, Vijay worried about his finances. His accountancy experience told him that, if he was successful, he would be worth a lot of money in twenty years' time and have a comfortable lifestyle along the way, but he had a large debt to service to achieve this. He had to hope that hard work and determination would see him through.

He started his insurance job in January 1953 after a short, two-day training course. The company had arranged a few appointments for his first week. Vijay was only successful with three of the ten clients he visited that first week.

However, the arrangement fees for these three sales worked out to be more than his weekly wage at BSA and then there was the ongoing commission, so he now knew that he could make a substantial income if he secured more sales, so in order to achieve this, he decided on a twofold plan.

Firstly, he honed his sales pitch on Anshula to improve his chances and secondly, he revisited the clients who had bought a policy, taking a small gift for them. While they were in this favourable mood, he then offered them the chance of a larger gift every time they recommended a client who then went on to purchase a policy.

Meanwhile, following posters at the ports in London and Southampton and adverts in the local Indian and West Indian shops, the boarding house was becoming very busy. Anshula was in charge and they employed two cleaners/maids to do the housework, charging the clients extra for these services, and one cook.

Vijay tried to make as many evening appointments as possible for his insurance work, thereby allowing him to spend time with Meena during the day, which gave Anshula time to carry out her duties for the boarding house. He also ran any errands that needed to be done, taking Meena with him.

Within months, the boarding house was at full capacity with the average lodger staying nine months.

By September 1954, the boarding house was constantly turning away clients. Their management plan had also changed as London changed. The opening of more Indian and Pakistani restaurants, providing takeaway meals as well as seated dining meant the evening meal option at the boarding house was not being taken up as much as before, especially as the guests could socialise more by eating out, so they removed this optional extra from their services.

Meanwhile, Vijay's income from selling life insurance was reaping great rewards, especially with the fortnightly weekend trips to Birmingham adding to his number of sales. Meena was also now five years old and ready to start school, so further changes were planned by Vijay and Anshula.

The last two years had also changed Britain as the people wanted post-war spending to improve their quality of life, with women leading the demands, having been given more freedom and responsibility during the war. The building trade was extremely busy as the government offered lucrative contracts to companies up and down the country, with the result that bribing officials became commonplace in order to secure them.

Depending on the size of the contract the 'sweeteners', as they liked to call the bribes, varied from gold watches, and briefcases full of money to, it was rumoured in one case, a saloon car. Was the bottle of whisky he had given to the planning officer two years earlier a bribe or a present? Vijay now asked himself. He reconciled to himself that his project was too small for a bribe and also that he had given the bottle before the planning permission was granted, telling the officer that it was a gift for all his hard work, irrespective of the outcome.

Also, as there had been no other interested parties or any objections with regard to his project, there had been no need to bribe the officer, so as far as he was concerned, he reassured himself, the planning permission would have been granted irrespectively.

His new plan now was for them to buy a house for themselves to live in as a family and to convert the ground floor of the boarding house, their present living quarters, into bedrooms and a bathroom, with the kitchen becoming a communal one with limited facilities.

This meant they could rent out nine bedrooms, offer a shared bathroom on each floor and a communal kitchen. The number of maids was increased to three.

As was the case before, Vijay would collect the rent every Friday evening and Anshula would still be in charge of the management.

They bought a detached house in the up-and-coming area of Sudbury, only a couple of miles from their boarding house in Wembley. The main reason for choosing this location was schooling for Meena as there was a well-established infant school very close to the house. Having lived in Handsworth Wood for over seven years, Vijay was not concerned with regard to buying a house in a professional, middle-class, predominantly white area as his aspiration had always been that he wanted to fit in with this section of British society.

Having researched the area, he discovered that his family was the first Indian residents on this street in Sudbury, although there was a small number living on other streets in the borough, all professionals, either doctors or lawyers.

They were also now wealthy enough to buy the latest appliances such as washing machines, televisions, telephones and refrigerators. Vijay had also changed the Ford Prefect he had bought in 1948 for a Rover 95 as this car was widely regarded as the car for doctors, bank managers, solicitors and successful businessmen.

Anshula was supportive of Vijay's aspirations but tried to caution him, explaining to him that some of these white people would be envious of his success, and also reminded him that on a number of occasions Meena had been racially taunted by older children when she had been playing outside the house or in the park. Vijay, whilst agreeing with her concerns, countered her worries with a more optimistic view of the future telling her that his vision was still one of an integrated society with equality for all by the turn of the century.

Hemant and Rupal had visited a number of times over the last twenty one months and they disclosed that they had worries about their future. Hemant had closed down the lorry delivery part of the business some months ago because a number of shops had now opened in the Black Country towns and this had resulted in a fall in revenue.

He had reluctantly dismissed the driver he had hired and had returned to his London trips with Rupal running the shop. The shop was making a healthy profit but he needed to expand or change his business. They narrowed their plans down to one of two options. First would be to buy a warehouse and import the goods and sell to the local shops directly, removing the London trips for both himself and the owners of the other shops.

Second, favoured by the sisters, would be to sell the shop and then Hemant and his family would move to London and they could all work together and expand the rental business. The second option made more business sense as the Indian, Pakistani and West Indian population in London was increasing rapidly and more families were arriving instead of individuals or couples, needing houses rather than rooms.

The decision having been made to opt for the second choice, they began to implement the plan, by putting the shop up for sale. Once the shop sold, which it did quickly, Hemant and Rupal bought a house in Wembley, a cheaper area than Sudbury and Vijay and Hemant formed a joint company to buy houses to rent.

Vijay was to be the guarantor, as he had the equity required to qualify for a secured loan from the bank, a much cheaper way to borrow money than an unsecured loan.

They bought their first house, a mid-terrace, in Neasden, a residential area just over three miles from Wembley, as this area was cheaper than Wembley and more industrialised, meaning that workers could either walk to their place of work or their journey would be no more than a short bus ride.

Hard work and frugal living saw the company grow with both families becoming very wealthy and by June 1964 they had 156 houses, all now paid for. Anshula remained in charge of the boarding house, which still belonged to her and Vijay, whilst Rupal managed the book keeping of the house rental business.

Vijay had overall control of the accounting of the company. Hemant, in the role he enjoyed doing, was the gopher; finding properties, renovating them, organising tradesmen and generally carrying out the day-to-day duties needed to run a property rental business.

They all had salaries based on their job titles, the amount being agreed on the rate applicable to similar jobs in the general society and calculated on an hourly basis, with time sheets submitted by each of them, hoping that by being remunerated this way, friction and disagreement could be avoided.

The profits were re-invested into the business for expansion. Vijay still had his insurance job, which as the rental business grew, increased also by him targeting his rental clients, thus, reaping rewards from the ongoing commission when they moved on. The rental company now leased an office on the 23rd floor of an office block in the heart of the city and employed five staff.

The joint wealth of the two families was now over £1,000,000.

Vijay, once they had bought their twentieth house, invited Eulet and his family to come to London and for Eulet to work for the company, registered as West London Homes, as a repairman to help Hemant in the maintenance of the properties. Also, because Hemant had been threatened on a small number of occasions when collecting the rent, Eulet was to accompany Hemant as protection as his size and build were such that people would fear him.

A bonus would be awarded to him annually if the company made a profit, even though he did not have a share in the business, in recognition of both his kindness and friendship when Vijay arrived in Birmingham and also for his services as a bodyguard for Hemant. Eulet accepted the offer and moved to London in 1957 with his family.

True to their word, Vijay and Anshula paid for her parents to visit England, although it did not happen until 1956. They came for three weeks during the summer and were delighted to see their granddaughter. Were it not for Gita and her family back in India, they would have considered the option to live in England permanently.

Sunila came to visit in 1957 and stayed for seven weeks, from mid-May to early July. She was so happy to see the success that her son had made of his life and repeatedly told him how proud his father would have been. She was not impressed with the music and freedom that the young generation was enjoying and was happy to go back to her quiet village life.

Vijay had kept in touch with Florence over the years, by letters initially and then by telephone and had visited her and her parents once since he moved to London. Anshula was aware of the enormous financial and supportive help that Florence had given Vijay and was completely in favour of his idea to visit her at Christmas 1960 and to take an expensive gift as a 'thank you' for her kindness and generosity.

After much thought, they decided to buy her an engraved gold bracelet with the inscription 'FLORENCE: A KIND AND GENEROUS WOMAN.' They also bought the newest model of television for the family. They set off early on Friday 23 December and returned that evening. Florence, Jim and Doris were touched by their gifts and thanked them for their thoughtfulness in the choices they had made, although Florence made light of what she had done and said all the credit should be given to Vijay for being so determined and hard working.

Fortunately, knowing of the visit, she had bought a Christmas present for Meena, now eleven and at grammar school, of a leather satchel similar in colour and style to the briefcase she had bought Vijay and was relieved she had done so, otherwise, she would have felt extremely embarrassed. After a pleasant day, including refreshments, Vijay, Anshula and Meena left early afternoon and returned home to London.

Time moved on as it does. As the business grew in size, parallel to the rapidly increasing commonwealth immigrant population in the area, both Vijay and Hemant became highly regarded pillars of the Asian community and were regularly sought out for advice, which they gave freely.

They sourced and then funded the purchase and refurbishment of a large building in Wembley to convert it into a temple for the use of the local Hindu's, but soon it became a place of worship for the wider Hindu population with some people travelling many miles to attend the weekend services.

The popularity of the temple grew and it became the hub of the Asian community, hosting many celebrations in the religious calendar and social events such as weddings.

Both Vinod and Meena were progressing well at school and were happy, with Vinod having just finished his 0-levels and Meena preparing to take hers in June 1965. Both sets of parents had decided to have no more children.

Life for the Patels' was very good.

Chapter 38

Robert Sinclair was a war baby as was his father Simon, who was born on 15 March 1918. His father, Robert's grandfather, had suffered appalling injuries in October 1916 during the battle of the Somme and had been repatriated home after having his right leg amputated at the knee, on the battlefield by an army surgeon, leaving him with terrible nerve pain and an ugly stump.

As well as the severe physical trauma that had been inflicted on him, he also suffered from horrendous mental problems because of the dreadful sights he had seen during his time on the front line and had returned to England a broken and bitter man.

Due to these horrific mental and physical health issues, he felt useless and worthless and consequently made no effort to find himself a job, relying on his disability pension as his only source of income. His wife of four years, Ruth, worked at the local mill to bolster their finances, whom he treated very cruelly by beating her with his crutch, shouting at her using profanities and often reducing her to tears by verbally abusing her in public and generally made her life a misery, with no remorse on his part.

He drank a great amount of beer at the local pub, leaving Ruth with little money to manage the home and then when there was no food on the table, he would accuse her of spending money on herself.

Simon was conceived following an act of abuse rather than one of love.

The death of Simon's father was never fully investigated or explained by the police. The official explanation given was that his crutch slipped from under him, causing him to fall as he tried to open his front door following one of his drunken nights out and his head hit the stone step and he died when he fell, from a brain haemorrhage.

The rumour and gossip amongst the local community was that his wife was waiting for him, hidden in the shadows, and kicked his crutch from under him, causing the same result.

Ruth was adamant that she was fast asleep in bed and had not heard a thing. Simon was three when his father died and had no recollection of him.

He was lovingly brought up by his mother and what he lacked in material wealth was amply compensated for by her care and devotion.

Simon in return was a model son.

Robert was born in Sheffield on 19 May 1942 and was the son of Mary and Simon Sinclair. He was an average baby in every physical aspect, whether it was size, build or looks and this status of physical averageness did not change throughout his life. Before the Second World War, Simon, starting at the age of fourteen, worked in the steel industry first as a labourer and then forging steel for cutlery.

He met Mary at a local dance and after a short courtship, they were married in 1938. She worked as a part-time cleaner and housekeeper for the owner of the factory and had to continue this job to compensate for the many sick days Simon had to take off work because of a congenital heart defect.

Simon was classified unfit for military service as a result of his medical condition and could not serve his country as a soldier, as his father had done, so continued to work in the factory, which had been converted to help the war effort, producing artillery for the armed forces.

They lived in a two-bedroom terraced house in the city, which had an outside toilet and washroom, as tenants. Simon's mother, Ruth, who had never remarried following the death of her husband, lived with them, on the insistence of Simon and helped to look after Robert, moving in six months after Robert was born, having given up her job in the mill, which meant she also had to give up her home, as it belonged to the mill owner and was rented out to mill workers only. She shared one bedroom with her grandson and her son and daughter-in-law slept in the other.

They all survived the war.

Ruth and Mary developed a wonderful relationship with each other, to the extent that sometimes, when family decisions had to be made, they would discuss the matter between themselves first, come to a conclusion and then they would gang up together against Simon to achieve their goal, much to his displayed annoyance, although most times he agreed with them.

Although poor, they were happy with their lives.

Robert started at primary school after the Easter holidays in 1947, just before his 5th birthday, as it was customary that children started school at the beginning of the term in which they had their fifth birthday. The school was two streets away from where he lived, which was in a working-class area of Sheffield.

Regularly playing on the streets, most of the young children in his neighbourhood knew each other and although they all had very little in the way of toys, they shared what little they did have and they all went to the same school.

His parents and his grandmother were very keen that he should have a good education and home-schooled him in reading, writing and arithmetic before he started. As a consequence of this, he was always top of his class in all the end-of-year exams from 1948 to 1953, both in primary and junior school.

Popular with the teachers because of his enthusiasm and drive, he thrived in all his studies and was given excellent school reports at the end of each year and was also very good at sports, especially football and cricket. He passed his eleven-plus in February 1953, thereby gaining a place at Sheffield City Grammar School, an all-boys school, to start in September 1953.

This school was across the city and required him to travel on two buses, changing in the city centre but he was happy to do this as he believed what his parents had constantly told him, which was that a good education always gave you a good start to your adult life.

At the end of the first term at the school, as a Christmas present, his parents bought him a second-hand bicycle to use for both school and pleasure and also, unknown to him, so that they could save on his bus fares. He was proud of his bicycle as no other boys or girls on his street had one; however, the problem that developed for him from this overall situation was that he was no longer considered a member of the children's street community, as he was the only child in the street to go to grammar school and to have a bicycle.

The boys now bullied him, ridiculing him about his uniform, physically pushing him around, taking his cap off his head and hanging it on the street lamp and often kicking their football at him as he rode down the street. On one occasion, the ball struck him on his head causing him to fall off his bicycle, after which he stopped riding it down the street, dismounting and walking with it once he reached the corner of his road.

All the boys on his street joined gangs as they became teenagers, which Robert did not want to do, resulting in him becoming fully and completely ostracised. The girls ignored him. He no longer played outside as he had no one to play with and was also wary of going anywhere on his own in case he was assaulted. He had witnessed a number of street fights from his bedroom window and on one occasion, a stabbing.

He lived a life of fear.

The husband of the woman next door on his left was in prison for GBH (Grievous Bodily Harm) and she was now a prostitute and their son, who was fourteen, was in Borstal after having assaulted and robbed a little old lady. The people who lived next door on the right were a retired, childless couple, who had spent their lives working in a factory.

All the houses on the street were owned by the council.

Robert only started to understand his situation as he grew up and met people from other walks of life through his achievement of passing his eleven-plus, and going to grammar school had shown him a different life to which he could aspire.

Life at home was hard and difficult.

Grammar school was also very different to his primary and junior school days. His parents could not afford the school uniform from the recommended suppliers, so they purchased the cap and tie from there and then bought a plain black jacket, grey trousers and white shirts from the market and his mother stitched the closest matching blue-coloured braiding she could find on to the jacket.

He felt very self-conscious that he was from a poor background whereas all the rest of the boys were from middle-class families. This was very obvious to him in many aspects such as; they had satchels and sports bags, whereas he had a second-hand army rucksack; they talked about trips out in their cars, holidays during the summer, shopping and fun activities they could partake in, all conversations he could not join in, and he also struggled to fit in academically with the other pupils because they had all come from good junior schools and had been taught French and Art as well as the basic maths, reading and writing. He now had homework every evening and his parents could no longer help him, unlike the parents of the other boys.

To make his studying easier from a practical point of view, he went to the local scrapyard and retrieved the wooden legs from an old bed and a board of wood and made himself a makeshift desk to fit into the alcove of his bedroom, and while he was there, he also found an old three-legged stool, which he used as a chair, all very generously given to him for free by the owner of the yard, once he had explained his situation.

Every Saturday, he went to the library and borrowed three books, the maximum allowed, and had read them by the following Thursday, choosing books recommended by his English teacher.

He now had a lonely existence with no friends at school and none at home.

Grammar school also was different in the way the teachers taught the pupils, which now changed from having one friendly teacher who taught one class and who developed a relationship with all the pupils, the situation in primary and junior schools, to now where the students had a different teacher for each of their subjects.

The masters, as they had to be described, were all dressed in black graduation robes over their suits and were all in possession of a degree in the subject they taught and most were aloof and formal, with the boys being addressed by their surnames only.

He felt intimidated.

With no one to help him, he focused on the fact that, as his parents kept reminding him, a good education would ultimately give him a good life, at least from a financial viewpoint. He was also now aware that, as his primary and junior schools were not of a very high standard, his belief that he was a clever boy because he had always been top of his class was not true and in his present school, he was below average at the moment.

He managed to achieve eighteenth position in a class of thirty at the end of his first year, having worked hard at home, but his parents were disappointed that he was not top of his class, a situation they had become used to expecting and although Mary, his mother, tried to be understanding, his father, Simon was not.

He started punishing Robert during the summer holidays, either by setting him extra studies or giving him domestic chores such as washing the paintwork and windows. Robert spent most of his little spare time in his shared bedroom, usually reading or learning to play chess, by competing with himself, using a second-hand chess set his grandmother had bought him from a church jumble sale.

By the time school restarted in September 1954, Robert had resigned himself to the fact that his father must hate him. When he had voiced his thoughts to his mother and grandmother, they had both tried to reassure him that his father did love him and he was behaving in this manner because he wanted him to succeed in life and that education was the best way to achieve this.

Robert reluctantly accepted this and worked even harder with the result that by the end of his second year at the grammar school, he had climbed to 9th position in his class. His parents were pleased with this improvement but his father told him he could 'still do better.' During his second year, he also became short-sighted and started wearing National Health Service spectacles, which resulted in more bullying.

Robert's sporting levels were also not the best any more. He managed to secure places in both the football and cricket teams for his year but he was no longer an automatic choice. He was not the best player anymore and sometimes he would have to accept being a reserve on the football team or 'twelfth man' on the cricket team. He was, however, a regular player for his 'house'; the boys all became members of a 'house' when they joined the school; at chess and he also ran for the relay team in the inter-house field and athletics competition. During these first two years, he had not made any close friends and was not invited to any events such as birthday parties or to any other boy's houses to play. Most of the boys made no effort to be friendly as they were already in groups when they came to the school.

He was also now being bullied every school day by a small group of three boys, mostly verbally, by reference to his 'homemade' uniform and his parent's jobs but also on three occasions, physically. On the first occasion, he retaliated and ended up with a bloody nose and bruising to his face. They also broke his spectacles, meaning he was unable to read the blackboard and had to ask to be moved nearer to the front until they could be repaired.

On the other two, he did not retaliate and accepted the pushing and punching to his body in order to protect his face with his arms. This lack of retaliation stopped the physical bullying but the verbal continued. The teachers, all male, were disinterested and told him to 'behave like a man.'

He never told his parents about the bullying and physical abuse, making up reasons for the bruises that could be seen following the first beating. He avoided the bullies as much as he could by hiding away at break times and eating his homemade packed lunch in a corner of any empty classroom he could find when it was lunchtime.

During his third year, his academic position was such that other pupils in his class and his teachers started to notice him as he was achieving high marks in all his subjects and gained first position in some, so that, overall, he was always in the top five pupils in his year.

Unfortunately, however, because of his parent's financial situation, when the other boys reached puberty and grew taller and larger, as did Robert, they all were bought new uniforms, whereas his parents could not afford to keep up with buying him new uniforms, meaning he was even more ridiculed by the other boys, which made him even more embarrassed and reclusive.

Fortunately for him, however, this did mean that the bullying decreased for two reasons. Firstly, the hormonal changes meant that some boys, including the bullies, began to become interested in girls and started to spend their lunchtimes congregating around the girls' school, which was only half a mile away, and therefore bullying him became a secondary pastime for them, and secondly the teachers were more interested and friendlier with him because of his academic improvements, so the bullies had to be more careful.

During the first term of the third year, he had made a good friend, Geoffrey Davis and they spent a lot of time together studying. Geoffrey, who was a plump boy and not at all sporty, was one of the cleverest boys in the class, if not the cleverest, usually coming top in most subjects. The other boys in the class, including the bullies, ignored him, and, as he was comfortable with his own company, he spent most of his time on his own.

During the second year, he helped Robert deal with the bullying by giving him advice and guidance, which Robert suspected came from Geoffrey's father who was a doctor and they started to become friends. This friendship strengthened and flourished and they became very close from the start of the third year. The two boys spent most lunchtimes together, playing chess and chatting about their future plans.

This also meant that Robert now had a friend with whom he could spend time during the school holidays, especially the long seven week summer break. He would cycle over to Geoffrey's house in the morning and then, dependent on the weather, they would plan their day. On the odd occasions that Geoffrey came to his house, Robert insistently requested that he be dropped off and picked up, not wanting to risk any confrontations with the local gangs.

They would stay indoors with Ruth, who would supervise them and also make lunch for them, whilst they entertained themselves by playing board games or other activities that could be undertaken in the house.

During the summer breaks when the weather was good, they would quite often set off cycling for the day, visiting local interesting sights or visiting the Peak District. Geoffrey's parents were very hospitable and welcoming to Robert and the way he was treated by them, and their influence and guidance, was very important to him as he tried to prepare himself for a future life in middle-class England, which is what he hoped would be his destination. This enormous help was much appreciated by him.

By September 1957, the start of his 0-Level year, Robert was consistently one of the top pupils in his year and the top places in his class in all subjects were always shared between himself and Geoffrey. He decided that he would be taking 9 0-Levels: English Language, English Literature, Mathematics, Geography, Chemistry, Physics, Biology, French and Latin and if he achieved good enough grades, he planned to stay on and take his A-Levels and hopefully go to university. Geoffrey took the same subjects and had the same aspiration.

Robert would never have said that his schooldays at grammar school up to his 0-levels were 'the best days of his life' because they weren't.

If he had been asked, he would have described them as 'survival training.'

The 0-Level examinations finished in mid-June 1958, approximately one month after Robert's sixteenth birthday with the results scheduled to be posted out to reach their homes on the third Thursday in August, which meant that there were nine weeks to wait. Both Robert and Geoffrey decided that they would get summer jobs for six weeks and then have a one week holiday together. The other two weeks would be 'lazy time'.

Casual work, especially poorly paid seasonal labouring, was easy to find, so, without much difficulty, they secured jobs loading lorries at the local fizzy drinks factory near to where Robert lived. This was hard manual labour and they were both glad this type of work would not be their future jobs. Six weeks later, they had saved enough money to afford to go camping for a week in the Peak District.

Geoffrey's father owned a four man tent, sleeping bags, a camp stove and utensils they could use, so all Robert needed to buy was a pair of good walking shoes and some outdoor clothes, all of which he procured from the army surplus store in the city centre.

They decided to go from Saturday 9th August to Saturday 16th, as the 0-Level results were due on Thursday 21st and would need to be collected from their school, so with the help of Geoffrey's parents, they booked a pitch on a campsite near a town called Hope. This campsite was in a field adjacent to a small lake and had a large number of country walks nearby. Geoffrey's father agreed to drive them there and then pick them up a week later.

The campsite had a clubhouse and, importantly for both sets of parents, a telephone, which meant that if there were any problems, they were to telephone Geoffrey's parents, who would try to rectify them if they could and would also keep Robert's parents informed, if necessary, as they did not have a telephone.

Geoffrey, having been camping with his parents on a number of occasions and also been with both the cubs and scouts did not anticipate any problems. After his father had left, Geoffrey with the help of Robert erected the tent and organised their space, and once they were set up they explored the site, then after lunch went for a short walk, discussing their plans for the week and the treks they would go on.

As directed by his father, Geoffrey then informed the site manager of the treks they would be taking and on which day they would be undertaken so, if they became lost, at least he would know where they were walking and therefore where to send any search party.

The holiday was a great success. Not only did their friendship develop and grow, but they also initiated themselves into the world of alcohol and girls. The first experience, alcohol, was on Sunday evening. After having returned from a six mile circular walk, they washed in the shower block, changed, cooked and ate a meal and then went to the clubhouse.

Acting nonchalantly, they entered the clubhouse and sauntered up to the bar.

"Two pints of bitter, please," said Geoffrey and then gazed round the room as he was looking for someone.

The two pints of beer were pulled and served without question. The ease with which they had bought their first alcoholic drinks swelled them with pride and this then became a regular evening treat.

They went on a different walk every day, setting off after breakfast, usually six to eight miles, always in a circular route, planning to arrive back early afternoon. They would then wash, change, cook and eat dinner and then go to the clubhouse. They would buy one round of drinks each and play table tennis, snooker or darts, sometimes competing with other residents of the campsite.

The second initiation was on Friday, the last evening of their holiday and also the same weekday for the clubhouse's weekly dance for its guests. Geoffrey and Robert had noticed two young girls earlier in the week and had chatted to them and found out that they were with their parents and younger siblings and were similarly awaiting their 0-Level results. They agreed to meet in the clubhouse on Friday for the weekly dance night.

After a couple of dances and a few drinks, they split into two couples and then when the clubhouse closed they went outside and, away from each other and out of sight, they kissed. Robert walked his companion back to her tent and Geoffrey did the same to his. Back in their tent, the boys excitedly exchanged their experiences, both very similar, and then having exhausted their stories they eventually fell asleep, happy and contented.

The following morning, they sought out their respective companions and wished them well in their examination results and in response, their wishes were reciprocated by the girls. Tentative arrangements were made for future contact with Geoffrey giving his phone number to his companion and Robert giving the same number, explaining that he didn't have a phone himself, but no time or date was arranged for the call.

They never saw or spoke to the girls again.

Robert gained nine grade 1's in his O-levels as did Geoffrey, which, being the highest grades achievable, meant that they were able to stay on at the school and go into the sixth form to take their 'A' Levels. Robert decided to take Mathematics, Further Mathematics, Geography and Chemistry with a view to applying for a place at a redbrick university to study Mathematics to then become a stockbroker. Geoffrey decided to take Chemistry, Physics, Biology and Maths with a view to studying Medicine, which could only be studied at a redbrick university.

On hearing about his excellent results, Geoffrey's parents organised a celebration party at their home and invited Robert and his family, including his grandmother, to attend. At the request of Geoffrey, in order not to cause any embarrassment to Robert's parents, his parents invited only family and no friends.

Simon and Mary had never been to Geoffrey's house and were very apprehensive. A five-bedroom detached house in one of the exclusive suburbs of Sheffield, they were awed by it. Mary, having cleaned at the factory owner's house had seen wealth before but that house was an old mansion handed down over the years. The Davis's house was a modern house, with up-to-date decor, furniture and fittings.

"Haven't the boys done well and made us proud?" said Mrs Davis as she gave Mary a glass of wine. "Come on, let's sit down and have a chat as we have not really done that yet, because the few times when we have met, I have been dropping Geoffrey off, so we have not spoken much. As you work, it is usually Ruth I meet when I come."

"You have a lovely home," said Mary, "and, yes, both boys have done extremely well. Both Simon and I are very pleased that Robert has found such a good friend as Geoffrey. He has been a changed boy since they became friends and we are so glad that you and your husband Desmond allowed that friendship as it would have been easy for you to have stopped it."

"Why do you think we would have tried to stop the friendship?" asked Marjorie Davis.

"We are a working-class family from the poor end of Sheffield and it is difficult for us to fit into your level of society. I know that Robert has suffered at school because of his poverty, although he has never told me directly, because I can tell from the way he talks about school that he is not accepted by most of the boys." replied Mary.

"Well, he has certainly shown that he is better than them academically, and this will set him up for the future. His children will be the ones like the boys at the school, talking about holidays, cars and the like, except, because you, Simon and Robert will bring them up to understand your lives, they will look after the less fortunate boys and girls rather than make fun of them, which is how a good and fair society will develop," said Marjorie. "Now, come on, let's go and enjoy the party."

On the way home, Mary told Simon about her conversation with Marjorie and they both agreed that Robert had made friends with a nice family, who they hoped, could also guide him in his future life.

The three bullies all achieved good grades as well, not as outstanding as Robert and Geoffrey but not far behind. Only one of them stayed on to do A-Levels as he wanted to become a solicitor, the other two went to work for their fathers, both starting as junior clerks, one in the office of the department store that his father owned in the city and which he would inherit as his father had and the other in the office of his father's biscuit factory, again a business he would inherit.

Robert did not meet either ever again.

Apart from having to play on the same cricket team, Robert had no contact with the third bully, although the boy did try to make a half-hearted apology, citing youth and peer pressure as the reasons for his behaviour and also saying he was only following the others. Robert refused to accept the apology and the excuses and made sure their paths only crossed on the cricket pitch.

Other boys who stayed on at the school to do their 'A' levels and had been indifferent towards him in earlier years now started to behave in a more friendly manner towards him, though he did not know why, which intrigued him, but he did not forget that no one except Geoffrey had shown him any kindness or had ever invited him to their home, so he accepted the new friends with some reservation.

He reconciled himself to the fact that these new friends would be 'here today, gone tomorrow' persons during his 'A' level years and were young men, who because they were now six formers, felt that they should behave more maturely.

Now he was in the sixth form and had achieved excellent '0' Level results, his parents did allow him to go out occasionally to meet up with other sixth formers from his school on Saturday evenings, usually in a pub if they could get in.

Robert's sixth-form days were better than his previous five years.

Also, his parents were now financially better off and had bought their own terraced house in a better part of the city. The relationship between him and his father had improved considerably, in parallel with his successful academic performance, with his father now becoming much more lenient with him following his 0-Level results. He would proudly boast about his son's achievements to all his family and friends.

Robert and Geoffrey were both excelling at school with their studies and the relationship between the students and the teachers was now different. The sixth form staff now treated the pupils as adults and would engage in social conversation with them. The sixth form tie was more discreet, they no longer had to wear caps, the blazers had just the school badge on the breast pocket and no braiding and the students had their own common room.

The other costly change was that they now had to have briefcases. Robert's parents, knowing this, had bought him one, a cheap, light brown artificial leather one, as a congratulatory present for achieving such good grades in his 0-Levels. Geoffrey had been given his grandfather's genuine leather briefcase, who had sadly died some years ago, used by him when he was an accountant at a bank in Manchester.

When the time came for them to discuss their university choices, their headmaster, an Oxford-educated man, suggested they both apply for places at Oxford or Cambridge, although this would mean they had to stay on after their A-Levels to take the entrance exams for those universities, but he felt they would both be capable of obtaining places at either.

Geoffrey and his parents acquiesced without hesitation. Robert was in favour of applying but when he discussed the matter with his parents, they were much more apprehensive.

Mary was worried about him leaving and having to manage on his own and said that she would prefer him to stay at home and go to Sheffield University, whereas his father Simon was more concerned that Robert would not fit into the world of public school educated men, especially those from Eton, Harrow, Rugby, Winchester and other similar establishments, but eventually, with a great deal of persuasion and reassurance from Geoffrey and his parents, who emphasised the possibilities and prestige of this opportunity, they finally relented.

The boys both worked hard and achieved grade A's in all their subjects. During the summer holidays of both A-Level years, they did the same as before, working for six weeks at the fizzy drinks factory and then having a one-week camping holiday.

Only six boys stayed on at the school to apply for Oxbridge, of which four passed their entrance examinations and were offered places. Three of the four, which included Geoffrey and Robert decided to accept Oxford, possibly heavily influenced by their headmaster, the other going to Cambridge. Having secured their places, they left school at the end of the first term and celebrated Christmas 1960 in style. They now had nine months to wait before starting at Oxford in September 1961.

Geoffrey's father, through a friend in his Rotary Club, arranged for them to work in a distribution warehouse stacking shelves and loading lorries for those nine months. This was extremely beneficial to Robert as it meant he would have some money before going to Oxford.

He already knew that his tuition fees were to be paid for by the government and because of his parent's low income, he would receive a small maintenance grant, but extra funds would never go amiss, so the money he earned from this job would be very useful. He also hoped to work every summer at the fizzy drinks factory, which would help to subsidise him during his time at Oxford.

Chapter 39

Robert went to a different college than Geoffrey, who had decided to study medicine at St Catherine's. Studying mathematics at Merton College, he hoped to achieve a first, thereby enabling him to work in London as a stockbroker. Because of their different colleges and timetables, although they travelled home to Sheffield together and spent time there together, their time together in Oxford was limited.

Studying, college life and sport, having joined the fencing team, was taking up much of Geoffrey's time, whereas Robert was only studying, because as his father had predicted, he found it difficult to be accepted into college life, not for any other reason than the fact that he had not grown up in their world of social graces and etiquette, so it became far easier for him to refuse invitations than to subject himself to the trauma of inadequacy. Added to this was the cost of many of the functions.

With rugby being the predominant winter sport and not football, he was again in a position where he was unable to participate, as football was the only winter sport he played. The other winter sports of rowing and hockey did not cater for beginners. When it came to playing summer sports, his cricketing skills were no match for the public school boys, who had benefited from professional tuition.

Lonely and bored, he joined the debating society and found an interest he had not expected, discovering a sharpness in his thought patterns he did not know he had. With this new interest, he enthusiastically spent many hours researching topics that were programmed for debate to ensure he knew his subjects well, so much so, that he would decide minutes before a debate which stance he would take, sometimes on a whim, depending on who the adversary was.

He never volunteered to be the chairman or to be on the committee as he much preferred to take up the argument from the assembly. He became well known by staff and students as a fierce debater and on a few occasions, if the topic was of interest to them, senior lecturers and professors also attended.

By September 1963, the start of his final year, he had earned himself a respected place in the university debating circles. Because of these debates, he also became knowledgeable on many topics, including apartheid, racism, poverty, wealth, war and politics. On one occasion, in acknowledgement of his debating prowess and the recognition it brought to his college, he was invited to his college ball as a guest of honour, meaning he did not have to purchase a ticket.

He now also had a girlfriend, a fellow mathematics student called Annabelle Bailey, daughter of Sir Harold Bailey and Lady Margaret Bailey. Sir Harold was a Conservative cabinet minister, having taken up politics after a short time in the army, that commission having more to do with character building than a career, as it was always planned that he would take over the family business, which was the manufacture of bricks for the building industry.

His company owned many quarries throughout the country and had over three thousand employees. His incredible wealth, both earned and inherited, made him one of the wealthiest men in England. He and his family lived on his two thousand-acre estate, which he had inherited from his father who had been an importer of goods, mostly from Europe; however, the original origins of their wealth lay in the slave trade. He also owned a house in Belgravia.

Annabelle was a slim, average height, young woman with beautiful features, accentuated by high cheekbones, long dark hair and soft green eyes. A modelling career could easily have been an alternative choice for her. She was the eldest child in the family by virtue of having a younger sister, Caroline.

Her earlier education had been at Godolphin Girls School, a boarding school overlooking Salisbury Cathedral, following in the footsteps of her mother, who had excelled there in many aspects and also had been head girl as had Annabelle.

Starting as a boarder at eight years old, she was now a strong independent young woman, determined to make her own way in life, having fought hard to pursue an academic career, because her parents, as her mother had done, wanted her to leave school and become a debutante, socialising and mixing with high society.

Their choice would have been for her to leave Godolphin after her 'O' Levels and then attend finishing school in Switzerland, returning to join in the Debutante's circuit of Grand Balls to find herself a husband from a similar background to herself.

Annabelle, who wanted to choose her own path in life and achieve success for herself, mistakenly believed that her privileged life and heritage would not play any part in her future, because she was adamant to herself that she could succeed on her own merits.

Her first day at Oxford proved how wrong she was.

Through the fame of her parents, many staff and students recognised who she was and so, consequently, she had no shortage of people trying to become her friends. Those who did not recognise or know who she was soon found out as she was pointed out by those who did.

Robert, who did not know or recognise her and knew little about her father, had met Annabelle at their first lecture in September 1961, they randomly having sat next to each other, entering the row of seats in the lecture theatre from opposite ends and ending up together in the middle, and introduced themselves.

Following that first encounter, they had nodded in acknowledgement to each other in other lectures or seminars but socially, their paths never crossed, for two very obvious reasons.

Firstly, Annabelle, a well-dressed and immaculately groomed young woman, had many male admirers and suitors, all of whom she had rejected without exception, so much so that the inevitable rumours of her sexual bias proliferated, such that by the end of her first year, she was free from the advances of young men. Robert made no effort to attract her attention as he felt he was in no position to compete with the other men from wealthy backgrounds and then because of the rumours he had heard, he believed that she was a homosexual and therefore, any romantic relationship was out of the question.

Secondly, because she could also afford to attend all the dinners, dances, dine out at the best restaurants and buy suitable clothes to attend all those occasions and Robert could not, he never came across her socially.

During the second year, she and Robert were allocated to the same study group for seminars and on one occasion, they were paired and assigned to the same project. A romantic liaison, in Robert's case because of their extremely different backgrounds and the rumours he had heard and in Annabelle's case as she wanted to be successful in her studies and did not want any distractions, was never a consideration for either of them when they were assigned together, so they were relaxed in their behaviour towards each other, often only discussing their backgrounds as a subject for conversation when they had become exhausted with their academic work and were relaxing with a cup of tea or coffee.

Annabelle, in an eloquent, neutral accent, described her life at boarding school saying that she was much closer to her school friends than her parents, whom she loved very dearly, but because they were not easily or readily available for help or advice, her friends were whom she turned to for support. It was not that her parents were not caring or supportive but the fact was that telephone conversations were not the same as personal contact.

The advantage this situation provided was that she became a very independent and strong woman. Whilst at boarding school, she had learned to play the piano and the violin, could read music and was quite knowledgeable about art and culture.

She explained to Robert that she was expected to marry into an upper-class family or even aristocracy.

Following these conversations, Robert started to appreciate some of the difficulties of upper-class life and understood why Annabelle had been so reluctant to become involved in any romantic relationships, because she felt, rightly or wrongly, that all the young male students were more interested in her father, his wealth and his connections than in her.

She did accept this was inevitable, although she had secretly hoped that this would not be the case and resigned herself to this inevitability even more so when Robert reiterated what so many people had previously said, which was that her father was a well-known politician and businessman and that most people are interested in the rich and famous, with him citing the interest in film stars as an example.

She also, by chatting to Robert, developed a more informed knowledge of life for working-class families, their financial worries and their poor housing and was genuinely appalled when he told her about the 'poverty bullying' he had experienced at grammar school. By the summer term of the second year, they had become very close friends and started dating, finding they had similar views in some things, diverse in others but could respectfully debate them without anger or rudeness.

Politics was always the most difficult debate initially but as time went on, they accepted and agreed that no political party could be the one for all citizens and winners and losers were always going to be had. There can be no equal society when it is made up of individuals who are all unique, becoming their eventual assessment and agreement.

The first debate of the 1963 academic year was very controversial. The introduction of the contraceptive pill in 1961 but only for married women, had made many young women across the country very angry and because of their very public protestations and rallies, the debating society programmed this subject as the first debate because of its high profile.

Annabelle firmly believed the contraceptive pill should be available for all women and urged Robert to take that side in the debate, which he did. After a long and volatile debate, the vote ended in favour of the universal availability of the contraceptive pill for all women.

This had ramifications for both Robert and Annabelle. Those on their side celebrated the win, whereas some on the losing side became rude and abusive. They accused the winners of encouraging promiscuity and because the majority of students were male, of pressurising women by promoting sex before marriage, a sin in the eyes of God, they claimed.

When one of them called Annabelle a 'slut', Robert stormed over and punched him in the face, the first violent act he had committed since his aggression at school with the bullies, when he had tried to defend himself and had retaliated to their aggression.

This time, however, he was not the one with the bloody nose. Annabelle quickly dragged him away and they left the building. What upset Annabelle the most was that she was still a virgin and did not advocate sex before marriage for herself but believed in women's rights to choose for themselves the path they wished to take.

Robert resigned from the debating society the following day explaining that he had disgraced both himself and it by his actions. His resignation was accepted unanimously and without equivocation. Robert also wrote a short apologetic letter to his victim and offered no excuse for his behaviour.

Robert and Annabelle's attention now became focused on the final exams as the highest grades were essential to be offered a good job in London. Representatives from many city firms visited the university to promote themselves to the students. The firms all had favourable relationships with the staff, so with their help, they chose and then targeted those students they felt best suited to their working practices.

Robert and Annabelle were both 'wined and dined' by a number of companies, in order to secure their services, as they were both expected to achieve the highest possible grades. Robert was delighted with the level of interest in him and enjoyed the experience of dining in some of the most exclusive restaurants in both London and Oxford.

He preferred to go to London for his meetings if he could, because this also meant that the company would pay for him to stay overnight at a top London hotel for at least one night, although on one occasion the company paid for two nights, which delighted him, as this allowed him to explore the city during his spare time.

When Annabelle was invited for meetings in London, she always stayed at her parents' home in Belgravia.

Annabelle and Robert had already agreed to work together and after a few meetings with different firms, they accepted positions with a medium-sized, friendly, family firm, Brunswick Stockbrokers, in the heart of the city, agreeing to start work on the first Monday in July 1964, which would give them a month to relax after their exams.

Brunswick Stockbrokers had been started over one hundred and fifty years ago by John Brunswick and was now managed by his great-grandson Charles. The company had grown and expanded over the years and now employed seventy-five staff, of which two-thirds were brokers and the rest administrative, and prided itself on safe, careful management of its client's funds and was a well-trusted company.

Charles, his wife Christine and their three children lived in a seven bedroom house in Surrey, set in two acres of land. They employed a full-time gardener whose wife also worked for them as their full-time housekeeper. These employees lived with their children in a cottage in the nearby village.

Charles's eldest son and firstborn child, James, had joined the firm two years earlier having been educated through Eton and Oxford, as had his father. Their daughter, Rebecca, had lived at home and attended the local primary and junior schools until the age of eleven, after which she moved school and became a boarder at Wispers, a girls' school in Midhurst, East Sussex.

At present, she was at Cambridge studying history and their third child and youngest son, John, was in the first year of his A-Levels at Eton. The company's clients were all long-standing and well-established, with any new ones only being accepted on recommendation, either by an existing client or by personal friends of Charles.

They were a happy and contented family enjoying their upper-middle-class life.

As expected, both Robert and Annabelle achieved 1st's and with honours. To celebrate their excellent results, they went out 'on the town' with all the other graduates and Oxford was filled with the noise of happy students. Annabelle's parents bought her an apartment in Sloane Square as a present, and Robert's parents bought him a Parker pen for his desk.

Chapter 40

Robert rented a one-bedroom flat a short distance away from where Annabelle lived in her new apartment. They always met after work to have a drink and at weekends would go out together, usually for a meal. Once a month, Geoffrey would come to London and stay with Robert for the weekend, sleeping on his couch, so that he could watch his favourite football team Arsenal and also catch up with Robert and his life.

He had a girlfriend named Catherine, a fellow medical student, with whom he had been in a relationship for over eighteen months and they lived with four other medical students, in an old Victorian house on the outskirts of Oxford. Although they both had their own rooms, they would spend some nights together, mostly at weekends.

She would occasionally visit London with Geoffrey in the early days but, once she had become a good friend of Annabelle's, she became a regular visitor and stayed with her in her apartment, leaving Geoffrey to stay with Robert. Catherine's father was an optician and her mother a pharmacist and they lived in Bristol, which is where Catherine's parents had met when they were students at Bristol University.

When Robert and Geoffrey went to watch Arsenal play football, Annabelle and Catherine would go shopping, which suited all parties.

Both Geoffrey and Catherine were well supported financially and otherwise, by their parents.

True to her beliefs, Annabelle was still a virgin and Robert respected her wishes, which meant that he also was still a virgin but they were intimate in every other way. Robert had broached the subject of marriage and told her that, once he had saved enough money, he would propose to her and buy her an engagement ring, an arrangement that she was very happy with.

The one concern for both of them was how and when to tell their parents as neither set of parents had any inkling or knowledge of their relationship. They had both denied, to their respective parents, having had any romantic involvement with anyone during their time at university.

Annabelle had decided to specialise her stockbroking work in the retail industry and acted for clients who wanted shares in companies such as Marks and Spencer, Woolworth's, Debenhams and many other similar high street names.

Robert chose the industrial sector, acting for manufacturing companies and was under the supervision of James. An arrangement was made for them both to meet every Thursday and to have lunch together at James' favourite restaurant, Normans, which was a short walk from the office, to discuss Robert's work and progress.

The company, which had a reserved table there on a permanent basis, would be paying. They both liked each other and developed a friendship as well as a good working relationship with James being very impressed with Robert when he told him about the incident at the debating society meeting, assuring him that his behaviour had been both chivalrous and honourable with regard to the punch, followed by integrity with regard to his resignation.

They talked about their lives and James told Robert that he should be extremely proud of his achievements. He, on the other hand, had benefitted from a privileged life and had been given opportunities very few people have, adding that the pressure on him was to be more successful than his father.

The observation that he did make was that, if success was measured by 'doing better' than your father, then it is easier to succeed from Robert's starting point than his. Similarly, Robert's children would find it harder to 'do better' than him. Robert was in complete agreement with James's analysis of their differing personal situations.

After a couple of months, James invited them to his family home for a weekend, reassuring Annabelle that they would have separate bedrooms. The three of them all travelled down to Surrey together on a Friday afternoon after work, taking the train, and once settled in they had a family meal with Charles and Christine, after which, especially as it was a Friday evening which marked the end of the working week, James took Robert and Annabelle to the village pub, a fifteen minute walk from the house.

The pub was full of James's friends who were all from similar backgrounds.

The clothes they all wore and the cars parked outside demonstrated that they were all very wealthy. Robert felt reasonably comfortable because he knew that from an income point of view, he could afford to be there but also knew that having no wealth to inherit as the others did, he was no match for them financially.

Hopefully, his children and grandchildren will have an inheritance, he told himself. Annabelle, as expected, felt at ease. They had a very pleasant evening and strolled home after closing time.

The following morning Charles, James, Robert and John, who had arrived late the previous evening from Eton and was staying for the week, as it was half term, played tennis; there were two courts in the garden; whilst Annabelle sat in the house with James's mother and chatted. Christine knew of Annabelle's parents and had seen them from a distance at a charity dinner in London but they had never met, she told her. After lunch, they all went for a walk through the beautiful countryside.

Saturday evening the whole family, including Rebecca, who had come home for one night, Robert and Annabelle went to a local restaurant for a meal. At the end of the evening, Charles insisted on paying for everyone, even though Robert and Annabelle offered to pay for their share.

Nightcap drinks were had back at the house by all but Christine, who retired to bed. On Sunday, after breakfast, Robert and Annabelle thanked the family for their very generous welcome and hospitality and gave Christine a box of chocolates from Fortnum and Mason and Charles a bottle of wine from Berry Brothers, both presents suggested by Annabelle because of her experience of etiquette, and then they left Surrey and returned to London, after having had a wonderful time at the Brunswick's family home.

Robert had wistfully admired the wealth of his employer and struggled to comprehend what it was like to have so much money. He became even more anxious about meeting Annabelle's parents knowing that they were considerably wealthier.

Christmas 1964 was very different for the Sinclair family. Robert was now earning more than three times his parents' joint income, so, humbly stressing how appreciative he was for all they had done for him, he told them that he wanted to buy them presents that they would like but would never have bought for themselves. They said this was not necessary as they had only behaved like any other parents, but after much persuasion they finally agreed to his request, with his grandmother asking for a pair of comfortable winter shoes and his parents asking for winter coats.

Having succeeded in his wish, he bought them day return train tickets to London for the Saturday before Christmas, the 19th of December, in order to take them shopping and also booked them all in for afternoon tea at the Savoy. His parents and grandmother felt somewhat uncomfortable about this latter arrangement but Robert assured them that there was nothing to worry about and everything would be fine.

Annabelle similarly asked her parents to come to London on the same day and also booked the three of them into the Savoy for afternoon tea at the same time as Robert and his family. Already well known there, she made sure that hers and Robert's tables were next to each other, by means of a request and a five-pound tip to the manager.

The day arrived.

Mary and Simon dressed in their finest clothes, the ones they had bought for Robert's graduation and Simon's mother, Ruth, put on her 'Sunday Best.' They were still very apprehensive about afternoon tea at the Savoy, especially as the occasion of his graduation had been quite traumatic for them and they had felt isolated and uncomfortable amongst the other parents.

In fairness, they had admitted afterwards, no one had been rude or aloof to them; on the contrary, the parents sat on either side of them during the ceremony had been friendly and chatty and very complimentary about Robert's achievements and had praised them for their part in his success.

The isolation and uncomfortableness had more to do with their personal feelings of inferiority than anything else, as they believed, incorrectly, that they were being constantly observed and scrutinised by everyone around them to see if they made any behavioural mistakes. This situation of being on edge and full of anxiety meant that they could not enjoy the occasion, feeling out of place even though they had every right to be there.

Robert, his parents and his grandmother had an enjoyable day shopping and, as promised, he bought them the items they had decided on, all from shops on Oxford Street. His grandmother chose knee-length leather boots trimmed with fur, a surprising choice as she had never worn boots before, his mother a wool coat with fur collar and cuffs and his father a navy blue knee-length wool coat.

Robert insisted his parents had the matching scarves and gloves to complement their coats. They each wore their new presents and bagged their old shoes and coats respectively, looking very smart when they arrived at the Savoy at 2.55 p.m. for their 3.00 p.m. booking and were directed by the receptionist to the restaurant where they were greeted by a member of the restaurant staff who then escorted them to their table.

They sat down and then surveyed the grandeur of the room. They had been to Geoffrey's parent's house and thought that was grand but this was much grander and beyond their comprehension. They were lost for words. As they were looking around, Annabelle and her parents came in, escorted by the restaurant manager. The Sinclairs noticed the difference immediately.

Their staff member had been very polite and courteous and formal with them and they could not fault him in any aspect. In contrast, however, the manager himself escorted the Bailey's to their table and although still polite and courteous, was much more informal, inquiring about their health, how long they were in London for and just generally chatting as friends would.

Suddenly, as if taken by surprise, Annabelle halted her stride and exclaimed, "Hello Robert, I didn't know you would be here."

She then introduced Robert to her parents and told them that he was a fellow student from Oxford and now a work colleague. After she had finished, Robert introduced his parents and grandmother.

The introductions and niceties having been completed, the Bailey's sat down at their table, made themselves comfortable and engaged in relaxed conversation as if they were at home.

Annabelle had asked Robert previously whether she should suggest that they join up but he had intimated to her that it was probably not a good idea as he felt his family would feel very uncomfortable having afternoon tea with her titled parents, explaining that it would probably spoil their day, although he strongly reassured her that this was no reflection on her parents as he felt sure they were very nice, friendly people.

He tried to convince her by giving her the analogy of how her father must have felt when he waiting for the queen to knight him, nervous and apprehensive and definitely worried about making any mistakes.

She completely understood.

Afternoon tea was nervously enjoyed by the Sinclair family. Even though Robert had passed on Annabelle's guidance on etiquette, his parents and grandmother constantly glanced around to check that they were 'in harmony' with the other guests, making him question his decision to arrange the event.

They also asked him if they should have bowed or curtsied to the Bailey's. He reassured them that they had behaved completely correctly.

Perhaps, he thought to himself, he and Annabelle had been too preoccupied with planning a surreptitious way of meeting each other's parents, that he had not considered the implications on his family. Annabelle, he knew, would not have any concerns as dining at the Savoy was a regular occurrence for her and her family.

They had arranged to meet that evening until he heard Annabelle say, loud enough for him to hear, "Thank you for arranging a table at Claridge's tonight for eight o'clock, I would love to come; however, I will have to be home by six o'clock at the latest to get ready."

Afternoon tea was over by 4.30 p.m. for the Sinclairs. Outside the Savoy, they all said their goodbyes and then Robert went straight to Annabelle's flat, let himself in and waited until she arrived, which was at ten past six. They greeted each other with a kiss and then flopped down onto the sofa and chatted, both politely agreeing that the other's parents were 'very nice' and that the mothers were 'very pretty', knowing that no meaningful views could be expressed on such a short interaction.

Robert was ushered off home at 6.30 p.m. as Annabelle needed to get ready to go out, so they arranged to meet for a drink and a 'bite to eat' at a nearby pub at lunchtime on the following day, which was when they had a more in-depth conversation about the previous day.

Annabelle gave an understanding smile when Robert told her about the bowing or curtsying and said that she was pleased that his family had not done so, as it would have embarrassed her parents. They both agreed that there was no need to involve their parents again until they were definitely sure about their future together, especially as they needed to concentrate on their careers.

Robert went home to Sheffield for Christmas, leaving London on the 23rd and once there, he arranged to meet up with Geoffrey on Christmas Eve for a drink. They met in the city and joined in with the festivities until 11 p.m. and then returned home. Geoffrey was going to his uncle's house for Christmas dinner this year as it was his turn and the family were staying over, so they agreed to meet again on the day after Boxing Day.

Robert was spending a week with his parents and grandmother and enjoyed his rest from the stresses of stockbroking. He returned to London on the 31st and relaxed, sorting out his flat and watching television to pass the time before going to a New Year's Eve party, which James Brunswick had invited him to at his parent's flat.

Annabelle was spending Christmas and New Year at her parent's estate with her family.

Chapter 41

The next twelve months, Robert and Annabelle's relationship flourished and grew stronger and they became the best of friends as well as emotionally attached, to the extent that they both agreed that a life together as a married couple was what they both wanted and if fortune was on their side, they would be blessed with children. They made plans for their future lives together, discussing houses, children, pets and many other topics.

Robert and James also became good friends and close working colleagues over the eighteen months he had now been working for Brunswick's and Charles had expressed his approval on many occasions on how well he was performing.

Robert was very pleased with the way his life was progressing.

By Christmas 1965, Robert had his own list of clients, over two hundred and fifty of them, and all of them, without exception, were pleased with his recommendations and work ethic. He had, over this period, made them all more profit than loss and because of this, he received a generous bonus from his company for which he had also made significant profits.

Annabelle, a slightly more cautious person, had not made such high profits and was, therefore, given a more moderate bonus. Robert had already decided that his bonus would be used to buy an engagement ring, a single diamond set in a 24-carat yellow-gold ring, which he had seen at Tiffany's, and when he bought it, it became the most expensive item he had ever purchased.

He decided to propose to Annabelle on Saturday, 8 January 1966, and booked a table at Claridge's, knowing that Annabelle liked to dine there, and made sure the restaurant manager was aware of his intentions thereby ensuring that they had a table in a private and secluded part of the room.

Much to his regret afterwards, because he felt he had abused his future father-in-law's place in society, he did tell the manager who his future fiancée was, hoping that this would ensure the best possible table and excellent service. Sure enough, as he had hoped, his action did serve its purpose as they were escorted to a very discreet table and the service could not be faulted.

He proposed to her after they had sat down and their champagne had been served, placing the box containing the ring on the table as they clinked their goblets.

Not a complete surprise to Annabelle, she accepted without hesitation and was absolutely delighted with his choice of ring. They then planned, over the course of the meal, how to tell their parents, not only about the engagement but also about their longer relationship. Annabelle did not want to discuss a date for the wedding until after she had spoken to her parents as she suspected that they would want to be very involved with the planning.

As she was their eldest daughter and the first to marry, she knew that they would want a big wedding; although, no doubt, Caroline would also have a big wedding; but the first of anything is always a more special event, she believed.

They decided that the most sensible way of announcing their engagement to their parents would be to tell them all together, on neutral ground and in a public place. Their plan was that each would tell their parents that, as a 'thank you' for the support given to them during their lives, most especially during their time at Oxford, they were treating them to an afternoon tea, dinner and an overnight stay followed by breakfast in a country house hotel in Buckinghamshire. They would each book a double room for their respective parents and a single room each for themselves.

They arranged the trip for 12 February 1966, the closest Saturday to Valentine's Day, hoping that none of the parents would become intrigued and start asking questions. On that day, Annabelle and Robert caught the earliest train they could and arrived at the hotel around midday. Robert had organised the travel plans for his parents to arrive at the station at approximately 1 p.m. whereas Annabelle's parents, who were driving from their estate, planned to arrive at about 1.30 p.m.

Afternoon tea for six people had already been arranged for 3 p.m. They also agreed that Robert would meet his parents at the station, accompany them back to the hotel in a taxi and guide them through the registration process as they were not accustomed to staying in hotels, this being only their second time, the first being when they had stayed overnight in Oxford on the day of his graduation.

Annabelle's parents had no such problems. They arrived, checked in, washed and changed and were sat in one of the lounges by 2.45 p.m., having pre-ordered drinks for themselves and their daughter. Annabelle joined them a few minutes later. Robert had arranged to meet his parents in the lobby just before 3 p.m. giving them time to rest, wash and change.

At two minutes to three, they all arrived at the restaurant door and stopped in their tracks. No one said a word for a few seconds. Finally, after what seemed an eternity, Harold held out his hand and said, with a large grin,

"Good afternoon Mr and Mrs Sinclair, I think we are victims of a conspiracy." The four parents exchanged handshakes and then turned their gazes towards Robert and Annabelle. The pair sheepishly smiled, took hold of each other's hand, then turned and walked into the restaurant and sat down at the only table laid out for six people, a round one nestling in the bay window overlooking the lawned gardens. All the other tables had couples sitting at them who were all celebrating Valentine's Day, the most romantic day of the year.

The conversation at the Bailey's and Sinclair's table was all about Robert and Annabelle and their relationship. Sometime during the afternoon tea, Annabelle reached into her handbag, retrieved her ring from the zip pocket she had safely placed it in that morning, put it on and then proudly displayed it to both sets of parents.

After some discussion, taking into account work commitments, the time needed to arrange the wedding, the World Cup and other factors such as the dress, the flowers, invitations and so on, the date for the wedding was provisionally and tentatively set for Saturday 24th September that year.

Both Robert and Annabelle knew that many a private discussion was going to take place with their own parents before that day, with reservations being held by both sides about the suitability of the marriage. They had already prepared for these difficult conversations as best they could. The evening meal that day would be the first test.

As expected, as soon as afternoon tea was over, the families separated. The country house had two lounges, both with comfortable sofas and chairs, so Robert and his parents settled down in one and Annabelle and her parents in the other. The two groups talked about the class divide and the social differences from opposite standpoints, with both Harold and Simon becoming very agitated and vocal.

Both sets of parents avoided the financial discussion. After an hour, as agreed privately the night before by Annabelle and Robert, the engaged couple called an end to their individual group discussions and said that they could all carry on the conversation at dinner. Robert and Annabelle went for a walk in the gardens, wrapped up in their winter coats, hats, scarves and gloves and exchanged their experiences of the discussions before returning to their rooms to rest and gather their thoughts prior to dinner.

The two sets of parents went straight to their rooms and talked. Simon, once in the privacy of their room, told Mary in no uncertain terms, that he was totally against the idea and that there was no chance of the marriage working. A very similar outburst was made by Harold to his wife, Margaret. The wives said very little in response to their husband's rantings and got on with getting themselves ready for dinner.

On the insistence of Margaret, Harold contacted the hotel manager and arranged for a bottle of champagne to be served when they sat down for dinner so that they could all toast the happy couple and wish them well in their future lives together as a married couple.

The first half of the evening meal was difficult, with many minutes of silence interspersed by innocuous conversations about the weather, football [England was hosting the World Cup that year] and work. Sir Harold, now a shadow minister, the conservatives having lost the general election on 15 October 1964, although he had retained his seat, did broach the cost of the wedding by simply stating that he would pay for the wedding in its entirety, as Annabelle was his daughter and tradition stated that the 'father of the bride' does this and that the only cost to Robert and his family would be their outfits.

The tense atmosphere could be felt by all six of them.

During the meal, as women do, Margaret excused herself and asked if Mary would 'like to powder her nose too.' Annabelle offered to go with them but her mother firmly refused her suggestion. The two women left to go to the bathroom and were away for at least twenty minutes. During that time, more awkward and uncomfortable innocuous conversations took place at the table, with periods of silence.

When the mothers returned, they were both smiling and were in a more relaxed and happier mood. They sat down and Margaret said,

"Please, no interruptions or comments while I speak as I have something to say. Mary and I have been talking and we think that the happiness of our children is of paramount importance. As we all know, there will be difficulties, especially in terms of our backgrounds but they can and will be overcome.

"If we work together with a united approach and compromise when we need to, all will be fine. With this in mind, I have asked Mary to be involved in all the planning, as not having a daughter means this is the only chance she will have to be involved in the planning of a wedding. All final decisions will, of course, be Annabelle's.

"Mary will be invited to every meeting, dress shopping day and any other events with regard to the wedding and will be made very welcome at all those that she wishes to attend. As mothers, we would like to make this wedding the happiest day of our children's lives so far. Is there anything you would like to add, Mary?" Mary nodded her head from side to side.

The rest of the meal was much more relaxed and the conversations flowed more easily, with Harry, Simon and Robert discussing England's chances of success in the World Cup as well as their own teams, Sheffield United for the Sinclair's and Chelsea for Harry, and the women talked about the wedding as well as the courtship between Robert and Annabelle.

After breakfast the following day, they all said their goodbyes. Harold drove Simon and Mary to the station in his Rolls Royce, as theirs was the first train, after which he and Margaret dropped off Robert and Annabelle an hour later for their train and then continued their journey home.

True to her word, Margaret constantly updated Mary on the progress of the wedding and very generously paid for Mary to travel to London for any fittings or appointments, insisting that she stay in her Belgravia house. They had decided that the church ceremony for the wedding was to take place in the local village, two miles from their estate followed by the wedding breakfast which would take place in a marquee in the grounds of the estate.

Robert's parents and grandmother would stay in the house, arriving the day before the wedding and leaving the day after whilst Robert, with Geoffrey who was to be his best man, would travel up from London on the day and the married couple would then return to London and spend their wedding night in Annabelle's flat in Sloane Square, after which they would go on their honeymoon on Monday 26th September, which they would organise themselves.

Annabelle would arrive at the house on Thursday 22nd September. A hotel in the nearby town was block-booked by Harold to accommodate the guests and a minivan and driver was contracted to be used to ferry guests to and from the wedding with a maximum of fifty guests per family being agreed upon. All was running so smoothly with the wedding plans that by the end of June, there was very little left to arrange.

11 July 1966 heralded the start of the football World Cup.

Chapter 42

8 December 1961, Vijay's 40th birthday, passed without celebration. His only important thought on that day was his renewed determination to seek out and wreak revenge on his father's murderer. Having spent, on and off, the last twenty-eight and a half years thinking about it, he was now in a position to devote time and energy to actually doing something about it, as his life was in a stable and successful position.

During all this time, his family knew that the murder of his father was never to be mentioned or discussed with him as it was a subject that only evoked negative and painful emotions and memories. If they talked about Ramesh, they were only to reminisce on his life and not on the tragic circumstances of his death, even though they knew every detail about that terrible event. Because of this insistence of Vijay's not to discuss the murder of his father, they did not know how he felt or what, if anything, he would do.

Sadly, earlier in the year, his grandmother had passed away after a short illness, diagnosed as heart problems. He had travelled back to India with Anshula for the funeral, leaving Meena with Hemant and his family, because this time they could afford to travel by aeroplane, so could arrive in time.

He again lit the funeral pyre and the day after made the same journey to the coast to disperse the ashes, deciding to drive rather than walk on this occasion, borrowing a car from the same doctor who had lent them a car on his wedding day.

He had communicated with William Grundy during his visit asking him for his help with regard to the regiments that were stationed in Bombay when his father had been murdered, without explaining his reasons for wanting that information.

When he returned to England, he hired a private detective to search for any records that might help him discover the identity of his father's killer, which meant that, as a result of all this heightened activity, by mid-1962 he knew the name of the regiment that was stationed in Bombay in June 1933 and the name of the general in charge, both of which had been provided by William along with the fact that any further information would not be forthcoming without a personal interview with the Ministry of Defence, and subsequently, according to the detective, he was told that it was very unlikely that they would disclose any names. Armed with this limited information, he knew he needed to find a ruse to explain why he needed the name.

He contacted Thomas Goddard to ask him for the contact telephone number of Mrs Oakenshaw who, once he had explained his predicament by lying to her, invited him to her office to discuss the matter, arranging an appointment for him to meet her at Leconfield House, the headquarters of MI5, on Friday, 20 July 1962 at 3 p.m. and also asked him to come an hour early to allow time to clear security.

When he arrived, he was treated with great suspicion by the security staff, even though he told them he had an appointment, and was taken to a small room to be rigorously searched after which he was taken to an office to be questioned.

He was both surprised and shocked when the officer came in to question him.

Mrs Constance Sayers sat down opposite him, also with a surprised look on her face. They shook hands and then she explained that at the time they first met, her husband worked for the foreign office and was posted to Brazil; however, after the birth of her first child, the family had returned to England and she and her husband now worked in London, she as an interrogation officer for MI5 and her husband still at the foreign office. She now had two children and lived 'south of the river', evidently not wanting to disclose her exact location.

Vijay, whilst speculating whether Constance had been an MI6 officer in Brazil, told her about his life and why he was there but deliberately did not mention his time with MI5, pretending that he did not know Mrs Oakenshaw. Constance reassured him that, "She was a lovely person and would help if she could." Eventually, after their chat, he was cleared and taken to Mrs Oakenshaw's office for his appointment.

His lie was that the father of a friend of his had been helped by an officer on that day and this friend wished to meet and thank the officer personally. All that was known was the officer held the rank of a second lieutenant [the detective had confirmed what William Grundy had said the rank was, from the description he had given of the shoulder epaulette, known as the Bath Star].

They reminisced about their time at BSA and then his chance meeting with Constance in Southampton and both agreed that she did not need to know about his work during the war; however, because of her husband's position at work, which meant he could be of some use, they agreed to ask for her help if it became necessary.

Then he told her his lie in more detail, being as vague as he could about any specifics. Mrs Oakenshaw agreed to help but made no promise that she would be able to find this person, and also made it clear that she would not disclose any information to Vijay without consent from the soldier in question.

Two months later she contacted him and informed him that, on the day in the question, 13 June 1933, there had been three officers of that rank stationed in Bombay, one of which had been on leave and another one was off duty leaving only one who could have been his friend's benefactor.

She had contacted this person who did remember a number of incidents when his patrol had helped men whose carts had overturned but he could not remember the exact dates, so he could not be sure if that was one of the dates or not as carts were always overturning and he had helped on a number of occasions.

He confirmed that he was stationed in Bombay at that time but did not want to be contacted or thanked as he only gave the order to his patrol to help the men. He suggested a donation to an army charity would be thanks enough and much appreciated.

Vijay contemplated the situation, now knowing that this man was the murderer of his father and decided on the next course of action as he was determined to find out the identity of his father's killer. After a week, he contacted Mrs Oakenshaw again and asked her if she would forward a letter to the soldier from his friend, saying that villagers often did not exactly know dates and it was obviously this man who had helped but it was probably a day or so before or after the 13th June.

She agreed to his request.

Vijay wrote a letter calling himself Mr Joshi, a well-known high caste [Brahmin], name, profusely thanking the soldier, explaining that his father, whose cart it had been, would have lost his leg had it not been for the actions of the patrol [Vijay hoped memories had faded as he was describing an incident that he had no knowledge about or any of the circumstances associated with it] and that one of his father's dying wishes had been for his son to trace the officer in charge and reward him for his actions.

The reason for the long delay of nearly thirty years was that the man had left the request in his personal belongings, which were only examined after his death earlier this year. He finished the letter by asking for a reply, insisting that the soldier name the charity of his choice. Three weeks later, he received a reply.

Vijay sent a cheque for £100 to the charity and then forwarded the receipt to the address of the soldier's place of work, which was on the top of the letter he had received.

A personal 'thank you' letter was sent back to Mr Joshi.

Armed with this knowledge, Vijay instructed the private detective, Mr Bernard Close, to gather as much information about this man and his family as soon as he could. Months later, Vijay knew the identity of the man who had murdered his father, all his family members, his home address, his workplace and his daily routines.

By Christmas 1962, he had formulated a plan for his revenge based on the facts he had been given. His intention was to hurt the man as much as he could, using any means possible but without committing a criminal offence.

Chapter 43

Vijay and Hemant, after Vijay had made the suggestion, agreed to have lunch together every alternate Thursday at a restaurant in the city. From February 1963, except for the odd occasion when circumstances prevented this, they met at Normans, a well-established eating place in the heart of the financial district of London.

On the occasion of their first two visits, they booked a table for 12.30 p.m. but then Vijay changed the time to 1.00 p.m., saying it suited him better. Much to Hemant's annoyance, he always left a larger-than-average tip. By September 1963, they were well known and accepted at the restaurant, regularly chatting to the manager.

Vijay had, by this time also established, through watching and listening, which table was reserved for Brunswick Stockbrokers. He then made a request to the manager for him to have a regular table next to it, on the grounds that it was a more suitable private one for him and Hemant to talk, adding that he would pay a retainer for the table, with the extra persuasion that if he cancelled without forty eight hours' notice and the table did not get booked, he would pay an extra charge. The manager agreed to this arrangement, having nothing to lose.

James Brunswick had been dining at Normans every Thursday lunchtime since he started working for his father in August 1962, who in turn, had been dining there for the previous five years with colleagues and clients. For the first twelve months, it was always only with his father, Charles, but as he became more experienced his father's place was substituted on some occasions by other senior members of the firm so that he received a more varied and diverse view of the work carried out by it.

This was to allow him to develop a full understanding of the company in preparation for his future as the owner when his father handed over to him as had happened to previous generations. By August 1964, his father thought him ready to have a junior to work for him and appointed Robert Sinclair. James asked if he could have his Thursday lunches with Robert.

His father agreed, spoke to the manager and changed his day to a Wednesday so that James and Robert could continue to lunch at 1.00 p.m. on Thursdays, the regular time the table was reserved for. Vijay noticed the change of persons but decided to continue with his plan irrespectively.

By September 1965, the four occupants of the two tables were on nodding terms, greeting each other when they arrived and saying goodbye when they left. It was obvious to James that the two Indians were men of considerable wealth and he could see them as potential clients. The company already had one Indian client.

James had started to listen to their conversations because Vijay spoke loudly enough to ensure that he could just be heard, initially talking about the rental business, discussing the profit it was making and how fast it was expanding.

James was very impressed.

Then, some months on, Vijay started talking about his time at BSA in the accounts department, mentioning Arnold Robinson, who was now well known in the city as he had left BSA to work for an international investment bank, as a close friend and ex-colleague and a person he was still in contact with, the last statement not quite true he knew, as he had not spoken with him for a number of years. He also dropped the name of Christopher Kingham into his conversations, another well-known name in the city and in this case, someone he was still in contact with.

Vijay had decided to start his plan in January 1966 in the belief that he felt that three years of regular attendance at Normans was sufficient time to present himself and Hemant as decent, upstanding and honourable members of society. He regularly donated to charities, making sure that he told Hemant loudly enough for others in the restaurant to hear. Hemant did question his behaviour but Vijay just kept reassuring him that all was well.

Chapter 44

20 January 1966, a Thursday, saw Vijay and Hemant at their table in Normans as usual, with the adjacent table again being occupied by James and Robert. The four of them had already exchanged nods and were chatting to their respective companions while waiting for their lunches.

Vijay then, slightly turning away from James and Robert, beckoned Hemant towards him and in an audible whisper, said,

"I have some exciting news for you. I have been speaking to Arnold Robinson and he has told me that the researchers at Thawtin Engineering and Scartel have developed a product that could see the end of having to solder metal tubing together by forming a watertight joint that will revolutionise plumbing.

"They plan to release the news on Monday, August 1st, once they are in a position to mass-produce the item. Their shares are cheap now, about £1, but will rise exponentially once the news is out. I want you to buy 10,000 shares in each company every week for the next six months, which will ensure that no suspicion is aroused, otherwise, we could have bought a lot all at once.

"By May, brokers will notice the increase of activity and the share price will rise quickly but by then, we will have over 200,000 shares in each company. The overall cost to us will be no more than £500,000, even with any small rises in the share price over that time. We already have more than £700,000 in our funds, so we are in a position to do this without jeopardising our company.

"We should be able to sell them at three times the price once the news breaks or we could keep them as an investment. I want you to start buying them on February 3rd using our regular brokers. Do not discuss this with anyone, not even Anshula or Rupal."

Over the next week, both James and Robert extensively researched both Thawtin Engineering and Scartel and they concluded that both companies were legitimate and trade was steady with no unusual or past problems that could be identified.

James debated with himself whether he should discuss the matter with his father or whether to impress him with the final profits and, after much deliberation, he decided on the latter course of action. He instructed Robert to inform all his clients and he would do the same for his own, about their recommendations and hopefully, guide them into buying shares in the two companies. He also suggested to Robert,

"Those of your clients who like to take a risk should buy shares 'on account' and you should persuade them to buy a substantial number of shares on Thursday, July 21st, which will then cover the announcement date as the payment date will be a fortnight later, on August 4th. Some of these clients could speculate large amounts of money, £10,000 or more and then a fortnight later when the payment is due, sell the shares, which means that if the share price goes up, as we expect, during that period, they will make a large profit. This way they make a profit without actually having to physically buy the shares. Brunswick Stockbrokers would also make a healthy profit with its commission and in this particular case, when the news breaks, they will be held in high esteem by all the other firms because of the advice and subsequent profit they have provided for their clients. As no link will or can be found between Brunswick, Thawtin and Scartel, there is no risk of any investigation into the trading actions advised by us."

Robert enthusiastically replied,

"I think you are right James, and I are going to do exactly that."

In the next few weeks, Hemant bought the shares as instructed by Vijay. The price of the shares did not move for a month but as more shares were bought, the price started to slowly climb. Robert and James started advising their clients to buy shares in the two companies and then bought the shares for those clients who accepted their advice.

The board of directors at Thawtin and Scartel were surprised and baffled at what was happening but were pleased. The companies were not large enough to cause any concern at the Stock Exchange about their rising share prices, so no alarm bells were heard.

By May, as predicted by Vijay, the price started to increase more dramatically as other stockbrokers, although still wary as there was no plausible explanation for this upward movement in price, did start buying small numbers of shares for their clients, so that by the end of June, the price exceeded £1 and 10 shilling per share.

The fortnightly lunches were more exhilarating as the cousins watched their investments grow and they excitedly talked about how much profit they might make when the announcement was made and how they might use it to expand their business. James and Robert, pretending to be disinterested, now listened more intently than ever.

July 21st arrived and the four of them were having their lunches at Norman's.

Vijay said to Hemant, "We have now already made over £200,000 in profit and when the announcement of the revolutionary product is made, I expect the amount to double, meaning we will have made an overall profit on our investments of approximately 80%. Let's have a celebratory drink." The cousins finished their lunch and left having celebrated their success with a bottle of champagne.

James and Robert went back to their office and started to instruct their clients to buy more shares in the two companies. They encouraged their 'on account' clients to also buy heavily. With the previous trading and the final surge late in July, their total investment for their clients was in excess of £2,500,000.

By Wednesday 27th July, the cousins had approximately £650,000 in shares in the two companies. At precisely nine o'clock on Thursday 28th July, Vijay contacted his stockbroker and instructed him to immediately sell all the shares they had in Thawtin Engineering and Scartel.

Although he had made a large profit, that was not part of his plan, just a bonus.

He was, more importantly to him, hoping his information was correct and that Brunswick's had bought heavily into the shares of the two companies and would therefore lose substantial amounts of money when the price dropped. At ten o'clock, he permanently cancelled his table at Norman's. By eleven o'clock, the share price in both companies had plummeted and more than 90% of the gains made over the previous six months had disappeared.

The companies, when questioned by the Standards Authority, could not explain why their shares had risen in value over the previous few months and categorically denied ever having developed any product to replace soldering or spreading any such rumour. James and Robert tried to sell once they heard about the fall but no one was buying. The total loss to their clients was in the region of £1,700,000.

They were both devastated and sat at their desks with their heads in their hands, desperately trying to fathom out what had happened. The rest of the office staff kept well away from them, knowing that nothing could be said or done to improve the situation. A few minutes later a very angry Charles called them into his office and demanded an explanation.

They told him the sequence of events and tried to justify their actions by saying that they had thoroughly researched both companies but admitted having not contacted the companies directly, as they assumed they would deny the development of the product and might ask questions as to where they had heard such rumours.

Charles vaguely remembered Vijay and Hemant from his days of having lunch on Thursdays. He was livid with James and Robert for not telling him what they were doing and told them in no uncertain terms that the damage to the reputation of the firm was incalculable and that the huge financial loss would have to be borne by the clients who had taken the advice and bought shares in the two companies.

They would, of course, demand an investigation and if a culprit could be found, ask for recompense for all or some of their losses. Both James and Robert explained that they too would have also bought shares but had refrained in case they were accused of insider dealing or fraud.

Disinterested in their woeful explanations, he dismissed them from his office and told them to take the rest of the week off and return to work on Monday. Robert was absolutely distraught and shunned all contact with everyone including Annabelle. His office colleagues, understanding the seriousness of the situation and the despondency that Robert would be feeling, kept their heads down and left him alone.

Charles had decided to take all the calls from the very angry and upset clients and tried to calm them down and was very distressed to learn that many of the 'on account' ones had been financially ruined and could end up being declared bankrupt. Those who had bought their shares requested their immediate sale to try and mitigate further losses.

By the end of the day, Charles was mentally drained and exhausted but had managed, by being apologetic and conciliatory, to reassure his clients that this was not the fault of the company and that he would do all he could to help them.

Chapter 45

Robert went back to his rental flat and spent the rest of the day contemplating his situation, eventually retiring to bed just after midnight. After a disturbed night of sleep, he finally came to a decision. The following day, he wrote four letters. He wrote a letter to his parents saying how sorry he was and that he had 'let them down'. He wrote a resignation letter to Charles with a similar apology. He wrote a letter to Annabelle, calling off the wedding and wishing her every happiness for the future. He wrote a letter to the Financial Times, asking them to print it, outlining what had happened and why he felt he had to take the action he would have taken by the time they received his letter, and finished it with an apology to all the clients of Brunswick Stockbrokers. He did not sign or give his name on this letter.

He put as many of his affairs in order as he could. He spent the evening of Friday, 29 July 1966 consuming a bottle of whisky, ignoring all telephone calls and then fell asleep in a stupor on his sofa, waking up the next day with a terrible hangover.

Saturday, 30 July 1966 was World Cup Final day, with England playing against West Germany at Wembley Stadium. The whole country was buzzing with excitement. Robert spent the morning in his flat. Early in the afternoon, he walked to the offices of the Financial Times and delivered his letter, hoping it would be printed in the Monday morning edition of the paper. He then returned to his flat.

At 4:45 pm, he left and walked to London Bridge posting his other letters on the way. He walked with hunched shoulders due to the extra weight of the stones in both his trousers and coat pockets. The almost deserted streets meant that he drew very little attention otherwise people may have stared at his appearance, a young man in a heavy coat on a summer's day. A long walk, he knew it would take him over twenty minutes.

He arrived at the centre of the deserted bridge, as virtually everyone in the whole country was listening to or watching the game, climbed onto the guard rail and jumped into the waters below without a moment's hesitation.

Had he been nearer to Wembley, the sound of the splash as he hit the water would have been drowned out by the great roar of the crowd as Geoff Hurst scored his third goal that sealed the win for England.

A little old woman walking her dog on the river path had stopped when she saw him climb onto the guard rail. Her screams for him not to jump were to no avail as he was too far away and too high up to hear her. When she saw that he had not surfaced, she ran to the nearest phone box and called the police.

The desk sergeant, who was in a state of elation with England's win, joyfully asked if he could help. The little old woman told him what she had seen, causing him to immediately stop his celebrations and become very professional and set a protocol in motion.

By seven o'clock that evening, police divers had found and winched up Robert's body. The heaviness of the stones had resulted in the body sinking straight down from where it had hit the water and therefore, had not been difficult to locate. News bulletins about the suicide were broadcast on television and radio but were overshadowed by England's victorious World Cup win.

Annabelle, on seeing the broadcast on television, went to Robert's flat and let herself in, calling his name as she entered and when she received no reply and saw the empty rooms, the untidiness of the flat and the empty whisky bottle, her mind went into a panic, fearing the outcome she had suspected when she saw the news. She telephoned her mother.

The noise in the background told her that her parents were still hosting the party they had laid on for the day of the match, planned whether England won or lost. Her mother reassured her that Robert was probably celebrating with friends in a pub somewhere and not to worry. She went to the local police station and explained her worries to the desk sergeant.

After a few phone calls, arrangements were made for her to view the body on Wednesday 3rd August as, with it being the weekend now, nothing would be started until Monday and then time was needed for the pathologists to do their investigation, which meant Wednesday was the earliest possible time. In the meantime, he suggested, she should contact his friends to find out if he was there.

Annabelle went home, worried and distraught.

Her mother rang her on Sunday morning and she told her what she had found out. No one, of all the people she had contacted, had seen Robert or heard from him. She was very upset and anxious, so her mother told her she was coming over. They went back to the police but they were of no further help and asked her to wait until Wednesday.

On page five of The Financial Times on Monday 1 August 1966, the tragic story of 'John Doe' and his suicide was recounted in a few lines, with a brief explanation.

Robert's actual letter was not printed.

The other three letters all arrived at their various destinations on Tuesday 2nd August. Charles also received another letter later that day, with a folded note attached to it, delivered by a courier. The note when opened, simply said, in capital letters:

YOU MURDERED MY FATHER, NOW YOU HAVE LOST YOUR SON

Charles did not understand what was happening as he had spoken to James earlier and knew he was in his office. He telephoned his home and John answered and said all was well.

He opened the envelope and unfolded the letter. It was a copy.

He recognised the contents immediately. He read it out to himself.

19 June 1933

To whom it may concern,

Following an attack on our army barracks by a thug, I chased him. Having him in my vision I fired a shot. Unfortunately, he was only injured. I continued to chase him and fired another shot. This shot missed the thug and struck a civilian who died. Regrettably, his death has to be recorded as 'a casualty of war.' I was carrying out my duty to my country.

A British Officer.

Charles dropped down into his chair still holding the letter. After a few moments, he rose and went to his safe, opened it and drew out a pile of letters held together with a green ribbon. He returned to his chair, sat down and put his feet on his desk. Undoing the ribbon, he read through them in the chronological order that they were filed in.

The first was another copy of the letter he had just received. The next letter was to Sir Frederick Norbeck, Chairman of The Bombay City and Gujarat

Textile Company, dated a few weeks later. This letter requested a name for him to contact regarding the company's late employee, Ramesh Patel. The reply gave him the name of the British General Manager of the company in India, a Mr David Armstrong.

After an exchange of letters with him, he was given the name of Gurwinder Singh, a close friend and colleague of Ramesh's. Then there was a letter to Gurwinder Singh. This letter instructed Mr Singh to contact him if the family of Ramesh Patel were in need of any help in a practical or financial way.

A few years later, a series of letters were exchanged between Gurwinder, Charles and Florence culminating in a contract stating that Charles would fund Vijay and his education and all other expenses during his time studying in Bombay.

All of this was to be kept secret and in the strictest of confidence. The final letter dated 15 January 1942 was from Mrs Florence Baldwin stating that Vijay was now in England and was preparing himself to start university in Birmingham in September, and that he had secured a job at a factory in Birmingham for the next few months.

Attached to the letter was a series of accounts of the cost of Vijay's board whilst staying at her home in Bombay and all other associated costs. A number of receipts and bank statements proved that Charles had reimbursed Florence for all her costs with regard to Vijay's life from 15 August 1938 to 5 January 1942, including all travel costs, clothes, educational aids such as stationery and books as well as food and board.

Apart from the letters to Sir Frederick Norbeck and Mr David Armstrong, who both received their letters from Charles and were posted from the barracks in Bombay, the rest of the letters to Gurwinder and Florence were sent in the name of a Mr Frederick Simpson and the return address was a P.O. Box in London, which Charles had done in order to protect his identity.

He reflected on the chapter of his life whilst he had been stationed in India. Reluctantly, following in the footsteps and tradition of his father and grandfather, he had joined the army. As was also the norm, he, because of the status of his family, became an officer immediately upon joining. A young man with no experience, he had struggled to carry out his leadership duties.

On the day of Ramesh's death, he was in charge of the patrol guarding the gates of the barracks and when the thug had thrown the rock through the window, he saw an opportunity to prove himself to his superiors by apprehending or killing the thug.

This desire had made him throw caution to the wind in his pursuit and had resulted in the death of a civilian man who had left a widow and two sons. He had regretted his action and had, in his opinion, done his best to make amends. He threw the letters onto his desk, lowered his feet onto the floor, stood up walked to the window and stared out across the city.

Sir Harold Bailey and his wife, Margaret, sat either side of Annabelle on the settee in her flat, having travelled there from their home in Belgravia after she had called them regarding the contents of the letter from Robert, which she had received that morning.

She had called the office to say she would not be working that day, without giving any reason. After consoling her as best as they could, Margaret remained sitting, hugging her daughter whilst Harold got up, walked to the window and stared out across the road.

Mary and Ruth sat crying on the sofa as Simon walked around his living room, letter in hand, gritting his teeth. He had read the letter at least a dozen times, trying to accept and believe its contents. He finally stopped and stared out of the window at the houses on the opposite side of the street.

Vijay, having read the financial newspaper that morning and learned about the demise of Brunswick Stockbrokers, sent a courier with a letter to Charles Brunswick and then, with a smile on his face, slumped down in his chair in his office in the city.

He had already read the article in the Financial Times the day before about the young man who had committed suicide last Saturday and had assumed it was James Brunswick. After a few minutes, he walked to the window and stared out looking at the buildings of the financial district of the City of London.

Of the four faces looking out of their windows at various times during that day, one was full of anger, another full of rage, a third full of revenge and the fourth was full of self-gratification.

On Thursday, 4 August 1966, the newspapers printed the story of Robert Sinclair and his short life. Vijay read the article while he sat at his desk and was dismayed and shocked, and then his thoughts turned to the widespread extent and terrible outcome of his actions, all because he had not fully considered what could or might happen, resulting in events he had not expected, wanted or bargained for.

Vengeance can have immeasurable, unplanned and unexpected consequences, Vijay thought to himself. He contemplated his future and the possible repercussions that might come his way because of his actions.